THE BEAUTIFUL RISK

Also by Lynn Hightower

Novels

HIGH WATER
THE PIPER *
EVEN IN DARKNESS *
THE ENLIGHTENMENT PROJECT *

The Sonora Blair series

EYESHOT
FLASHPOINT
NO GOOD DEED
THE DEBT COLLECTOR

The David Silver series

ALIEN BLUES
ALIEN EYES
ALIEN HEAT
ALIEN RITES

The Lena Padget series

SATAN'S LAMBS
FORTUNES OF THE DEAD
WHEN SECRETS DIE

* available from Severn House

THE BEAUTIFUL RISK

Lynn Hightower

SEVERN
HOUSE

First world edition published in Great Britain and the USA in 2023
by Severn House, an imprint of Canongate Books Ltd,
14 High Street, Edinburgh EH1 1TE.

Trade paperback edition first published in Great Britain and the USA in 2024
by Severn House, an imprint of Canongate Books Ltd.

severnhouse.com

British Library Cataloguing-in-Publication Data
A CIP catalogue record for this title is available from the British Library.

ISBN-13: 978-1-4483-0993-1 (cased)
ISBN-13: 978-1-4483-1278-8 (trade paper)
ISBN-13: 978-1-4483-0994-8 (e-book)

Typeset by Palimpsest Book Production Ltd.,
Falkirk, Stirlingshire, Scotland.

Praise for Lynn Hightower

"Lynn Hightower is a brave, bold writer – and this spooky, suspenseful masterpiece could be her best yet. Super-recommended!"
Lee Child, #1 international bestselling author of the Jack Reacher thrillers, on *The Enlightenment Project*

"Sensitive characterizations match the imaginative plot. Readers will compulsively turn the pages to see how it all ends"
Publishers Weekly Starred Review of *The Enlightenment Project*

"Establishing unsettling tones early on, the book's tension mounts, even during its quiet, tender moments. Both the medical and supernatural elements are detailed in engrossing terms. But human connections are at the heart of the novel's draw"
Foreword Reviews on *The Enlightenment Project*

"This taut psychological page-turner has a gripping, tightly woven plot and is jam-packed with head-spinning twists and an overwhelming sense of menace that will keep readers riveted"
Booklist on *Even in Darkness*

"Psychologically compelling"
Kirkus Reviews on *Even in Darkness*

"Fast pacing, a strong and sympathetic main character, and a genuinely frightening supernatural being keep the pages turning in this ghostly thriller"
Booklist on *The Piper*

"A stand-alone nightmare that will keep you awake till
the last page and maybe even afterward"
Kirkus Reviews on *The Piper*

About the author

Lynn Hightower is the internationally bestselling author of numerous thrillers including the Sonora Blair and Lena Padget detective series. She has won the Shamus Award for Best First Private Eye novel and a WHSmith Fresh Talent Award. Lynn lives in Kentucky, in a small Victorian cottage with a writing parlor.

www.lynnhightower.com

Pour Robert, je t'aime pour toujours.

ACKNOWLEDGMENTS

Thank you, thank you . . . Patrice Rayssac, for conversations on the novel, and insight on all things French. Wendy Katz, dog whisperer and trainer extraordinaire, who helped me train my very own dog, Leah, and had excellent insights on how to find a German Shepherd like Leo, lost and alone on Mont Blanc. My good friends, Marc and Nadine Kissel, who let me hang out with them in Annecy. To Gaëlle Dunoyer of Taxi Massingy, who drove me everywhere I needed to go for research, and is the only reason I am not still lost somewhere in the French Alps.

To Marla Carlton of Specto Design, and Axel Muench, photographer, brilliant professionals and good friends. Carl Moses, LSW and Dr Alessia de Paola Gottlieb for character insights and story spitballing, and their thoughts on trauma and what might drive my terrorist, Mae Yvonne McDermott. To my agent, Matt Bialer, my publishers at Severn House, particularly to my editor, Rachel Slatter. My fabulous and hardworking publicist Kim Dower of Kim-From-LA.

For musical inspiration . . . my gratitude to the brilliant guitarists Charo and Dolly Parton, and the Penny Dreadful band of Athens, Greece, for their incredible album, *Dead Wood*.

And to the beautiful city and people of Annecy, France.

ONE

The night Olivier died – before it felt real, as I lay curled up in a chair by the fire, worn out by the agony of hope – he came to me.

What woke me was the lamp beside the chair. A sudden flash of light. I opened my eyes, frowning. The light flared and dimmed, and flared yet again. And then I saw . . . *myself*.

My face, tear-streaked, mascara drying on my cheeks. Hair mussed, the open collar of my red-and-black checked flannel shirt, the way I was curled sideways in the chair. And I saw myself in a way I could never have imagined. And I laughed because I was so utterly beautiful, in a way I cannot describe. It was the beauty of all of me. My physical self. My soul.

And then I saw *him*. Olivier.

'*Junie*,' he whispered.

I felt his hand as he caressed my cheek, as he leaned over me. 'Hello, my beautiful wife.'

He bent close and kissed me, and I felt the rough three-day beard on his unshaven cheeks. He was wearing his old brown leather bomber jacket and brought with him a breath of cool fresh air, and the scent of the spruce, larch and conifers of Chamonix.

It is impossible to describe how happy I was. Because that night . . . he was there. And he was real. And he was there not to tell me goodbye. He was there to show me how much he loved me. In a way that would stay with me forever.

He kissed me hard.

And then he was gone.

I scrambled up out of the chair. Wide awake. I could still feel his hand on my cheek.

'Olivier?' I whispered. But I was alone.

And I knew so many things then. How my husband truly saw me, how much my husband loved me. And that there was no longer any hope. Olivier was dead.

And so came the abyss. And the dark, sick knowledge that I would never see him again.

And yet . . . love does not die. It cannot be swept away in the tides of death that come to us all. And grief? Grief is a dark and magical journey.

TWO

Nine months later

I have always thought that it was no coincidence that I was hesitating in the doorway of our little Victorian cottage, touching Leo's old leather leash, when the call came in with that +33 country code from France. The man introduced himself as investigating judicial officer Capitaine Philippe Brevard, who had a letter from *Le juge*, and who was temporarily assigned to Chamonix, investigating the death of Olivier and the pilot, Madame Fournier, who had a husband, a young daughter and three cats.

I really didn't understand. Not then.

But it was one of those phone calls that changes your life, that shakes you to the core. At the time, I thought I was bulletproof. I did not want the life that I had. I was a widow, navigating the new phase of my marriage, where my beloved was somehow gone and somehow here.

The worst had happened, and no one could hurt me anymore.

So I thought.

But at the time . . . at the time, I was relieved. The call was a reprieve from the daily routine where I was going to have to make myself walk out that door, steeped in the sick and too-familiar feeling that I was once again headed out for a walk alone. When what I really wanted to do was run up and down the street calling for Olivier. *Where are you? Where did you go?*

Routine is how you navigate grief. Walk in the morning, go to sleep at night, hoping never to wake up. Death for me would be a rescue mission.

I was a high achiever in the Grief Olympics, which all of the bereaved are subjected to. The endless stream of advice from people who didn't have a clue. Who had no possible way of understanding how alone I was. Going for a walk every day was not going to make it all better. Nothing was going to make it all better. I regret to inform you that you cannot fix grief.

I had lost everything. My husband, Olivier, and our dog, who used to keep me safe in the world.

Leo. Our German Shepherd rescue, who came to us at ten months old, wild, neglected, twenty-five pounds underweight, ready for his next adventure. Nine months ago, he was one hundred pounds of pure muscle, eight years old, intense, high-strung, always on the job. Leo had been with Olivier in France that afternoon when the Cessna 172 had gone down – slamming into a crevasse over Mont Blanc, bursting into flame upon impact. It's not the crash that kills you. It's the fire that comes from the faulty carburetor.

Mont Blanc is not the highest mountain in the world, and is by no means the most difficult to climb. It is simply the deadliest. It takes an average of one hundred hikers a year. Eight thousand people have lost their lives on Mont Blanc, and the number keeps rising.

Mont Blanc has everything that scares me. Extreme heights, freezing temperatures, heavy snow, narrow footpaths over steep drops, falling rocks along the Goûter Route – death avalanches that take out anything in their path, human or animal. Skiers, climbers, chamois, roe deer, ibex. And deep endless crevasses that lay in wait.

Olivier loved it. He loved snow, cross-country skiing, mountain biking. And me.

He had been there doing a safety assessment of the Mont Blanc Tunnel, his skill set a unique and high-demand combination of manufacturing background, steel mill processes, degrees in metallurgy and mechanical engineering, and ASO Black Belt Quality certification, which used to be all the rage. He spoke French, German and, pretty much, English. He could walk into a manufacturing plant, figure out the problems in the process that were causing quality issues and come up with a short-term plan that would correct the issue and a long-term plan for a permanent fix. He would bring the factory up to specs – train the workers in the new processes, repair, replace or just deep-clean the machinery, look for efficiency issues and scrap salvage that would save time and huge sums of money, and, most of all, do all of this while not shutting down the lines. Shutting down the lines could cost a manufacturing plant millions. For the smaller ones in the supply chain, where profit margins were razor-thin, it could take them under. Olivier was much in demand.

He also pissed people off. And he had grown weary of manufacturing plants. He would not compromise on quality or safety, or fudge inspections. He greeted the cagey, good ole boys of American manufacturing with a stony face and a small shrug, and was prompt in initiating safety recalls for products that posed a risk. This got him fired regularly until he set up his own consulting firm. Most of his work in the last eight years was for European-owned companies – the French, the Germans. He was highly in demand with the Japanese.

And now he was on to something new. Tunnel safety. Hired by Prometheus – an international consulting firm, out of Glasgow. Hired for his skill set in evaluating the stuff that burns in a fire, he was moving into new territory. Fire suppression in tunnels had always been about chemicals and foam, the fear being that a mist of water from a sprinkler system would heat up and cause scalding and steam and be as dangerous as the fire it was supposed to suppress. But that was not how it worked. Because the mist of water reduced the temperatures drastically. Sprinkler systems in tunnels would save lives and a great deal of money, and Olivier was a genius at cost–benefit analysis. He had become an evangelist for using water for fire suppression.

Olivier had delayed his flight home from Geneva to get on the four-seater Cessna 172, taking a short one-hour flight out of Chambéry to fly over the Mont Blanc massif and its glaciers. The job had kept him there longer than we'd planned. He had told me the night before that there was something he wanted to look into. I knew that, overall, the tunnel assessment had gone well, and he was impressed with the Mont Blanc safety set-up. Since the terrible 1999 Mont Blanc Tunnel fire, safety was state of the art and impressive, and Olivier was thrilled to have the chance to do the assessment. His specialty was the quality of the concrete and steel and how it stood up to extreme temperatures.

Because it was never about *if* there would be a tunnel fire. It was always about *when*.

Olivier had been tired. I thought there was something on his mind, but I knew he would not discuss it with me until he was home. Sitting beside me on the battered leather couch, sharing a glass of cognac.

My husband was a master of compartmentalization. Work and family were two separate categories for Olivier. I rarely knew about work problems unless they blew up.

It had been a beautiful day, sunny, cold. A patch of fog had caused the pilot of the Cessna to become disoriented, and the plane had gone down. Leo had survived the crash. He had pulled Olivier and the pilot out of the wreckage, and he was there when the rescue came. They had spooked him, and he'd run away. I had been on the first plane out, arriving in France twenty-one hours later, and I had looked for Leo for weeks. Gone home to arrange Olivier's funeral and come back. Kept track of sightings. I had set traps to catch him – crates with food inside that would close when he went in. I had spent hours trekking over slopes and in the forest.

And then the sightings faltered. Spring came, then summer. Soon the weather would turn. Winter in the Alps is brutal, and storms can rage for days. I had given up.

The first thing that I noticed about Capitaine Philippe Brevard was his voice. It was deep and mellow with a resonance that made him easy for me to hear. The second time I asked him to repeat what he said, he paused.

'I will speak English with you?'

'Yes, thank you. I am confused as to why you are now investigating the death of my husband. I thought the investigation was done by the BEA.' Any accident in French airspace was scrutinized and analyzed by the Bureau of Enquiry and Analysis for Civil Aviation Safety. My back was up. I knew I sounded formal and cold.

'Yes, they also investigate. They are concerned with aviation safety. But there is also a judicial . . . a criminal investigation into the crash if there is a fatality. So in that circumstance, there are always two investigations. Both have been ongoing from the beginning. But there have been developments, and I have been called in.'

'I see,' I said. But I didn't. 'What do you mean, "developments"?'

'Madame, *je suis désolé*, there is no easy way to say this. There has been a sighting on the trails near the Parc de Merlet. Drone footage they have forwarded to me.'

I immediately thought of Leo. The Parc was an animal sanctuary. Leo could not get in – the fence was too high and electrified on top. But there was a breeding operation nearby for St Bernards. He might gravitate to the area. 'Has someone found my dog? You know about him, he—'

'*Oui*, Madame, we know about your dog. Everyone here does.'

'Good to know.' Sans tourists, Chamonix is a small town. The American wife of a Frenchman cannot fly under the radar in France, no matter how much she thinks she can. They watch discreetly, but they watch.

'He is the service dog for your hearing loss – that is correct?'

'That is correct.'

I had a cookie bite hearing loss, fairly rare, but it ran in my family. It was odd in that I could hear acutely at the top and bottom range of sound frequency. Birdsong woke me up in the morning. I could always hear the wind in the trees. A barking dog. A siren. Quite a lot of music. My issues were with mid-range frequencies. Which was most conversation. I could hear but not always catch the words, so I had to concentrate hard to understand. People with resonant voices were a blessing. Hearing aids helped. A lot. But turning up the volume meant I could hear the hum of a refrigerator in the next room as well as what people were trying to say. The technology was supposed to account for that, but, like most tech, it was way overrated. This Capitaine Brevard – he had the kind of voice that I could hear.

'We know that he is your special service animal. People have been aware of him. Mountain Rescue has been keeping watch. It must be difficult for you without your dog.'

'I do OK. It's just better with Leo.' People never quite got that hearing loss was not all or nothing or about volume control. That hearing dogs don't just alert you to sounds you need to hear or things you should pay attention to. They keep you engaged in the world. How easy it is, when you have to work hard to hear, to retreat to an inner world, where people are not impatient, do not give you annoyed or confused looks, do not talk down to you as if you are a child. Your dog gets you out in the world, encourages people to smile at you and keeps you from feeling isolated.

'I shouldn't have left him behind, but—'

'He had an issue with his leg, yes?

'He'd injured his psoas muscle; it's a chronic problem for him. The vet said a couple more weeks of rest in France would be best for him, so he stayed behind with Olivier. And I had to get back. There was a forensic accounting dispute between one of my high-dollar clients and a law firm, and I needed to be face to face for a deposition. But how did you know that?'

He paused. 'You told me this, Madame. The day I took you to the morgue to see your husband.'

'Did you? Take me to the morgue?'

'Yes, I drove you there and took you inside, and waited for you while you identified him. You asked for time alone with him, and I waited for you in the hallway. You do not remember this?'

I shut my eyes tight. I had no memory of this whatsoever. Just me, alone with Olivier. That was seared into my memory. 'No, I don't.'

His voice was steady and kind. 'Yes, you were very much in shock; it does not surprise me you do not remember.'

'It's so *odd* to have no memory of this.'

'But very normal, Madame; do not let it worry you.'

I pictured him nodding his head. Taking notes.

'Madame, there is something else, and it is going to upset you. You are alone? Is there someone—?'

'There is no one; please just tell me.'

There was a long pause. 'I have been sent some drone footage that was taken near the Parc de Merlet eight days ago, by French Biodiversity Officers. We are losing animals there to wolf attacks. And they filmed what they thought was a lone wolf circling the Parc, but they have decided after looking at several sections of footage, what they think is a wolf, they decide is a dog.'

I clutched the worn leather of Leo's leash. If I could have my dog back . . . the surge of hope was so strong that my hands were trembling.

And it made sense. Leo was tall for a Shepherd, all gray and black, marbled together. He did not have the traditional GSD saddle markings, and Olivier and I often got stopped when we walked through town by people who wanted to know if he was a wolf. Some people would see him and cross to the other side of the street.

'This does not upset me, Capitaine Brevard. I'm thrilled. If this is my dog, I am coming to get him.'

He hesitated. 'You see . . . in one segment of the drone footage, there is also a man.'

I began to feel that familiar sick, grieving dread in the pit of my stomach.

'Now, we know, you and I, that he cannot be your husband. But he is holding the dog on a rope. A dog that looks like a wolf. It is the same dog in all of the footage we have.'

I leaned back against the wall and slid down to the floor.

'Madame?'

'Yes, I'm here.'

'This man, he seems to me too tall to be your husband, but there is a resemblance we find very strange. Like a man who is trying to look like your husband. And the dog, he looks like your dog. I would like you to look at this footage. I have sent it already to your email. Please look at this and tell me if this is your Leo. And we know this man is not your husband, but maybe you might know who he is. A friend, someone in the family.'

My breath was coming hard and fast. 'Capitaine Brevard, I identified my husband after the crash. I took the wedding ring off his finger, and I wear it on my left hand, right next to my own. I don't know who or what this is, but it's cruel, and . . . and—' Shit, I was crying. I did not want to cry.

'Yes, Madame. I understand you. I agree with you as well.'

'You sound pretty calm about it.'

'It is my job to be calm. I have sent you the email with the link. Look at the video, then please call me back. Inside the email will be my personal mobile number; you will reach me directly.'

I didn't want to let him go. I was going to have a million questions. I wanted an explanation; I wanted answers and I wanted them now. 'Maybe just stay on the line?'

'It would be better for you, I think, to take your time with this, then call me back.'

'And you'll be there? You'll answer right away? You won't just . . . get busy and not answer the phone?'

'I would not be so cruel.'

I took a breath. Thought about it. 'There is more to this than the sighting of a man with a dog. There has to be a reason you are so . . . all over this.'

'All over this?' He sounded puzzled. 'Ah, yes, I understand you. I will tell you the reason.'

I took a deep breath.

'Madame, we have established beyond a doubt that your husband's plane was sabotaged.'

THREE

The video was all wrong. This man was nobody I knew. He was too tall, heavier than my husband, but his black wool coat was exactly like the one that had disappeared from Olivier's office a couple of years ago during a consulting job. It had been a birthday gift from me, and he'd been upset about losing it. The man also wore a thick gray scarf just like the one Olivier wore. And his hair – same exact haircut, but where Olivier's hair was thick with gray-black waves and curl, this man's was straight, dark. I could not see him close up, but I could see enough.

I enlarged the picture and saw the coat had a small tear on the left sleeve where Olivier had caught it in the door of our car. This was my husband's coat. Had this man taken it out of Olivier's office? Was he someone my husband worked with?

And the dog on the video. I knew my dog. It was Leo. And Leo was alive.

I looked at the video in wonder. So this was where Leo had been. This man had taken him. And the fury rose inside me.

And I saw everything I needed to know in how they walked together.

The body language of a dog, their energy – how they walk, the set of their ears, the way they hold their tail. This will tell you everything. Leo was turned away from the man, straining to get free. If you had ever seen Olivier and Leo walking together, you would know. Because Leo and Olivier, they were always in sync, almost a dance. With horses in dressage, they call it *the float*. Leo rising up on the balls of his feet, moving with a grace that made him look as if his feet barely touched the ground, completely in tune with Olivier's stride. Head turning from side to side, watchful, because Leo was always on the job.

I saw none of this on the video. I saw a stressed dog, who wanted to get free. Limping – that left-side psoas muscle giving him trouble. He had blackened burns on his skin. He had lost a lot of weight. But there was no doubt in my mind. This was my Very Good Boy.

I watched the video over and over, sick to my stomach, frozen in my heart, as anger surged so strong it made me tremble.

And I thought of my husband. How he had come to me the night that he died. I thought of crying softly in the plane on the way to France, turning my face to the window so no one could see.

Identifying Olivier's body had not traumatized me. I had shut out the world, turned my hearing aids off. The time I spent with him then was surreal, gentle and precious. Just the two of us. I remembered how the flesh on his chest and neck and the left side of his face had been scorched and burned. How I had kissed my fingertips and touched that ravaged skin. The face so familiar, so different, so still.

How I sat beside my husband, telling him over and over how much I loved him. Held his hand tight, knowing it was the last time. I had bent my head close to his shoulder, soaking him with my tears.

Why did I even have this slight flicker of hope that somehow . . . some way . . . he was still alive? I knew better. Whoever did this . . . I could not fathom such cruelty. Someone had sabotaged the plane. Olivier had been murdered. It was too hard to think about. I had no idea what I should do.

But Leo. Leo was alive. And I laughed and I cried. I was going to France. I was going to find my Leo. I was going to bring him home.

FOUR

I arrived in Geneva thirty-seven hours later. I had called my big brother and his husband, left them a message. My brother and I ran a business together – forensic accounting, lucrative. I was behind with my clients, and I was going to be even more behind. I had brought my laptop. I made promises to my brother that I knew I wouldn't keep. It was not because I could not concentrate on the work. It was because I concentrated too well. It took me longer, much longer to do the work now, and I was missing deadlines. My brother did not understand that this was a good thing. He just knew that if I said I'd be done in a week . . . I wasn't. But I was strangely better than I'd ever been before. I could see the pathways of money being hidden and moved around as if I was following a throbbing neon trail. I had always been an intuitive forensic accountant, which is a rare thing. And now I saw everything. All the twisty little layers of deceit.

I exchanged money at the airport and was met at the curb outside baggage claim by Olivier's best friend, Eugene. We exchanged two *bises*, right cheek, left cheek. He took my hand in both of his and studied me. He was a sturdy man, thinning chestnut hair that flipped to one side, eyes very brown. Unshaven for about a week, which was four days more than I liked. People looked at me carefully since Olivier died. Searching out my grief.

'You are looking good, Junie. But I am worried about you now, with this weird thing going on. I watched that video you sent me, and so did Annette. No, this is not Olivier. This man with your dog – how can that happen?'

'You don't know who he is?'

He hesitated. Shrugged. 'It's best for you to talk to Laurent about this – you talk to him, OK?'

Eugene knew things, then. And so did Laurent – another good friend. He and Olivier were roommates in college. 'I just want my Leo. I'm not going to think about anything else until I find him.'

He nodded, then smiled, showing dimples. 'I see you have brought the guitar. That is good for you.'

I raised an eyebrow. 'Essential.'

I had brought my Alhambra Flamenco Acoustic guitar and left the Ortega at home. I had brought it safely through on a direct flight from Dulles, tucked in a hard-shell case in a storage closet at the front of the plane, courtesy of an understanding steward, who was a musician himself. He played the cello.

Three hours' practice a day, more now that Olivier was gone. The only time I felt like me again. When I could get lost in the music and be almost content. My heroes, my role models, were Charo and Dolly Parton, two of the most talented guitar players alive.

We were strangely quiet, Eugene and I, on the drive from Geneva to Annecy. The weather was clear. I could see the Alps when we drove past Lake Geneva. We took the A1. It was thirty-nine kilometers to Annecy, and dark out, windy. The neat, manicured countryside made me feel easy in my heart.

It was good to be back in France, and I stared out of the window into the darkness so Eugene would not see my face. I had arrived looking for something I would not find. No Olivier waiting just outside security, searching the crowd till he found me. No shy smile and kiss, Olivier holding my hand tightly, taking my briefcase and guitar, leading me through the airport because if it was possible to take a wrong turn, he knew that I would.

Just me now. And if I was lucky, I would have Leo. That was all that kept me going. I was not yet ready to think about that other thing.

Olivier and I had a tiny apartment on the second floor of Chez Eugene, in Old Town Annecy, the Haute-Savoie in France, about a forty-minute drive from Geneva, forty-five from Mont Blanc. Eugene and his wife Annette owned the building, and the apartment there was small and perfect – space in Annecy was in high demand. We were lucky to get it.

Old Town – they call it the Venice of France. Small canals

ran beside the cobbled streets, the water clean and shimmery. And we were a block from the market.

It felt like home, coming back again. Annecy is an exquisite and popular holiday town on the banks of the Thou River and Lake Annecy. It's medium-sized – two hundred thousand plus residents in the urban area. Not counting the tourists, many of them French, a happy place for the family vacation. Close to Geneva, close to Italy, cosmopolitan, energetic. Olivier and I used to walk our regular promenade around the lake with Leo, and, to me, this was the most perfect city in France. And it was my kind of place. Narrow streets, bistros, food and antique markets. For me, Annecy is heaven on earth.

Or it was when Olivier and I were there together.

The city was well lit, the light reflecting up from the water, which was very low. There had been a drought. There was plenty of nightlife here. I like a city with nightlife, even though I rarely go out. I like having that energy all around me.

Eugene pulled up in front of the café. It was busy but not overflowing, late-night dinner, the buzz of conversation. I felt guilty for taking him away from his kitchen.

'Tell Annette I am sorry about my timing.'

'Oh, no, Junie, she wanted to come as well, but this was not possible.' He bustled out of the car, pulling my briefcase out of the trunk. Next came the guitar case, which Eugene handled carefully, with a nervous look at me over one shoulder. He knocked on the passenger's window and cocked his head to one side. 'Junie? You are coming?'

I wondered if it would ever get easier to come back here, alone, without Olivier.

I scrambled out of the car after Eugene, who was heading through a doorway to the side of the bistro, lumbering up a narrow flight of steep stairs, carrying the briefcase with my computer and the guitar.

'You need your own Sherpa, Junie. You have always so much stuff.' He gave me a quick look over his shoulder to see if I would smile.

I cocked my head at him and nodded, giving him a twisty half-smile. Olivier said this exact thing every single time I arrived, and when Eugene was there, he would laugh at me and help to carry all my bags up the stairs. I had never mastered the art of packing light.

I followed Eugene up the worn, creaky wooden steps. There was no railing – it was too narrow – but I ran a hand along the whitewashed plaster walls as I headed up.

The smells coming from the restaurant were enough to make your knees go weak. Shallots and garlic simmering in olive oil, and some kind of stew that had been bubbling for hours.

Eugene's shoulders were tense, and he waited for me at the top of the steps, standing to one side of the landing. The lines in his face looked deep and settled. He was worried.

'There are things you're not telling me, Eugene.'

He frowned at me. 'We will do it this way. I will come in and we will make coffee. I will not go down to the kitchen, or I will get caught up in work. And yes, there is something we need to discuss. But first I must ask if you have had dinner.'

I hadn't. 'I'm not hungry, Eugene.'

He made a noise. 'If you have been eating airport food all day, you must be hungry.'

'What I want is for you to tell me what is on your mind. Is it about Olivier? That man in the video?'

He nodded.

I unlocked the door and he followed me in.

FIVE

I was OK as soon as I was inside. I snapped on lamps. The shutters were open, and streetlights shone in through the windows.

It was small and cozy, full of light in the mornings, old stone floors and a bank of windows with flower boxes, white-washed plaster walls, our books mingled together on the shelves. Olivier's collection of hardbound *Thorgal* comics, his tomes on quality management, tunnel fire safety, books on chess strategy, histories of the American Revolution, which he was obsessed with.

Leo's empty food and water bowls were still tucked by the back wall in the kitchen.

Eugene settled at the kitchen table – a retro yellow lino-leum table that seated four. Hideous but practical. Olivier had made noises when I wanted to replace it with something more French bistro.

'Please, can we live in the real word and not your fantasy of France 1952?'

I had told him that table was the reality of 1952 and I'd prefer the fantasy, and he had laughed. We kept it. For economy, you could not beat it, and I knew it would easily last another hundred years. Ugly goes on forever.

I took coffee beans out of the freezer, ran them through the grinder and put grounds and water in the old aluminum mocha pot that Olivier and I found at an antique market. It cost us two euros. The old two-burner gas stove heated the pot up quickly, coffee bubbling up to the top, thick and black. Just enough for two tiny cups. I missed my coffee maker from home. I never got used to mocha pot coffee with the consistency of syrup.

I sat across from Eugene who nodded when I handed him his cup of coffee, and I set out the sugar.

Eugene sipped coffee. 'Junie, I have been in touch with

Laurent. I sent him the video, but he had already seen it. He has talked to the police.'

I tried to unwrap one of the big cubes of sugar, but my fingers were trembling. Eugene took it from me, peeled it open and dropped it gently into the cup.

'You know that Laurent, he sometimes does volunteer work with Mountain Rescue, and he has many friends, including people at the Parc de Merlet.'

I nodded. 'I'm not even sure where to start looking. And if that man has him—'

'What? *No, no*. There is more footage, you see; that is what I want to tell you. This Brevard, he did not give you everything. Leo was seen three days ago along the road beside the park. He had a broken rope he was dragging; it looked like he got away from that man who tries to dress like Olivier. Laurent, he says you should come to him tomorrow. He spent yesterday trying to find Leo; he set out a trap. He would like you to go to him in Chamonix; he is close to the Parc and this forest where Leo was seen. He will take some time from his work to help you find him. He tried to call you but you were already on the plane. This is happening very fast.'

Laurent was intense about work, just like Olivier. He ran his own NGO. A non-profit, non-governmental entity, usually with a humanitarian cause. People trust them. They shouldn't. It's a Wild West show. For every NGO that is trying to do good in the world, there is another that fronts a lobbyist group for a corporation that is actively greenwashing – which is all about marketing spin. Green PR and green advertising to let the world know their goals and policies are improving the environment when the opposite is true. A corporation can claim to be working for climate change when they are really sucking up grants and government contracts while conducting business as usual. The only change they make is the spin.

Combine that with poor oversite and the usual toothless regulations and there is a lot of money to be made. The Volkswagen 'clean diesel' emissions scandal earned a place in the Greenwashing Hall of Shame.

Laurent's NGO was operational as well as advocacy. There was a lot of money to be had on the operational side, big money interest in green manufacturing processes. And Laurent was moving from researching to setting up projects and stirring up a lot of interest – which meant grants, subsidies and government contracts.

Laurent had the same steel mill process and metallurgy background as Olivier, but he was working in climate change, researching the cost–benefit analysis of using hydrogen instead of carbon to fuel steel production – which would reduce the carbon footprint astronomically. Right now, the process was expensive enough to take a company under, but that was now. He had been trying to get Olivier on board – Olivier would have been perfect for this kind of work. Olivier had been considering it, but he had become a fire suppression evangelist, and I had the feeling he did not want to work with Laurent. We had discussed it, and I admit I loved the idea. Working for the environment, spending most of our time in France. With tunnel safety, Olivier would be all over the world. But he said we could sell the cottage in the US and move our base to France, and I was very much on board with that. All those plans we had made.

Laurent and Olivier had been friends since college. At first, Laurent and I had not gotten along, but we tolerated each other, for Olivier's sake. And then Olivier died, and Laurent came to the funeral and helped me look for Leo, and I had bonded to him like a little lost dog.

'And he'll help me look? That's awesome.' I took a breath. I got lost easily, and a forest could swallow me up. 'That's so kind of him, to round up all that footage. He helped me look, you know, at first, when Leo went missing.'

He nodded. He did not meet my eyes.

'What is it, Eugene?'

'Annette's cousin works in the office of the BEA, and they know things about the judicial investigation. It is not their side of things, but still they know.'

I nodded.

'I can tell you how the sabotage was done.'

I set my coffee cup down and put my hands very carefully in my lap. 'I promise not to cry.'

He shrugged and patted my hand. 'What happened is the

pilot's seat was all the way back and stuck. If it slides back while they are in the air, the pilot, she would not be able to get to the controls. That is why the plane went down; this can happen very fast. This is a thing that causes a lot of crashes in small planes – wear and tear on the slides is always causing problems, and the pilot, she knew this. She was very smart and conscientious. She replaced the slides recently so that this would not happen.'

'And yet it did.'

'Two of the four steel bolts in the fail-safe broke. The bolts were tampered with. Cut almost through. It was done the night before the flight.'

Just the kind of thing Olivier would have picked up in an inspection. Just the kind of thing Olivier looked for in his assessments.

'That sounds . . . targeted. To Olivier.'

He shrugged. 'I am not a manufacturing guy. But' – he put his hand over mine – 'you know Laurent was supposed to be on the plane with Olivier?'

'Yeah, I know. Laurent told me; we talked about it at Olivier's funeral. He felt terrible about it.'

Eugene shrugged. 'There is no sense in both of them dying. But that has made this Capitaine Brevard guy suspicious.'

'Of Laurent?'

Eugene nodded. 'I have known Laurent for years; we three were at school – me and Olivier and Laurent.'

I watched him.

'Laurent did not have anything to do with this, but he helped Madame Fournier with the repair.'

'Seriously?'

'Yes, he was friends with Madame Fournier, and he was there to arrange the flight and pay her for it, and she was doing the repair, so he lent a hand. He is good at this kind of thing. Not like Olivier.'

'Oh, God, please tell me Olivier didn't help him with this.'

Olivier was good at spotting problems in our ancient little cottage – sometimes too good – but he was clumsy, and his attempts so often ended in a trip to the ER that I forbade him to ever work around the house again. We hired it out.

Everything except the gardening, which Olivier always did. He used to take me to garden centers and tell me to pick out anything I thought was pretty. Then he'd take it home and plant it and make it grow. We only argued about *where* he planted things. Evidently, some things need sun, some things need shade, and Olivier felt that kind of thing was important.

'No, no, no. No one lets Olivier do this kind of repair; we know him too well. Junie? Where did you go?'

'I am here, sorry.'

'OK, so Laurent . . . him helping with the repair, and him not going on the flight at the last minute . . . this Brevard, he has had many questions for Laurent, and he is clearly suspicious of him. I felt you must know.'

I thought about this. Laurent helping me find Leo. So kind at Olivier's funeral. So guilty he was not on the flight. I didn't think he did it. It didn't feel right. And what possible motive could he have? To also kill the pilot? And hell, if he helped with the repair, he'd be an idiot to set it up this way. It put suspicion right on him. And Laurent was almost as smart as my husband.

But I did not like the doubt in my head. My gut said *be careful*. My brain said *ridiculous*. I tended to go with my gut but maybe I should just be . . . watchful.

'Junie, Laurent would never hurt Olivier. He and Laurent used to work together, before you and Olivier met. Olivier was a good friend to him, years ago, when his wife Violette died. You know about Violette?'

'I know. Olivier told me.'

'Tomorrow, you go to Laurent in Chamonix. Laurent is a good guy; he was devastated when Olivier died – you saw him at the funeral.'

I nodded. It was true.

'This Brevard, he came to Laurent a few days ago about the video, and Laurent told him everything he wanted to know. Laurent is pragmatic and was very honest with him. Junie? You still want to meet with Laurent tomorrow? This is still OK?'

I nodded. 'He knows the sightings, where Leo is. He knows

the trails around the Parc. So yes, I'd meet with the devil if it got me and Leo home.'

'Laurent is not the devil.'

I would meet with him tomorrow. I would make up my own mind.

Eugene looked away from me. 'He is not the same since Olivier died. None of us are, I guess. But you will be OK with him.'

I shrugged. I didn't want to think anymore. Grief wears you down, and I just wanted to put a blanket over my head and go to sleep.

Eugene put his hand over mine. 'Olivier talked about you so much. He loved you, Junie.'

'I know.'

But I was still thinking. Had the killer been after Olivier . . . or Laurent? Olivier was not supposed to be on the flight; it was a last-minute decision. Laurent was.

I thought then that Eugene had told me everything.

SIX

I was happy the next morning, up at five a.m., well before sunrise. I was going to find Leo. The sabotage, the malevolent stranger in the video footage – they changed nothing. Olivier was dead, I knew it, and that strange flicker of hope had burned out fast, then gone cold.

I knew better. I knew.

Today I would go to the forest by Parc de Merlet and I would find my dog. I had a quick hot shower under a trickling stream of water, and a bowl of thick black coffee with sugar, and then I gathered up everything I thought I would need. I admit it was a lot of stuff. I had planned carefully.

It would take me less than an hour to get to Laurent's place in Chamonix.

It was a pain getting everything down that tricky narrow staircase, my guitar and my little backpack with an extra sweater, treats for Leo, water. It was a short walk around the corner to the place we garaged the car. It was light enough now for me to see my way.

The alley, with its row of five wooden garages along one side, was not the most beautiful place in Annecy. There were weeds growing on the side of the pavement, which was cracked and crumbled in places. I stopped at the garage door that was second from the left. And froze.

The padlock was gone. Not open, or hanging, or smashed. Gone. I set my stuff down, grabbed the handle and pulled hard. The garage was narrow, the door heavy, the wood aging and splintered at the bottom, and it reminded me of the garage at my grandmother's old house in Danville, Kentucky.

Please, please, please.

I would not survive if our car was gone.

I lifted the heavy garage door, and there it was, and all of the tension in my shoulders melted, and I was once again able to breathe. I had brought the car back from Chamonix right after I had identified Olivier's body. Tucked it into the garage and had not been able to face driving it since. I had spent a fortune on hired cars.

This was Olivier's dream car. And Olivier was a terrible but enthusiastic driver, inciting furious shouts of *Belgian!* when we rambled along the backroads of France, which always puzzled me, because there were worse insults, surely. When I asked Olivier about it, he would give me that look of mischief and say, *What do you think it means, petite grenouille?* Which meant *Little Froggy*, which is what passes for flirting with a French engineer.

I had wanted another BMW Z3. I'd had an old one when I met Olivier, and he had loved it and promptly wrecked it. Then I had been cajoled and romanced to go along with Olivier's passion for the BMW Z4. Our first car together.

We had bought it to keep in France, where Olivier could get a switch installed to turn off the passenger-side airbag, so Leo would be safe riding shotgun.

This one was a beauty. Black, with a tan soft top, and caramel-colored heated leather seats, and Olivier made the ultimate and exquisitely painful compromise of ordering an automatic, not so easy in France. He had been teased about it. But he would smile slyly and say, *This is my wife's car; she just lets me drive it.* He had tried to teach me to drive a stick, but for the sake of our marriage, we had given that up. Not all things are possible.

Seeing the car made me happy, made me feel connected to my husband, as if I had been homesick and found my way back. I missed the life we had together, but I did still have the car. It was full of memories of the three of us bombing through Luxembourg. It was a two-seater, and Leo would sit in my lap, all one hundred pounds of him. He and Olivier had matching wraparound sunglasses.

I had sometimes felt a bit grumbly; I still preferred the Z3. But now . . . now I was glad I had gone ahead with the car Olivier loved. Glad it had made him so happy. I would drive it, and Leo would sit beside me. It would not be the same, but it would be good.

I clicked the lock on the key fob, relieved the car was still locked up tight, and piled everything into the trunk. My guitar I had put in the soft canvas bag, so if I laid it catty-cornered, it fit snugly and safe. Olivier was right: the trunk was superior to the Z3 trunk, which he would dismiss with a grimace as ridiculous. I slammed the lid shut, headed to the driver's side, and that is when I saw the bridal bouquet that had been carefully laid on the hood of the car.

I cursed and went very cold. I did not touch it.

It was the same. Just like the one I carried when Olivier and I got married. A small wedding in France, more like a dinner with friends that also included a marriage. The legal stuff we'd done the week before.

White roses, mixed with pink-blush roses, baby's breath. I picked it up carefully. The flowers were fresh. The white silk ribbon that trailed the flowers had picked up a smudge of dust from the hood of the car.

I sorted through the flowers gently, touching the soft petals with care, looking for the secret. The roses smelled sweet. They brought back memories; they made me sick to my stomach.

And they were there. *Les muguet.* Olivier's favorite flowers, the tiny delicate lily of the valley, so small and tucked so deeply that they could not even be seen in our wedding pictures. Not practical for the lapel of his sexy black tux, so we'd had them nestled softly in the middle of the bouquet. No one knew they were there but the two of us and the florist.

I took a hard breath. I gritted my teeth. This was a ten on the scale of creepy and fucked up. And I thought of the malevolent stranger who'd been holding my dog on a rope.

Bastard. I did not know why I was so sure it was him, but it made a creepy sort of sense. It certainly wasn't my husband.

I slammed the bouquet into the garbage pail Olivier had set up in the corner, empty now for months. Backed the car out carefully, fingers trembling. The alarm of the car chimed as I shut the garage door, leaving the driver's door wide, the engine running.

I found Olivier's old gray sweater in the trunk of the car. I snuggled into it, folding the sleeves back. Tucked my hair up into the ball cap that was on the passenger's seat, the old green one with the embroidered picture of a German Shepherd in a scarf on the front. I had given it as a gift to Olivier, then promptly stolen it. It was cold out, so I put the top down and turned the heat up full blast.

I would focus only on Leo. Not creepy bouquets, sabotaged safety bolts, planes on fire, Olivier's ravaged skin.

SEVEN

Laurent Valiente was not the man I remembered. If I saw him in a café, I might not know him.

Grandfather Spanish, grandmother American, met in France after WWII, and stayed. His parents were French.

It had only been four months since I saw him last.

Laurent's *petite maison* in Chamonix had begun life as a small barn, which he had converted himself after his wife died twelve years ago. They had spent holidays in Chamonix, away from their home in Dijon, and had found the land and the barn on a cross-country ski ramble and dreamed about buying it and converting the barn into their own snug space. A holiday home.

Violette had died suddenly, a traffic accident, and I knew that Laurent's friends had been worried about him after her death, the same way that mine now worried about me.

Two weeks after Violette's death, Laurent had bought the land and spent every spare moment converting the barn. His friends had been baffled and worried, but Olivier had told me he admired Laurent.

'He takes the rubble of his heart and creates a beautiful thing.'

It was a beautiful place. At the end of a narrow road, in an open space of tall green grass, thick woods on both sides, and in the distance . . . Mont Blanc.

Laurent came out of the front door as I parked the Z4, and he froze, standing on the wide wood planks of the front porch he had built.

And the look he gave me. As if he was meeting me for the first time but had known me always. Italians call it the thunderbolt. *Colpo di fulmine.* Love at first sight. In French, they say *le coup de foudre.* I had to be misreading this.

I held tight to the open car door. I felt numb. Wary.

He had changed so much. A handsome man, still. Tall,

strong shoulders, trim before, thin now. Thick dark hair waving over his collar had more gray now than black. The face was drawn and tight, cheeks hollow, and he had lost weight and muscle tone. The in-your-face confidence had faltered.

We stared at each other.

'Eugene told me everything,' I said. So much for subtlety. Olivier had loved it when I actually said what was on my mind.

Laurent nodded. 'He told me he would.'

This was a very French moment. Everyone speaking their mind. It could not happen in the US, not in the South, where I was from.

Laurent held out a hand. 'Come in please, Junie. Together, we will find Leo.' He came forward and pulled me close, a kiss on one cheek, then the other. He kept hold of my hand as he pulled me through the doorway.

All the wary suspicion that had kept me up the night before dissolved in a wave of guilt. Laurent had been my husband's close friend for years. He was my friend now.

EIGHT

nside the cabin, it was all open space. A heavy command post of a desk and computer beside the front door. A massive stone fireplace stretched across the back wall, flanked by windows on either side. In the corner, a steep open staircase, leading up to a loft.

Tile floors, worn throw rugs, stacks of books and papers on the desk.

The kitchen was to the far left, a mix of rough charm and compact pragmatic Euro attitude. A convection cooktop, which made me grimace. At home, I had a nonstop love affair with my sturdy Wolf gas range. Olivier said I bought it for the bright red knobs, and that might be true.

At the far right and a step up was a bedroom. Low platform bed, very French, bleached blonde wood with a thin mattress, and I remembered squabbling with Olivier over the bed in our apartment in Annecy. He had told me I was like the princess in a fairy tale, *The Princess and the Pea*, needing a stack of thick mattresses to get a good night's sleep. I said thank you for understanding, and he laughed. Our bed there was so high we'd had to tuck an ottoman on one side so Leo could jump up and sleep at our feet.

Laurent waved a hand toward the huge oak desk, circa 1950s. And along the wall to one side, a map full of push pins in two colors. Black and yellow. One that was red.

I headed over, studied the map. Touched that one red pin.

'Olivier's crash site?'

'Yes, Junie, place of origin. The hunt for Leo started there.'

'Why the different colors?'

'Black for the sightings of Leo after Olivier's crash. Then, you observe, he was not seen for a while, and you had to go home. This, I think, is when *le connard* in the video found him and took him. It is why we did not find him.'

'I thought he was dead. I was going to come back anyway just in case.'

'Yes, me, too, I thought he was gone. And we must find him, Junie, before the winter sets in. And we will do that. Eugene told you? That Leo has been spotted two times since he was with *le connard*. I have a friend on the staff at the Parc, Ailene Banville. She gave me drone footage of the last two sightings. She could not give me the footage of Leo with *le connard* – the police have told her not to show it – but you have sent it to Eugene, and he has sent it to me.' He hesitated. 'There is another thing I must tell you.'

I put my hands over my face. 'Good God, what now?'

He shook his head and gently pushed me toward the chair at the desk. 'You see, someone has put the video the police showed to you on YouTube, and it is now all over the place. The heading is this: *Man Killed in Plane Crash – GHOST OR FAKED DEATH?*'

I sat down hard. Tried to catch my breath. And the fury rose inside me and made my hands shake. 'The man is not Olivier. They need to leave me alone. Leave Olivier alone. *This is a private thing.*'

Laurent's look was stricken. 'I understand. Maybe you should not watch this. The one that has been posted, it is not exactly like the one Eugene sent me – in this one, the man looks more like Olivier. There is software for this, you know – the deepfake. I wanted to warn you.'

'Does Eugene know?'

'Yes. He says he did not tell you; it was too much for you last night. He called me after you talked.'

So that was why he hesitated last night.

'This video, Junie – it is getting many hits here in Chamonix and Mont Blanc. It has spread to the hiking community, and now it is viral all over France, Italy and Great Britain.'

'When did it go live?'

'Twelve hours ago.'

So after my call with Capitaine Brevard. Posted while I was on my way to France. I leaned against the wall. 'I don't know what to do with this.'

'You do nothing. And please, try not to look at it. You and

me, we will find Leo. I will ask Brevard to have this taken down, but, of course, that might come better from you.'

I chewed my bottom lip. 'Did your friend at the Parc put this up?'

'No, I think it was the man in the original. The man who took Leo. I know who he is.'

'*What?*'

'Yes, I know him, he is Charl St Priest; he worked with both me and Olivier two years ago, and I have told this to Brevard.'

'I know that name. *I know that name.* Isn't that . . . isn't that the guy that gave Olivier hell when he would not fire the engineer whose wife had breast cancer?'

Laurent nodded. '*Oui.* And St Priest was the big manager, so he had Olivier fired. And then there was a big heat and St Priest was demoted.'

And then I remembered. It would have played out very differently in the US. An engineer on a project whose wife was ill with breast cancer, who had missed weeks of work. The cancer had gone to her brain, and he was taking her to a specialist in Paris for a Hail Mary treatment. They had a five-year-old son. It was a US company, located in France, and he was an American worker, not protected like the locals. Olivier had been ordered to fire him, and Olivier had refused and caused a huge stink, and Charl, his high-up French boss who made the order to fire this engineer, had been busted down to Project Manager from Plant Manager, and was lucky to keep his job at all. Olivier, working as a consultant, was dismissed, and it was the last time he agreed to work for Americans.

'Good God, Laurent, that guy hates Olivier.'

'Yes, and he became very disliked locally after that business with the wife, who died three weeks later. They could not save her. And, of course, he did a flip-over. He got very weird about your husband, and told everyone that Olivier was right and he admired him and—'

'God, Laurent, stop. I don't want to . . . I want to find my dog. I can't think about this right now.'

'*D'accord.* Take this out of your head, OK? For now, Junie, let me show you the footage of Leo. I have two sightings to show you. Both here.' He pointed to the yellow pins. 'All on a trail that is right by the little road up to the *Le Parc Merlet*.'

'So he is staying in one place.' My hands were shaking. I twisted them together in my lap.

'It's a very big place. But it is an animal sanctuary, so it makes sense he would stay close. And everyone has been watching for him. Let me show you.'

He pulled the desk chair out for me. It was black leather, with no wheels on it, which I liked. Olivier and I got rid of all our rolling desk chairs; they were a danger to Leo's paws when he settled by our feet, which was always. Laurent leaned over me and touched the keyboard, and the first video began.

'This is the road to *Le Parc Merlet*. You see there, to the right. It is dusk and hard to see.'

It was late afternoon, the sun going down; a car was parked to one side of the road. I could see a shadow in the trees, and I looked hard, and I felt my stomach go tight and a sort of happy pressure in my chest. Yes, it was Leo. Looking out to the roadway. Watchful in that Shepherd way. I knew in my heart he was looking for me.

Then people came down the road, making noise and laughing. Leo looked up and took off. Limping a little, the swollen psoas muscle in his left hip area as usual. The rope had broken and was now about a foot long, hanging off his shoulder. Either that or he had chewed through it.

I laughed a little and brushed a tear off my cheek. 'Sweet boy.' I touched the screen.

Laurent touched the keyboard. 'Here is another. This one is the most recent.'

At first, I did not see him. The mountain of Mont Blanc on the horizon, green with trees, snow on top. The grass was high, a slope to the left, a trail, and trees to the right.

'I can't find him. Where is he?'

Laurent froze the screen, leaning close. I could smell the scent he used, faint, masculine. 'In the shadow there – see, on the left, by those three trees? His coat is like camouflage.'

'Ah, OK.' A gray ghost beside the trees. 'It's Leo. Look, enlarge that. You can see his collar. And that damn rope around his neck.'

Laurent nodded and pulled a chair up beside me at the desk, one hand on the back of my chair.

'How long ago were these taken?'

'That one there? Five days ago. It's the latest. And I know that spot. I can show you. They also think they have seen him near the fence, after hours, close to the gate. He would smell food from the restaurant, the trash cans. It would make sense. They are coming back, the wolves – do you know this?'

'Yes, Capitaine Brevard told me.'

'They are attacking animals, killing sheep; it is getting dangerous. So the Parc staff, they have trail cams, and this is why they were getting drone footage. The wolves cannot get in, but still they keep an eye out. And they have been watching out for Leo since the footage with St Priest.'

I nodded. 'OK, this is good. I need to go and get him. Can you—'

'Yes. I know the place and I will take you there and show you. I have the trap ready.'

The trap. A kennel with food inside, the door triggered to shut when Leo went after the food. Experts had told me to do this, but it had not worked, and I'd had doubts from the beginning. I didn't know what else to do. But anyone who knows Shepherds would know better. They are suspicious of food they don't already know and would be too suspicious to go into a kennel that was strange. We'd tried traps; they never worked. Trying to force a Shepherd could backfire. A trap would be just as likely to make him stay away. Shepherds did better with some autonomy. All dogs do.

'No trap, Laurent.'

He frowned at me.

'Look, I appreciate all the advice from dog handlers and all the rescue people, and those St Bernard breeders – they're all very smart, compassionate, and they know dogs. They do. I appreciate how they have been looking out for Leo, and looking out for me. But I know my dog. The traps have not worked, I don't think Leo will go in even for the food.'

'But maybe it is because *le connard* had him. That he never went into a trap.'

'Maybe. But he's a Shepherd. They're curious, but also,

even more, they are suspicious. Of everything. Of food and people they don't know. Of anything that is different from what they're used to. They like order and routine. They like to supervise. Leo won't take treats from anyone he does not know, and sometimes he won't take them from me till he's had time to check it over and think it through.'

Laurent nodded. 'OK, I see that. When he and Olivier stayed with me, it took a while before he would take food from me; even then, it had to be cheese. And that was only when Olivier was there to vouch for me.'

'Exactly. So we try this my way. Take me to that place where he was last seen.'

'What, are you going to sit and wait for him?'

I nodded. 'Every day. If I'm there, he'll pick up my scent. If we're lucky.'

'He may have gone feral, Junie, now he has been on his own.'

'Which is why he has to come to me. We have a scent bond. He'll know me that way. So I will go to a place he knows and is comfortable with. I will have Camembert cheese and beef jerky, both of which he loves, and he will pick up the scent of the cheese and of me. And I will play the guitar, and he will hear my music and know me that way, too.'

He frowned. 'How loud can you play? It seems like a long shot, Junie.'

'If there is one thing I trust, it's my dog. This is not about me finding Leo. This is about Leo finding me. He is going to be on the job, Laurent. He is going to be looking.'

NINE

I know why Olivier loved this countryside. Early October in the forests of Chamonix, sixty-six degrees Fahrenheit. I could see the fog-shrouded mountainside of Mont Blanc from where I sat, tucked under a handful of spruce trees, about three hundred feet into the forest. It was cold there, up on the mountainside. I could see snow on the peaks.

I was trying not to get my hopes up, but that wasn't working.

The Parc was closed for the season, winter was imminent, and the twisty narrow road up the mountain that Laurent and I had taken that morning would be treacherous if it snowed.

Laurent had driven me in and walked the trail with me, to show me the exact spot. He was reluctant to leave, but he had to work, and Leo was more likely to come if it was only me. Because he was right. Dogs can go feral when they are lost. There are times they don't recognize their owners. I would text Laurent when I was ready to leave, and he would come to pick me up.

I settled into the grass, propped against a tree. I kept my sweater on, one of Olivier's old ones; it was chilly in the shade, late in the morning. The air was crisp.

I wandered a bit and called out for Leo, and trampled around, but there was no sign of him. So I settled back in, opened the foil-wrapped Camembert that Leo loved, hoping he was close. Hoping the scent would bring him in.

I took my guitar out of the case, held it close to my heart and played. And thought of Leo. Leo who loved to curl up beside me when I practiced. Leo who loved my music. Leo who had a song of his very own. I played for three hours straight.

I am here. Come home to me.

Five hours later, the guitar snug in a soft bag, I settled back in once again at the foot of the trees. I had wandered, and circled, and called Leo's name. I had seen a mother and two adolescent roe deer off in the distance, which did not seem to me a good sign. Would they be so calm with Leo close? And yet they barely reacted to me.

It was not hard for me to wait, to be still. Before Olivier died, it would have been agony. These days, I spent long stretches of time sitting quietly, lost in my thoughts. I almost never remembered what I thought about.

And every now and then I got up, looked around, called Leo's name.

But Leo did not come. And the thought of going home to my empty house in the US without him, touching that leash hanging from the hook every time I went out . . . I didn't think I could do that anymore.

I would not go home without him.

If he did not come, well . . . the mountains were cold, I could get lost easily and curl up in the snow. The terrain of Mont Blanc frightened me. It was beautiful, brutal, harsh. So I would come here, to this coven of trees, when it was cold and snowy. Spend the day hoping Leo would come, and if not . . . go to sleep by the trees and not wake up. It only took an hour and a half to die of hypothermia, huddled alone in the snow. Sometimes not nearly that long.

I waited until dusk. The wind was coming up. I would be back tomorrow. I reached for my phone to text Laurent, then saw him, through the trees, coming to find me.

TEN

Laurent was much like a German Shepherd himself, the way he supervised me. He had a strong stride, and he ran a hand through the thick gray-black hair that curled over the top of his collar.

I grabbed my guitar, packed up my backpack and stood up slowly, back stiff and achy. The sun was going down, and it caught me through a gap in the trees. I felt the heat of it, bathing my face in light. I came out of the trees, and Laurent lifted a hand. He'd been watching me.

'No luck, Madame?'

I shook my head. I was going home without Leo. I did not want to leave. 'Did I miss your text?'

'No, I wanted to come and get you before it got dark.'

I bit my lip. If I tried to talk, I would cry. I wanted to find Leo *today*. I did not want to leave if he was there somewhere.

Laurent's look was kind. 'We will come back tomorrow, and he will come then. You told me he would find you and he will. He has maybe a girlfriend now. A wolf *femme* from Switzerland. Named Francine.'

I smiled. I couldn't help it. Laurent took the backpack and the guitar, and we headed down the path.

'Why Francine? That's not a Swiss name.'

'No, but it is what her *maman* named her. And they had babies. Three of them. All girls. And Leo, he will come to you tomorrow with Francine and the three pups, and we will pile them all in my car and take them home to dinner. And speaking of dinner, I hope you are hungry because I have cooked for you the *tartiflette*. You like the *tartiflette*?'

'I have seen it on every menu in Annecy, but I always get the mussels.'

'Potatoes, bacon, cheese. Baked. With bread and wine and salad and little pickles. You don't have the *tartiflette* in the US?'

'No, but we have barbecue. It sounds awesome, but you don't have to cook me dinner, Laurent.'

He shrugged. 'It is cooked already, so you will come and you will eat it.'

And while we walked, he told me stories of Leo and Francine and how the three puppies had tried to hunt a marmot, which was why Leo was busy today and did not come. But tomorrow . . . tomorrow they would come.

ELEVEN

I hesitated once we got to Laurent's place. He got out of the car and gave me a quizzical smile over one shoulder.

'Come in, Junie. I will build us a fire; it will be cold tonight.'

'It's a long drive back to Annecy. I should go, Laurent.'

'Dinner first. You are hungry?'

I was starved. 'OK, thanks then.'

I followed him in. It was warm inside, the desk cluttered, and I could see he'd been deep in his work today. Papers were stacked, some had fallen to the floor, and I had the sense of a man who had worked in frenzied frustration. Or maybe he was just messy. Dishes were piled in the sink and on the countertops, and I could smell the bacon, onions and cheese bubbling in the oven.

'It smells amazing in here.'

Laurent veered into the kitchen and opened the oven door. 'Another fifteen minutes and it will be ready.'

I tucked my guitar next to the backpack. Laurent waved a hand at the battered leather couch, and I sat on the edge, wishing I was already at the apartment in Annecy where I could take a long hot shower and curl up with a blanket. I was getting that feeling I always got since Olivier died. The need to be alone.

The fire was already laid, and Laurent lit a long match to a fire stick. The flame caught and took hold, and the wood crackled, and Laurent stood up and dusted his hands off.

'A glass of wine?'

I nodded. He opened a bottle of Gigondas. 'Every time we go out, you and me and Olivier and Eugene, you order red. Even with mussels.' He gave me a puzzled look over his shoulder. 'So we will go with the red.' He poured two glasses and sat beside me on the couch. He raised his glass.

'To Olivier. And to Leo, who will be here with us tomorrow night, eating leftover *tartiflette*.'

'To Olivier. And to Leo. And to *tartiflette*.'

I took a sip of wine and leaned back into the couch and sighed. I would limit myself to half a glass. I was dreading the drive back.

Laurent touched my shoulder. 'It has been a long day for you. Let me put the dinner out.' I followed him into the kitchen, watching as he bent down and took a bright yellow dish out of the oven, cheese bubbling and browned across the top. He set it on a thick pad in the center of the table, a rough wood farm table, the kind I had wanted for our apartment in Annecy.

'*Et voilà, Madame*. Please sit.' He circled behind me and pulled out my chair. He scooped some of the tart on to my plate and added three tiny pickles. He pulled a chunk off the bread and set it on the table beside my plate, and refilled my glass of wine.

I ran a finger around the rim of my wine glass. 'Thank you for this, Laurent.'

He was helping himself to tart, and he gave me a look. 'It is good to have you here. It took me some time to get used to eating alone, after my wife died. You know about Violette? Olivier told you?'

'Yes. Twelve years ago, wasn't it?'

'It was thirteen years last month. We were very much in love.' He gave me a steady look across the table. 'You are always going to miss him, Junie.'

'It doesn't get better?' I asked softly.

'Grief is love, and love does not go away. This is a forever pain. I am sorry. But . . . you somehow get used to it. People say to you stupid things, like move on, because they don't understand, and we must hope for their sake that they never will.'

'But you haven't been alone all this time. You have a steady girlfriend, don't you?'

'*Non*. That was over last year. I have tried, several times, but nothing has worked for me. But it has been OK, just not serious. I am open to it, and so should you be.'

'I am still so in love with Olivier.'

He nodded and took a bite. 'Of course, yes. Like me with Violette.' He shrugged. 'It does not mean with one you can't have the other.'

'Yes, so I've been told – like adding a new dog to the pack.'

He laughed. 'Yes, that is perfect. Do you talk to Olivier in your head?'

'All the time. You talk to Violette?'

He nodded.

'It doesn't stop?'

'Why should it? We are connected, she and I. Sometimes I even see her, slipping ahead of me in the woods when I walk.'

'I saw Olivier the night he died. I haven't told anybody. But he came to me and kissed me goodbye and told me he loved me. And he was wearing his old brown bomber jacket—'

Laurent's eyes widened. 'Junie, I will show you something.'

He jumped up and went to his desk, scrolled for a moment on his phone, then handed it to me. 'See? This was taken the morning of . . . the morning.'

Two dudes and a selfie. Olivier with that look of mischief in his eyes, smiling right at the camera, and Laurent was laughing about something. Laurent was in a loose white shirt and Olivier was kitted out in his bomber jacket, a gray scarf around his neck, the three-day growth of beard, and I took the phone and studied it. 'He was dressed exactly like that the night he . . .' I looked up at Laurent who was watching me. 'You think I'm crazy, right?'

He shook his head. 'No, Madame. I know he came to you. I know what this is like.'

'She comes to you, Violette? Still, after thirteen years?'

He hesitated. 'Not as often. But yes, she still comes.' He reached out and brushed the tears off my cheeks. 'Come back to dinner, I have made for you a *mousse au chocolat.*'

'I would love a *mousse au chocolat.*'

'You will have it, Madame, but first you must eat your tart and one pickle at least. Come, come, we are OK. And soon we will have Leo.'

*   *   *

The tartelette was perfect, the melted cheese soft and gooey, piquant.

Laurent soaked up the sauce with a chunk of bread and gave me a sideways look. 'I keep waiting for you to ask me, Junie.'

I studied another pickle and decided yes, one more. 'Ask you what?'

'About Olivier. And what happened to his plane.'

I shrugged. 'It's kind of a hard thing to bring up.'

'You do not have the poker face, Junie. Your thoughts are all over your face.'

I fiddled with the rim of my wine glass. 'Who do you think would do that? Sabotage Olivier's plane. This man Charl St Priest? Eugene said they . . . had suspicions of you, but it's ridiculous to think you would . . .' I grimaced. Articulate as always. 'You know. And I got the impression that there was something going on with that Mont Blanc safety evaluation.'

He frowned. 'Olivier's report was done; his consulting company had already turned it over to the client, so it's nothing to do with that.'

'But then why . . . why would someone go after Olivier? Why would St Priest go that far and wait this long? This does not make sense to me.'

'I do not think this was intended for Olivier. I think this was intended for both of us.'

I remembered his guilt at the funeral. And now that fell into place.

'You see, Junie, initially, only I was supposed to be on that plane, not Olivier. I was trying to recruit him to work with my NGO. Your husband . . . he had a way of seeing things, you know? Olivier was brilliant at analyzing outcomes, seeing what is now and what is possible. I had been trying to get him to come to work with me as a consultant for years. He told you about this?'

I nodded. 'He was always interested in working with you. He was so impressed when you started this up. But—'

'Yes,' he said with a grimace. 'The disagreement. On technology. Using blue hydrogen processes as a bridge to the green hydrogen processes. He always disagreed with that. And it turns out he was right all along. Sometimes I think Olivier could see the future. So this time we talked, we resolved the issues, and he was on board. With one condition. As soon as that got worked out, he was in.'

'He didn't tell me that.'

'It was not yet official.'

'What was the condition?'

'No more involvement with the group of oil and gas company investors represented by Charl St Priest.'

'*Oh God*. You work with that guy? After everything that happened with Olivier?'

'St Priest brought a lot of funding in. Believe me, it is huge, the investment money from gas and oil companies – something it would have been crazy for me to step away from. And their reason is to push blue hydrogen tech and infrastructure. At the time, I agreed with St Priest on this. You cannot like everyone you do business with.'

'But you have enough funding now to ditch him?'

Laurent shook his head. 'No, that is not the reason. I cannot accept his funding because he represents the blue hydrogen tech; he would expect me to keep pushing that as I have in the past. And I can no longer work toward anything but green hydrogen processes. This is not about the personal grudge with St Priest and Olivier. St Priest is a very smart man, and he understands the issues. But we disagree now, and I am in the process of cutting them loose. I can no longer use my influence that way.'

'Did St Priest know about the flight?'

'Yes. He already knew that I have been going up on those flights regularly for the last twelve years. To track and take pictures of changes in the glaciers, charting the melting, and I have done many flights, to go from the air, to look at the terrain. And this time, Olivier wanted to go, too. You know how he loved the mountains. He had already been looking at pictures I took, some drone footage, and analyzing metallurgy results from a lab.

'Only two people knew we were going up that day. The pilot, when I made arrangements – she and I have been doing this for years, and we were friends – and St Priest. He knew when I was going up, he knew about the flights I take; I have included some of the information I have gathered in my work with them. No one else knew. And then I could not go. It was an accident that I was not on the plane. I am so very sorry, Junie.' He shredded a chunk of bread. 'Whoever did this, they wanted to take both of us out. So it has to be something with the NGO, and St Priest is the obvious one. He tells somebody something he should not have or he is behind it himself.'

'And Capitaine Brevard, he knows this?'

'He knows.'

'And how exactly was it that you were not on the plane?'

He froze. 'A last-minute business call, for a presentation in Metz. For the climate change talks. It was essential to handle it immediately; we were looking to get a grant. It is a lot of money. And we were about to lose big money funding from St Priest's group of investors, so we needed it. Though I promise you, the money for the green hydrogen processes is getting enormous.'

'OK.' I broke off a piece of bread but did not eat it. 'Has Brevard said anything to you about this St Priest? His obsession with Olivier. That he knew about the flight. I mean, he did that insane deepfake video with Leo and put it up on YouTube – why haven't they arrested him already?'

'I agree with you that St Priest is involved, and I told this to Capitaine Brevard, and he asked a lot of questions and took a lot of notes, and so far nothing has happened. But I know this takes time. And posting the video after Olivier is dead? I think that has to be aimed at you. To get you here to look for your dog. It is not yet proven it was St Priest who posted it, but I think, of course, it was.'

'Why would he want *me* here? Although—' I told Laurent about the wedding bouquet on the hood of my car. That I thought St Priest put it there.

'How would he know you are here? The only ones who know are me, Eugene and Brevard. Unless St Priest was watching for you.' He frowned. 'Be careful, Junie.'

'I'm not going back home, if that's what you're thinking. I'm going to find Leo.'

He nodded and waved a hand toward his desk. 'I have been spending my days trying to figure this out. Even if St Priest goes after me and Olivier, how does that involve you? And I am thinking it is because, for St Priest, it is not enough to go after Olivier; he must also be after you. He has always had a very strange fixation on Olivier, and now that we are pushing his investors out of the NGO . . . it makes him furious, and that makes him worse. I am sorry, but I am worried about this. The NGO, me and Olivier, and you. All of this is mixed up together.'

'What are you working on that would cause so much trouble? Why don't they just take their investment money somewhere else? It can't be that hard to give money away.'

'Invest, Junie, not give. There is a big return for them. NGOs influence all the powerful people in the Brussels Bubble, and that is where the power is. These are the rich and influential people. They go to school together, they live in the same neighborhoods, and their thinking is lockstep together. We have a strong influence on these people, and they set policy – this is expected and accepted. I have been a big help to St Priest's investors. Now I am a threat.'

'How so?'

'This is a big climate change issue with carbon emissions and hydrogen. When I started out twelve years ago, after Violette's death, I was looking to find a way to transform the hydrogen process. It is crucial for steel mills, and the world is always hungry for steel, but the carbon emissions from making the hydrogen itself, and from using it to make steel, are huge. To make green hydrogen without using fossil fuels would reduce carbon emissions hugely in two ways – the making of the hydrogen itself and the making of the steel. Back when I was starting out twelve years ago, the debate was about using blue or green hydrogen. Green means no fossil fuels, so it is very clean. Blue uses fossil fuels in the process of making the hydrogen, and so causes almost as many emissions as it saves, and also there is so much leakage involved, which escalates emissions even more. So the thinking was to use blue hydrogen as a bridge to the green, which at the time had an astronomical expense. I thought then that blue hydrogen was the way to phase in the green.'

'Is this what you and Olivier disagreed on? Because I think I remember him talking about this, a long time ago. The green and the blue.'

Laurent nodded. 'Exactly that. Olivier's point was that using the blue hydrogen processes locked in the infrastructure for thirty years or more, and it allowed the gas and oil companies to do business as usual while appearing to be green. This is big money to them. No emission fines, no angry public, and they can make their money the same as always. And it is a lot of money, Junie.'

'And money is trouble, I get that. But . . . forgive me, this is only one NGO. Are you so very influential?'

'This is the EU. In your country, they influence with lobbyists. Here, the NGOs are seen as part of the . . . the civil contract. The moral side. It is an accepted thing, the influence we have, which cannot be underestimated. This affects government policy, laws, and it directs the way the money is spread around. And it turns out that Olivier was right all along. Before, it seemed like it would be decades before green hydrogen processes would be economical or efficient enough to work. But in the last two years . . . the tech is moving so fast that there are green energy hydrogen plants all over the EU. And all over the world, investors are pulling back from blue. Germany now has a policy of zero investment in blue. Right now, green hydrogen, to the investors, is looking like the opportunity of a lifetime – to get in on the ground floor and make huge sums of money while being on the side of the good guys in climate change. They are ecstatic.

'And St Priest's investors, they are on the side of the oil and gas companies who don't want to go with green, and they are scrambling hard. This is a war, Junie. You understand that? And they've made a lot of progress, and they have great power and influence – keep that in mind. In the US – West Virginia, the Gulf Coast and California – they are putting in the structure for the blue hydrogen, even with everything we know now. It is insane. And in the long run, the emissions are going to be worse than what is in place right now, *not better.*

And this infrastructure they are building locks them into blue hydrogen for decades.' He laughed, but it did not sound happy. 'And to do this, they pull in government monies, and everyone pats them on the back.'

This I understood. 'Greenwashing. It's brutal in the US. I thought it was better in the EU.'

Laurent nodded. 'Olivier used to call this your ridiculous faith in France.' But he was smiling at me. I could sense the energy and excitement he felt. 'I am going to stay in the fight on this, Junie. Only now I am on the right side.'

'What a thing this would have been, the two of you together.'

'We had such plans. To give companies a process timeline to gradually phase this in. Specific targets and a cost–benefit analysis. And to be there to consult when things get snarled up, which is always going to happen in manufacturing.' He rubbed his face with his hand. 'I promise you. After what happened to Olivier, I will fight that much harder. Because this is what keeps me going after losing Violette. Without it, I am nothing.'

I smiled at him and tried not to cry. I understood him completely.

TWELVE

We curled up on the couch for *mousse au chocolat*, and Laurent sat close to me. He made me feel safe.

He chuckled. 'You would not have pictured this, that first night, when we met at Chez Eugene.'

That was true. I had loathed him on sight. 'You stared at me and called me Barbie with a Guitar.'

He nodded. 'A terrible thing to say. I am sorry. I admit I was jealous.'

I thought about that. 'Of me and Olivier?'

'Yes, the two of you were so connected, even when you squabbled. It made me miss Violette, and I took it out on you. Olivier, he talked to me quietly in private, after that night. He said he understood my feelings, but I must not disrespect his wife. *You will not talk to my wife that way –* that's how he put it, and he was right.'

'I didn't know that. He never told me.'

Laurent nodded. 'He did not wish to embarrass me. But he was right, and I decided I could not be so angry, that I must see it as a beautiful thing. And now . . . oh, Junie, I am so very sorry this happened to you.'

I nodded. I had no yearning for anyone's relationship but my own.

'Olivier said you compose music?'

'I hear it in my head, so I write it down. I thought it might stop . . . the music I heard, when Olivier died. But just the opposite. I have not written so much music in my life. It comes to me in waves, one after the other. And it's the only time now that I am OK.'

He nodded and studied me. 'When did you start playing?'

'When I was seven. I had wanted a guitar since I was five, the moment I saw one, because I knew it was for me. It took me two years to talk my parents into buying me one. I also wanted a horse.'

'Did you get one?'

'Not yet.'

Laurent reached for the wine bottle.

I put a hand over my glass. 'I have to drive.'

'Tonight? *Non*. It is too far, this late; you can just stay here, and we'll get up early to go find Leo.'

'I told you, Leo will find me.' I had not been a good girl. I had had two glasses of wine, and I did not have great night vision. 'I can get a hotel.'

'Don't do that. It's late and cold, and we have this nice fire. You can have my bed. It is comfortable, my bed, and I will sleep on the couch and watch the fire die down.'

'I can't let you sleep on the couch. You're too tall – your feet will hang over.'

He shook his head and smiled at me. 'You will take the bed and not worry about my long legs.'

I love French men. It would never occur to them that they might not be right. 'OK, I'll take the bed. You are very kind, and I'm dead on my feet.'

And then . . . it happened again. That sick dread in the pit of my stomach, where everyone and everything around me felt wrong. Like I was Other. Not a part of the world anymore . . . just a ghost, haunting a life I used to have. The panic. The need to run, to get away.

There was no logic to this. It happened when I went to the grocery store. When I saw friends, had dinner with my brothers, Chris and his husband, Redmond. It happened when I went for a walk and people tried to say hello. There was no trying to analyze, no point in getting tied up with internal arguments. For me, now, there was nothing but gut instinct.

'*I have to go.*'

Laurent froze and pulled back. Studied me. 'I have done something wrong? If you really want the couch—'

'No, it's not that. I can't explain what I don't understand. *But I have to go.*'

Laurent nodded, and the open, smiling man retreated and turned serious. He helped me pack my guitar, my knapsack . . . I always had so much stuff. We loaded my car together,

and I gritted my teeth as we exchanged *bises*. I needed to go,
I needed to run; I could not be here anymore.

I breathed easier as soon as I pulled away in the darkness,
safe in my car. I pulled over and put on Olivier's sweater and
ballcap, turned the heat on full blast. I was no longer sleepy.
I felt sober and relieved and free, because solitude was my
comfort now, and I could only take people in small doses
before I had to get away. I wondered if I would be this way
forever. I didn't much care.

I drove home slowly, to the apartment in Annecy, in no
particular hurry, no sense of any place I had to be or any place
I belonged. My old life was falling away.

THIRTEEN

Today was colder in the woods near the Parc, and I snuggled into my sweater and huddled close to the base of a spruce tree. Everything was going according to plan. I had been texting with Laurent. He had taken my panicked exit last night in stride. Reminded me that he understood better than anyone, no offense taken, and did I need him to come with me today? I had turned him down; his presence might keep Leo away. He had asked exactly where I was and said to call if I needed him. The connection we had made me feel a little less alone, and I finally understood why he and Olivier had been close friends for so long.

It scared me how deep his grief was for Violette, and it comforted me, too. I didn't want to lose my grief for Olivier, and I did not want to face a future without him. His death had been a fast track to wisdom, and I knew what I wanted in life and that was Olivier and Leo and my music. I stopped thinking about the future because I did not want one. Life without Olivier? No.

I was a hot mess, and I knew it.

I'd been a hot mess when I met Olivier, too. I'd been cautious and wary, but there was a part of me that had known he was my guy from the moment I met him. The first time he had seen me, he looked stunned, and then he had smiled, so shyly and so warmly that I had taken a step backward. It took me a while to accept it was real, this connection. I had pushed him away in a panic more than once, but he had pursued relentlessly, and he was gentle, and he made me laugh, and he had no patience for throwing happiness away. When we took a crazy, impulse trip to Key West on our third date, we came back squabbling and laughing as if we'd been together since forever.

And Laurent . . . he had changed since my husband died.

Olivier's death had hit him hard. Perhaps because it so easily could have been his own.

For myself, I had one goal. Find Leo. Nothing else mattered, except those hours when I tucked myself around my guitar and lived in the music. If I could have Leo and play my guitar, I could make that a life.

I refused to be afraid of hope, not when it came to Leo. I opened the packages of the Camembert and salami that Leo loved. Leo had quite the nose for following scents, and the smell of salami would find him if he were as far away as Switzerland.

It was good weather for scenting, and Shepherds were gifted animals. He could find a scent nose to the ground, or circle and scent the air, allowing him to find an old scent that would lead him to a fresh one. Because Leo did not just have talent; he had brains.

Yesterday, I had tramped the trail to and from the parking lot of the Parc. This morning, before I'd left the house, I'd squeezed the cheese through my fingers, lacing my smell with the scent of the cheese, and though I'd washed my hands three times, the smell of the Camembert was still there. I might have to replace my guitar strings later.

And it was fall. A good time for picking up scents. The undergrowth was not as thick, and the ground was cooler than the air.

Dogs have a second nose, Jacobson's organ, located at the bottom of their nasal passage, honed to pick up pheromones. And a German Shepherd has 225 million scent receptors, compared to five to ten million for humans. The olfactory bulb in the canine brain is four times larger than in humans. Dogs pick up scents up to a hundred times better than we do.

Shepherds can track a human scent carried by the wind for days. I was counting on that. A front was moving in, and rain was predicted for late in the night. A bit of drizzle. A little wind. Today would be perfect. And Leo and I had a scent bond.

Come find me, Leo. Come find me.

FOURTEEN

By mid-afternoon, the temperature was dropping, and I could smell the rain. Mont Blanc was wreathed in smoky gray clouds. I huddled under my spruce tree and held the guitar close, my cheek resting on the curve of the wood. Olivier said my hearing loss had made my music better. He thought it was because of the way I had to wrap myself around the guitar now, feeling the vibration of the music, not just hearing it, but feeling it with my body and soul. He had smiled at me so big, as if my hearing loss was the best of good news. *You wrap yourself around the guitar like a lover, and the music you play is more beautiful now, more pure.*

And I had embraced it. The beautiful imperfection of my life. The new depths of play, letting it change my technique. And since Olivier died, I was better than ever. The grief had somehow focused me. I could hear and imagine layers, as I pushed to play the music the way I heard it in my head. I played for Olivier and for Leo, and it made them seem close, when they were both so far away.

My fingers were cold and a little stiff, which was annoying, and I was playing Niccolò Paganini's Sonata, Op.3, No. 6, a piece so steeped in perfection that I wondered why I ever bothered to compose. I moved into Sergei Rudnev's 'Fantasy on Crimson Moon' and was so deeply into the music that it was a while before I became aware, very slowly, of a slight movement, a presence, ten feet away, in the trees.

I kept playing, moving into the private little song I had written solely for *Leo the Lion*, and I sang the words softly, and saw movement out of the corner of my eye. Leo. Inching closer. My Leo, the same and so different. Wary.

I kept my movements slow and gentle, and kept singing the song, my heart beating hard, fingers starting to tremble. I set the guitar down and held my hand out, willing him closer.

'*Leo le Lion.* Come.'

He took a step towards me, and I saw that his beautiful nose was burned and scarred, as was his right shoulder, and I knew that nose burn came from dragging Olivier free of the flaming wreckage of the plane, and I fought the images in my head.

'*Avec moi, Leo. Avec moi.*'

He came forward, then hesitated, pulled his head back, moving slightly sideways, ready to bolt.

'*Au secours,*' I wailed. '*Au secours.*'

The emergency call. The one word that meant come quick, come quick, and was rewarded with a chunk of hotdog or deli meat. We had worked on this since we'd brought him home.

Leo sprang forward and ran to me, and I grabbed him, hugged him and fed him salami and cheese. And he whimpered and licked me all over my face. He knew me.

I cried a little and laughed, and fed him more salami, and wondered why I had not brought a tennis ball, because Leo was a typical ball-obsessed Shepherd and would do anything if you would only throw the ball, throw the ball, throw the ball.

I lured him into a down with a bit of meat, holding him tight. His collar was muddy and worn, and loose. He had lost so much weight. I clipped his collar to a leash, one that I wore snugly around my hips, leaving my hands free, and kept hold of him, petting him, speaking softly, while I gently tightened his collar.

He licked my fingers and talked to me in the way of dogs, whimpers and cries and those Shepherd-speak grumbles, and something inside of me healed, and I had my family back. We were two now, when we had been three.

My beautiful Leo had changed. Dirty and bedraggled. He had fleas. Ticks no doubt. I saw that his right flank had been burned, too, the skin scarred and black.

He was as thin as he was the day Olivier and I had found him, chained to a tree in the backyard behind a vacant house; from the looks of the weed-choked yard, the owners had been gone a long time. Olivier had gone for bolt cutters, and I had sat beside Leo, not too close, just sitting quietly and letting him bark, whimper, jump and whine, and eventually settle and approach me – on his terms. Which he did quickly, as if he had always known me and had been waiting for me to come. It wasn't a feeling of *Who are you?* More like *What took you so long?* Ever and always my dog.

Someone had been giving him food and water; there had been an empty, dirty food bowl, and the water bowl had a small amount at the bottom. The owner or a neighbor, I did not know, but they had left him chained to a tree, collar so tight we had to cut it off, and I consigned them to hell, and Olivier and I took him home.

It was clear when we got to our little cottage that he had never had regular meals, a toy, a bed of his own, or been inside a house, and he had gone wilding through, knocking over furniture. Ten months old and ready to rock. I had cried then, too, at his delight in a bed of his very own, and his first-ever teddy bear, which he took with him everywhere, dropping it into his water bowl to float while he ate. He carried it in his mouth, including on walks, until it had literally disintegrated.

He also had a taste for Olivier's black cashmere sweaters, my red leather gloves and my favorite leather travel bag. Olivier said Leo was a discerning dog who would not chew mere polyester, though cotton always appealed, and so this dog was clearly French. And in truth, Leo always responded best to commands in French.

Now, Leo settled in closer beside me with his head on my knee, and looked up at me, scarred black snout, and brown eyes with that particular mix of canine wisdom and love that said *I see you, I love you, I keep you safe. More cheese?*

And yes, there was more cheese.

I fed Leo everything I had, gave him water from the water bottle. He held it by the neck and tipped it back as I had taught him, the water trickling into his mouth. It was good just to be still for a while.

And slowly, building softly, like whispers all around me, I felt my husband close. I stroked Leo's ears and kissed his head, and I told Olivier thanks. I knew who had brought Leo home to me.

There was a break in the clouds, and I felt the sudden warmth of sunlight on my face, the warmth of it in Leo's fur.

Leo saw him before I did.

Your average service dogs are usually the easygoing types, ready to follow orders, creatures of laid-back emotions and the desire to remain alert while on the job.

Hearing dogs like Leo are different. They are born to it. Highly intelligent, they train themselves. Reactive and easily overwhelmed with sensory overload, which makes them anxious and hard to control. Add to that the protective instincts of a Shepherd.

But you cannot fight the heart of your dog; you embrace it and shape the behavior.

Leo knew I had a hearing loss before I did. It was hereditary and started small, and he began to alert me when he thought I didn't hear and was not aware. Usually with varying degrees of hysterical barking. With a hearing dog, it is not a matter of command, behavior, treat. A hearing dog initiates behavior, alerting consistently with or without treats and encouragement, until they train you to understand.

A lot of them don't do well in public, unable to manage their anxiety and reactive emotional responses, the way people expect service dogs to be robots who serve. But it is their heightened emotional responses that make them good at alerting you to things you need to hear, things you need to know.

It took me three years to get Leo calm in new situations. Using ERP – Exposure and Response Prevention, a cognitive behavioral therapy. A child psychiatrist might use this protocol for reactive children, children with extreme OCD, children overwhelmed by anxiety and fears. To teach their brains to handle the anxieties and emotions with steady, low-key exposures that kept them low on the reactive scale. Gradually increasing the exposures in small increments, every two weeks, with consistent exposure, and high-value rewards. The therapy worked for Leo, who used to be hysterical at anything new and slowly became so laid-back I sometimes checked to see if he was awake.

Still. His instinct to protect and to guard had never been tamped down. So when he saw the man coming down the hill toward us, he was on his feet, head lowered, completely silent.

Which is dog language for *I am going to fuck you up.*

I knew the man. I recognized him as I scrambled to my feet and he got closer; he was moving fast. Waving an arm as if we were old friends. Charl St Priest. The man on the video. The man who stole my dog.

I grabbed my phone and shoved it into the pocket of my jeans. Made sure I had my car keys. The rest I would have to leave.

'*Avec moi,*' I said to Leo.

He was crouching low. Reluctant.

'*Leo le Lion, avec moi, maintenant.*'

He hesitated, and I bolted into the woods, moving fast. Leo trotting easily beside me, attached to the leash at my waist. We ran.

St Priest shouted, but Leo and I kept going, moving off the trail and into the woods. Leo was leading now, me following, barely keeping up. We were making a lot of noise. It wasn't long before I was flagging, getting tired. Once we were out of sight, I ducked down behind a small hill of rock.

'Down-chill,' I whispered to Leo. 'Army crawl.' He scooted close to me on his belly, both of us now out of sight. 'Tuck tail,' I told him. 'Be small.' All my commands for getting underneath café tables. Also a good skill set when you were on the run and hiding.

My stomach was cold and tight, and my legs felt weak. I checked my phone for service.

I texted Laurent. 'In woods, found Leo, St Priest is chasing us. Hiding. Lost. *Au secours.*'

That should cover it. I waited. No response. The service bars faded in and out.

I did not know if the message had gone through. I did not know where the path was. If I went further in, I would get lost. If I could find the path, I would run right into St Priest.

And then it occurred to me that when you have a dog the size of a wolf, you are not the one who has to run.

FIFTEEN

I climbed up on the rock that had been my hiding place. I was somewhere deep in the forest. And I was totally lost. I scratched under Leo's chin. Catching my breath. Trying to focus. No sign of St Priest. Get to the car, I decided. Think of nothing else.

The trail made a loop, or so it had on the map Laurent had given me, and I was pretty sure it would get me back to the steep, twisty road where my car was parked, so I'd have to get back on the trail. There might be a shorter way, but being off the path would be a disaster for someone with my sense of direction. North, south, east, west . . . it all looked the same to me.

Laurent had not answered my text.

I was cold inside and shaky, but already starting to detach. That was the advantage of deep grief. You really don't give a shit.

Then the wind picked up and the rain started to fall. The irony was not lost on me. I had come to rescue Leo, and again, and as always, he had protected me. I gave him his head, and he led me on a circle and right back to the path. Good dog. I put *navigator* down on his job description. We rambled our way to the top of the hill, walking steadily.

We'd come a good way, and I was thinking we should be getting close to the road. The rain was falling softly, carried by the wind. We were shielded by the trees, but we were still pretty damp. Leo was limping – left hind leg, that old psoas muscle injury – so we stopped. I sat on a fallen tree that stretched along the side of the path, and Leo settled down beside me with a groan. A few minutes ago, I had gotten the second warning beep from my hearing aids. I had maybe fifteen more minutes, then the batteries would go. I would hear some. But I'd be vulnerable. Except, of course, I had Leo to hear for me. I looked over my shoulder. I could hear the wind in the trees.

Leo was panting, mouth wide. I pinched the flesh beneath his fur, and it stayed rigid. His gums were pinkish, the color fading to white. Definitely dehydrated. Probably had been for days.

Leo growled, low and menacing, and was back on his feet, head low. Something or someone was headed our way. He touched my thigh with his nose, an official alert, and I said *yes* softly. We were back in the groove. We were not prey; we were predators.

He was tense and watchful but quiet. His eyes were bright, and he was lethally still. This was the kind of day Leo lived for. In the game and on the job.

I took deep breaths and let them out slowly, heart slamming in my chest. This time, Leo and I heard him at the same time. The scuff of his feet, and he was breathing hard, moving more slowly than before. Well, I was tired, too.

Leo huffed low and deep and nudged my leg hard, and I said, *Alert*, and gave him a treat and kept a hand on his neck. I could just see St Priest coming down the path, waving a hand to get my attention. Which he had.

'*Junie*. Please, it is OK. It is just me.'

Just me?

'I see you have found Leo. That is wonderful, but please keep a tight hold on him.'

As if.

He wound towards us on the path. He was about five ten, broad shoulders, powerfully built. Jeans, boots, leaves caught in his hair, which was long and dark and straight, and tied back. And he was wearing the black wool dress coat, unbuttoned, hanging loose – the coat that belonged to Olivier, the same one he had worn in the video, the same gray scarf. He smiled at me. 'Don't be afraid of me, Junie.'

'I'm the one with the dog. And you are *le perdant* who stole my husband's coat and took my dog.'

He laughed, which I did not expect.

'Why are you dressed up like my husband?'

He shrugged. 'This is what I wear.'

'Why did you steal my dog? I saw the video. Because I know who you are. I know what happened between you and Olivier, so what the hell do you want?'

'Yes, I understand, this seems weird.'

'*You think?*'

He came closer, but Leo growled, and he froze.

'I suggest you back up about six steps. Leo has a space bubble he keeps in his head, and you don't want to get too close. Then I want you to sit down on the ground. If you don't do that now, or if you sit and get back up again, I'm going to let my dog loose. You don't want me to do that.'

'He does not seem to remember me.'

'I think maybe he does.'

'But I found him. Lost on the mountain. I tried to take him home with me, but he would not go. He got away.'

'You put a rope around his neck.'

He nodded. 'Yes, it is all I had. Do you know who I am?'

'I do, actually. You are Charl St Priest. You got my husband fired, and I don't like you.'

'No, no, *my name now*. Who I am *now*. Junie?' He held out a hand.

He was weird, which I expected, and off-the-charts creepy.

He stepped back six steps, as I had asked, and settled cross-legged on the ground. He gave me a smile full of longing, as though he had known me all my life. 'I will explain.'

It was disturbing. What he said and how he said it. How it made me feel to listen to his voice, to watch his mannerisms. Some of them reminded me of Olivier, as if St Priest had studied him, but they did not sit naturally with him and made him seem theatrical and *off*. He had taken up Olivier's way of pausing, looking to one side and thinking. With Olivier, it was subtle, quick – you might not notice. But with St Priest, it was broader, and the stare was long enough to interrupt the conversation. Then he gave me a studied look of affection that bordered on farce.

'You see, I knew your husband very well. You might not know this, but he and I, we worked out our differences, and became . . . in sync, I would say.'

'I wouldn't.' I laced my fingers through Leo's collar, and he pressed close to my leg, watching St Priest intently, head low. Silent.

'Yes, you would know about that, I am sure that I told you . . . the disagreement that I had with your husband. Back before.'

'Yes, the disagreement. When you tried to ditch one of your engineers whose wife was dying. Who had a five-year-old child. When you got my husband fired.'

He nodded. 'And I got demoted. I was supposed to act as liaison and prevent that sort of thing officially, but in truth I was just supposed to get rid of people when they wanted me to. I could usually find a way. Even in France. So long as the workers were American and not French. But Olivier was right to call management out on that. It is not the way of my country. I admit I was under the thumb of the Americans. But I am not that man anymore. I have changed.' He smiled when he said it, as if he had a secret he was dying to tell me. 'I lost a lot of friends over that. I had trouble on the job. Your husband – he may have been fired, but he was the hero. Many people at the company, who knew what happened, they admired your husband.'

I caught the flash of jealousy, a sick, angry jealousy that came off him in a toxic wave, then he smiled at me and shut it down.

'It was a turning point in my life. When I was young in business, I was so much like your husband that we could have been brothers. He helped me find my way back to the man I used to be. No, it is true, Junie; do not shake your head. Your husband and I were very much alike. We even look alike.'

'Don't say my name.'

'*Quoi?*'

'You heard me. Don't say my name. And you do not look like my husband. You are not handsome enough.'

He nodded. 'I understand you.' He reached out to me, but Leo growled, and I stepped backward. 'It brings on the grief when you see me. I remind you of him, the man you love. Did you get my flowers?'

I froze. I was right. It had been this video man who broke

into the garage and put that bouquet on the car. I shrugged. 'What flowers?'

'I left them on our car. A wedding bouquet, like you had when we got married.'

'*My car.* My marriage to Olivier, not to you. Dude, you have clearly lost your mind.'

He smiled at me kindly. 'I see you do not understand. It is a fantastical thing, what is happening.'

'What I see is not fantastical at all; it is common and boring. It is a poser. A man who was so envious of my husband that he wants to *be* him. A poor imitation of my husband's haircut, the coat you took out of his office, right? Who stole our family dog. None of this makes you remotely like my husband; it just makes you pathetic. No doubt there is a name for this in some list of mental illnesses. I am sure a therapist could help you out.'

'This . . . I did not steal your dog. I found him wandering. I kept him safe.'

'You tried to take him, and he escaped. Did he bite you?'

St Priest absently rubbed his forearm. Leo had never before bitten anyone, but I knew he had bitten St Priest.

'Junie, you do not understand. The dog was upset by the crash and the death of Olivier; he did not understand – he did not like the rope. I was trying to help him.'

'How did you know what my wedding bouquet looked like?'

He smiled at me, with just a hint of something dark, something malevolent. 'I kept our wedding picture on the desk in my office; everyone saw it.'

Of course. Olivier always had a double frame on his desk. A wedding picture, and one of me playing guitar. Still . . . you could not see those flowers in the picture. *So how did he know this? How did he know?*

'I was so proud of those pictures,' St Priest said. 'So jealous.'

The lines were blurred. He was Olivier one moment, the colleague with toxic envy the next.

'Why are you here? Why are you following me?'

'To make sure you found Leo, of course.'

'I don't believe you. How did you know I was here today? How did you know that?'

He gave me a puzzled look. 'But I always know where you are. Because of our connection – the connection of our souls. Junie, you must listen, you must understand. Something . . . something happened when Olivier died.'

My knees went wobbly, and I sat back down on the fallen tree. I wanted to stay on my feet, but I couldn't. 'Time for you to leave now. I want you to get up, turn around and walk away. Right now.' My hands were trembling. I felt sick to my stomach.

'Not before you understand.' He was up on his feet. 'Why don't you come home with me—'

'*Get away.*'

He stepped back. 'I see I must explain this to you. Have you ever heard of a *walk-in*? The walk-in of the soul, Junie?'

'I told you not to say my name.'

'When you understand, you will *want* me to say your name. The bad times are over, *mon amour.*'

I was back on my feet, shaky as hell, wondering if I should cut and run. Leo was resisting, lunging toward St Priest, and it took everything I had to hold him back. His gaze locked on to St Priest. And St Priest, who did not know dogs, did not understand that the longer Leo locked him down in that steady stare, the more trouble he was in. Leo was approaching the red zone, and I would not be able to hold him.

But St Priest was still talking. 'You see, I had lost all hope. I wanted to die. Olivier – he wanted to live. He loved you so much. *I* love you so much. Please, Junie, do you not know me? When Olivier died, he took me over. St Priest died, and Olivier, *he walked in*, a new soul in my body, a whole new life. It took some time, yes, to recalibrate to this new life, but it is me now, Junie. Olivier. I am your husband now. I have come back to you.'

And then he rushed me.

I unclipped Leo's leash from my waist, and things happened fast.

St Priest was close, but he never touched me. In a blur of movement, Leo had him down on the ground. St Priest screamed as Leo broke his arm, and ripped into the flesh of his shoulder, and shook him like the stuffed toys he had gutted and shredded since he was a pup. Practicing.

'*Au secours*,' I said.

Leo hesitated, then followed me as I ran for the woods. I got the final signal from my hearing-aid batteries, and the world became quiet. I could still hear the wind in the trees . . . but not much else.

This time, I stayed on the path. I did not care that St Priest was injured. I did not know if he followed, but I did know that a man so steeped in delusional, pathological envy was a dangerous man, injured or not. Olivier had been his target, and Olivier was now dead.

I had no doubt that St Priest had sabotaged that plane and killed my husband. I had seen that malevolent envious rage that came over him like darkness, and yet . . . the logic was flawed. How had he known Olivier would be on the plane? A last-minute decision between Olivier and . . . Laurent.

I stopped and held on to a tree, breathing hard.

How stupid I had been. How trusting.

Laurent had told him, of course. It was the only way St Priest could have known. Laurent, who had been steeped in guilt. Who had tried to look after me when Olivier died. Who had lost weight and changed so dramatically that I almost did not recognize him. Who used to dislike me intensely but could not do enough for me now.

Laurent who was the only one who knew exactly where I was today. Laurent who had not answered my text.

Of course Olivier's death had changed him. It was quite a reality shift to kill your good friend.

Part of me wanted to laugh. Part of me wanted to cry. Thank God I had cut and run last night.

I touched Leo's shoulder, and he looked up at me. I had my dog back. I would be OK. Leo was limping but, unlike me, he could go on forever. I would have to be Shepherd-tough like my dog.

And it occurred to me that if Laurent was involved in Olivier's death, there was a hell of a lot going on I didn't know about.

'Olivier, my love,' I said out loud. 'What the hell did you get yourself into?'

SIXTEEN

By the time Leo and I heard the voices of the men and saw them moving swiftly through the trees, I was pretty sure I was on the wrong path. I was nowhere near anywhere that seemed to lead anywhere but in circles through the woods.

I saw Laurent; I knew it was him, even with a glimpse from a distance. And he was not alone. I strained hard, trying to hear, but only caught murmurs, several men talking.

Leo growled, and I put a finger to my lips. A sign he knew. '*Silence.*'

The men were getting closer, speaking in rapid French, voices low and soft, sounding, to my impaired ears, as if they came from the bottom of a well. I had no chance of making out what they said. Just bits.

Blessé. Peur. Perdu.

Injured. Afraid. Lost.

And then, Laurent, shouting. 'Junie, *c'est moi*, Laurent. It's OK now. *Je t'ai eu.*'

I've got you.

Leo barked madly, and I held tight to his leash.

Laurent, back to us, turned at the sound of Leo's bark and smiled hugely when he saw us. He said something about finding Leo that I could not quite catch.

Two other men came swiftly out of the trees. One was in heavy boots, carrying a rucksack, kitted out in the garb of the Peloton de Gendarmerie de Haute Montagne. They called them the Angels of Mont Blanc. The other in jeans and a thick black sweater, hiking boots. His gaze locked on me.

'Madame Junie Lagarde?'

I nodded. I knew that resonant voice. I took a deep breath. I was safe.

He came to me swiftly and took my hands in his. 'Capitaine

Philippe Brevard. We have been talking on the phone.' He reached down absently and stroked Leo. '*Bonjour, fiston.*'

Leo leaped up and put his paws on Brevard's shoulder and gave him a kiss.

'Leo.' I grabbed him.

Brevard gave me a sideways smile. 'He likes me, of course. It is a wonderful thing that you have found him.'

'He found me. He usually does not like strange men.'

Brevard shrugged. 'But I am a man and I like him.'

It was a logic I could not argue with.

Brevard gave me a swift professional look. 'You are OK? We found your backpack and your guitar. We were very worried. You were running away, I think?'

I nodded. I had to concentrate, but I could hear him. His voice was in the deep range, so I could make out most of it. And he was standing very close. 'It was Charl St Priest. He showed up right after I found Leo. He . . . he came after me.'

'So you know who he is?'

Laurent moved close, giving me a tense smile. I caught some of his words. Something about a text and bad service and calling Brevard.

'What happened with St Priest?' Brevard asked.

'He's . . . three bricks shy of a load.'

'*Pardon?*'

'Crazy. He broke into the garage where I keep the car and left flowers on the hood. *A wedding bouquet* – how creepy is that? And he found me here. He said . . . he said disturbing things. He was aggressive and he came after me, and Leo broke his arm. And tore his shoulder open. *Defending me.*'

Brevard spoke rapid French to the man with the rucksack who had been studying Leo with a smile, and the man stepped away and spoke in low tones into the radio.

'You have the good dog,' Brevard said, and I nodded. Perhaps in France, this kind of thing was OK. Dogs were welcome in France, but they had to behave.

'My men will find him, this St Priest.'

'He's dangerous.'

Brevard gave me a look. 'Yes, Madame, he is, and I know

that. I understand you. You are very shaken, but soon you must
tell me exactly everything that has happened between the two
of you. And exactly the disturbing things he has said.'

Leo watched him, staying close to my thigh.

The man in uniform took a wary step forward, keeping an
eye on Leo, who held his ground, head low.

He paused and spoke to me, but I could not understand
what he said.

'I'm sorry, I can't really hear you.'

Brevard took it in stride. 'He asks if it is OK, Madame, for
him to come forward – your dog will allow?'

'I've got Leo. It's OK.'

'You are not injured?'

'No. My dog needs water.'

Laurent grinned and crouched down, spreading his arms,
talking softly to Leo.

Leo strained forward and whimpered, and I let him loose.
He ran to Laurent and put his paws on Laurent's shoulder and
whined and licked his face and nuzzled his neck.

The man in uniform grinned and held out his hand to Leo,
who bounded forward and leaped up and gave him a sloppy
doggie kiss on the cheek. Leo always had opinions about
people. Sometimes he loved them on sight.

So much for *Le Chien Commando*.

And then Laurent was on his feet, beside me in two quick
strides, wrapping his arms around me and holding me tight,
and close enough that I could hear him. '*Mon dieu*, Junie, I
thought he had you.'

I pushed him away. 'But this St Priest is really a good
friend of yours, isn't he, Laurent? Because otherwise, how
would he know I was here? I think maybe you told him. I
think maybe you told him I was here today, and before . . .
I think you told him Olivier would be on that plane.'

Laurent froze, and Brevard watched us closely. 'I did not
tell him you were here today, Junie; of course I would not do
that. But yes, I did tell him about the plane, at a business
dinner, and that Olivier and I were going together. I did not
know . . . I did not know what would happen.'

'So last night . . . you never mentioned that?'

Capitaine Brevard frowned, watching us.

Laurent hesitated. 'It is a hard thing to say. And I was not supposed to tell anyone about that. But I told Capitaine Brevard all of this, months ago.'

'*Months ago?*'

I looked at Brevard, who nodded. 'This is an ongoing investigation, Madame; he was told to share the information with no one else.'

Everyone knew everything except me. Olivier's actual wife.

'You are *fâchée*, Madame?'

'I'm *fine*.'

Brevard gave me a wary look. 'We will talk, Madame Lagarde, I assure you. But first you meet Michel Aubert, the one who talks too soft. He volunteers for Mountain Rescue, and he has helped to look for Leo since the crash.'

The man with the rucksack was scratching Leo behind the ears, but he gave me a nod and a serious smile. He raised his voice with the stilted tone that I often found useful but annoying. 'He looks very good for a dog who has been lost so long in terrain like this. I have water for him.'

'Thank you.'

Michel took a water bottle from his pack, then knelt down and called softly to Leo who was nosing the pack. He splashed water on his hand and rubbed Leo's face and head. Then pooled water in his palm and let Leo lap it up. Leo mouthed the lip of the bottle, grabbed it between his teeth, tipped it back and drank. The men laughed, and I felt a little smug.

'*Il est magnifique, ce garçon,*' Michel said.

Laurent smiled down at me. 'We know this.'

'But he is also in pain.' Michel lifted Leo with shocking ease and settled him up on his shoulders. Leo groaned and settled happily in. I had never seen such a thing and was impressed with both the dog and the man.

'It is a mile and a half to the car,' Brevard said. 'You can make this, Madame?'

'I can make this.'

SEVENTEEN

Seeing my car still tucked nicely to the side of the road was such a huge relief that my knees went weak. Michel carried Leo to the car and waited for me to open the door. I had my keys. He set Leo gently into the passenger's side of the Z4 and made some remark about the *sportif* dog that I could not hear. Leo groaned again, and he shut the door gently. Leo settled into his seat with palpable relief. All was right with his world.

Evidently, it was all a crime scene now, and there were already cars marked *Police* parked on the road, a handful of men and women. Brevard gave them swift orders, and they headed through the woods. I rummaged in the Z, the compartment between the seats, for batteries and replaced them in my hearing aids.

Brevard leaned close to the door, and I opened it wide.

'We have brought your things, Madame Lagarde. Your pack and your guitar. Will you unlatch the trunk?'

Brevard made sure everything was packed neatly into the car, the guitar settled into the soft case. I was not used to letting anyone handle my guitar, but for now I was past caring. I sat in the driver's seat, sideways, muddy shoes on the pavement. Brevard brought me a cup of coffee, very hot, black and sweet, and crouched down next to me.

'You must drink this, please. You seem very shaky to me. I would like to have one of my officers drive you home.'

'I . . . our apartment is in Annecy.'

'I know where you live. Also, we have found this beneath the trunk of your car.' He held up a small plastic evidence bag with a tiny bar of electronics inside. 'A tracker. You say St Priest broke into your garage and left flowers.'

'Yes.'

'OK. We think he put the tracker on your car then, and that

is how he found you. We will investigate and confirm. Are the flowers still there?'

'Yes. In the trashcan in the garage. I roughed them up a bit.'

He grinned, then nodded. 'Please would you leave everything as it is and not go back inside until my officers have time to take a look and collect evidence. You will comply?'

'I will comply.'

'Tell me the things St Priest said to you. Tell me what he did when he approached you.'

My hands were too shaky to hold the coffee, so I handed it back to Brevard and told him everything. It was hard to read his reaction. He listened and nodded and was annoyingly matter-of-fact.

'OK, Madame, that is what I need for now. Let's get you home. You may have to let us put you in our car and have someone drive yours back later. We will be happy to do this for you. Because there does not seem to be room for three in your car.' He called over his shoulder. 'Michel?'

'There's room, don't worry.' I stood up, then sat back down again.

Brevard steadied my shoulders. 'This is a normal reaction, Madame, but you must not drive.'

'OK. But I want to go home. With Leo. There is room in my car.' He handed me the cup of coffee again. 'Please.'

I took a minute or two to chug the coffee which was still hot and sweet and made me feel a great deal better. I got out of the car and moved into the passenger's side, and Leo knew what to do. He moved behind the steering wheel till I got settled, then climbed into my lap.

Brevard smiled at me. 'Most impressive, Madame, though I can barely see you behind this dog. I will come to you tomorrow morning, around nine – will that be OK? I will call and let you know when I am on my way. We must talk.'

I nodded. Michel folded himself into the driver's side and muttered softly. He was delighted to be driving the car but annoyed that it was an automatic. 'An American thing,' he said.

I nodded, and we were off. I did not look back.

EIGHTEEN

Michel was a chatty guy and talked fast and soft. I understood about seventy percent of what he said and guessed at the rest. He and I decided our first stop was Leo's vet. He called ahead, and she said she would keep the office open. Michel was a dog guy for sure. He also could not resist the car, and we made quick time toward Annecy.

As soon as we were on the road, I felt better. I could breathe. I could think. I could hardly believe I had found my Leo, and I hugged him and laid my head on his neck.

He licked my hand, then fell hard asleep, legs twitching as he dreamed.

The vet visit was almost more than I could handle. Michel carried Leo in on his shoulders; once inside, Leo greeted Dr LeClair, and Madame Lise and Madame Kelli, as if they were his entourage. It was a clinic designed by a dog whisperer, and instead of trembling and making himself small, the usual response to a vet clinic, Leo was greeted with utter delight by the staff who treated him like a rock star. Leo knew his people.

'You are OK now, Madame Lagarde?' Michel asked me. 'I can stay if you like.'

'No, I am OK now, but thank you.'

He nodded and gave the vet a long look and a smile, and then he headed out to the street, talking on his mobile.

There were no cold stainless steel exam tables here. We settled in a small room with a jar full of treats, and Leo sniffed and paced around, and Dr LeClair sat down on a thick fluffy mat on the floor and lined treats up, encouraging Leo to settle next to her, which he did. He gave her a kiss, and she laughed. She laid her instruments out on the floor and let Leo sniff them.

'Viens ici, mon vieux.'

She took her time with him, telling me he was stressed,

underweight; we would go gently with him, but he was tough stuff, always the Shepherd. All of this I knew, but it helped to hear her say it. There was swelling in the left psoas; she did not want to X-ray – it would stress him too much – but we would just treat it with anti-inflammatory and pain meds and see how he did. It did not seem too bad, so we would watch and manage. She knew he had a history with this. She clucked over the stairs in my apartment; it would slow his recovery, but there was no way around it. She shook her head at the patchy fur and blackened skin of healed-over burns, told him he was *le beau gosse.*

His heart worm test was negative, and I was given meds to treat the parasites he'd picked up. They were swift and gentle and practiced, washing him with a special shampoo to soothe and heal the ravaged skin, removing any ticks they found, and I was given strict instructions on his diet. Rice cooked in broth, boiled chicken, sweet potatoes, yogurt. Probiotics added to his food. We would get him back on dog food slowly.

Then home, at long last, to our place in Annecy.

I cried when we walked through the door of our apartment, and Leo ran around in circles, sniffing and whining, and both of us missing Olivier. But for the first time since Olivier died, I felt as though I had come home. I missed him. It was a forever pain. But I had Leo.

NINETEEN

That night I woke up three times, checking to see that Leo was really there. It did not feel real. But I was getting used to that; my life did not feel like my life anymore, and hadn't since Olivier died. I stroked Leo's fur, and he licked my hand. Neither one of us slept well, but we slept happy. It was good to be safe and snug in our little apartment. Just Leo and me.

When we woke late, with the sun streaming in, I saw that I had missed two calls from my brothers and a text from Brevard. Who was on his way. I put my hearing aids in, made sure I had a pack of fresh 312 batteries in my purse, and blocked any more calls from the bros. I did not have time for them right now.

It was not the relaxed breakfast on the balcony I had planned with Leo, but I gave him the leftover chicken from the fridge, and he ate every bite, and drank copiously from his water bowl. I did not even have time for coffee. My jeans were muddy and gross, and I slammed through the teeny armoire and found a red sundress I had forgotten about. One of Olivier's favorites, and it was sunny out, still warm. I could take a sweater. I wore tiny soft half booties, pretty and practical when you had a large dog on a short leash.

I had showered last night, and my hair was all over the place, so I twisted it up, sighed when it came tumbling back down in three places, smudged up some eyeliner, put on mascara and lipstick, and Leo and I headed out. We were late. Brevard was patiently waiting for us at a small table at the café a half block down from my apartment, as he had arranged in the text.

It was his stillness that intrigued me. How he watched Leo and me approach, with total focus. He stood up when he saw me, met my eyes and gave me a quiet smile that bespoke gravitas and compassion.

'Madame,' he said and pulled out my chair.

A waiter arrived with two tiny cups of coffee and a basket of croissants and went back to get a bowl of water for Leo.

Brevard looked freshly shaved and crisp, hair gelled back, white button-down shirt that looked ironed, with the cuffs rolled precisely back twice. There were two pens in his pocket, and I smiled.

'What amuses you, Junie?'

It was the first time he'd used my first name, and he had switched from *vous* to *tu*. Very familiar of him.

'The pens in your pocket. Are you sure you are an investigator and not an engineer? And a good investigator, *a super guy*, as I understand from Michel. In high demand. He is happy to be working with you on this.'

He placed his hand on top of mine for roughly three seconds. 'Laurent tells me you know about the video that went up on YouTube. Please know that it has been taken down.'

I took a deep breath.

He gave me a steady look. 'Did you see it?'

'*No.*'

'Do you want to?'

'*No.*'

He nodded. 'It was St Priest who posted it; that has been confirmed. He has admitted that. He used software to doctor the second one for the deepfake. It was not convincing by the way. It looked more like a doll man, not your husband. He is not very good with the software.'

'I don't get why he did it.'

'But I do. He wants the world to see him. And to see him as Olivier Lagarde, not Charl St Priest.'

'You found him, then? St Priest?'

'Oh, yes, Madame, we found him.'

'And how is he?' I looked at Leo and smiled.

'His arm is a clean break, and it will heal, and there are now many stitches in his shoulder. He does not wish to press charges regarding the dog attack, he tells us. Michel is *en liaison* with your vet to confirm Leo's rabies vaccinations and his overall good health.'

I was up on my feet and calling to Leo to go home, but

Brevard took my arm and pulled me back into my chair. 'Don't walk off, Madame, and do not take offense. There is no danger of any problem with your dog; I have seen to that.' He reached down and fluffed Leo on top of the head. It was no way to pet a Shepherd, but you would not know that from Leo's look of adoration.

Brevard pushed the basket of croissants to me, and I took one and put it on a small plate. 'You permit?' he said. 'For your dog?'

I nodded.

He took a croissant and broke off chunks of bread, discreetly passing them to Leo under the table where Leo had made himself small. 'You may use your garage again; we have made our investigation. The wedding bouquet – it is a creepy thing. We have traced it to a florist and to St Priest; there are no doubts on that.'

'Is St Priest under arrest or not?' I said.

Brevard shifted in his chair. 'Not exactly.'

'What does that mean? He is or he isn't.'

'He could be, but he is not yet. The judge wants us to gather more information. We are going to take this slow.'

'Slow? It's been nine months. Why is this taking so long?'

'I cannot give you the details of an ongoing investigation. What I can tell you is that we have only now had the test results that confirm the plane was sabotaged. But we had . . . certain information that made it clear the plane was tampered with early on. That is why we ran the test, to confirm exactly what was done. I must also confess to you that things have been slower than they should have. We have had many unhappy calls from Monsieur Fournier, the husband of the pilot who died. In truth, I had a heart attack three weeks after your husband died, and they handed the case off to someone else. When I returned, I found there had been no progress – it had been sitting – so it is back in my hands again. Also, though I am moving as quickly as I can, there are complications I cannot discuss. I would ask you to be patient.'

'Because you want him for more than harassing me; you want him for murdering my husband. What are the complications?'

Brevard gave me a shrug.

'I'm sorry about your heart attack.'

He gave me a smile that was hard to resist. 'I came back better than before.'

'And this is well in hand?' I asked him.

He nodded. 'You can trust me on that. But I did want you to be aware of the kind of man this St Priest is.'

'I'm very aware.'

'No, Madame, you must not underestimate how dangerous he is, how much he hated your husband. You see, this is a thing with him. This kind of malevolent obsession.'

'Malevolent?'

He nodded. 'He has a history.'

'So you are looking at a pattern. He's done this before?' I laid my hands flat on the table. I was not hungry anymore and set the croissant back down on my plate, and let my coffee get cold.

Brevard reached across the table and squeezed my hands. His skin was warm, his fingers strong. 'It seems to have started in childhood with his big brother, the oldest boy. St Priest was the youngest child and very spoiled. There were four of them – two girls, two boys. His brother was what you would call the high achiever. Very sporty, very smart, built the family business, which was a breeding farm for sheep. St Priest hated the farm, but he hated more that his brother loved it, and was good at it.'

'So what did St Priest do? How does this kind of thing play out?'

'It began with the typical little-brother things. Borrowing his brother's jacket, his clothes. His brother was very good at soccer, a striker, and St Priest would take his soccer jersey, then tell people that he was St Priest the soccer player. It was just a local thing; his brother blew it off, but it only got worse. St Priest had to have anything his brother had. Even things he did not want. His brother gets an old Land Rover – for the farm, you see – and St Priest, he has to get a new one. The brother gets married; St Priest gets married. The brother is divorced; St Priest is divorced. The brother builds a small house on the property – a cabin, leaving the main house for the parents – and St Priest is then building a cabin. It became ridiculous. And the brother marries again, this time to a woman who cannot stand St Priest. She is seeing the pattern and warning her husband, and St Priest and his brother become estranged.' Brevard looked away a moment. 'Five years ago, in order to heal the rift between them, the two of them went on a mountain-biking trip, St Priest supposedly apologizing, trying to have again the relationship with his brother. There was an accident.'

I froze. 'The brother *died*?'

'*Oui*. A crashed bike on a steep path, high speed, and a terrible head injury. The wife was suspicious, but there was nothing to prove.'

'But why kill him? If he was obsessed and needed his brother like that?'

'But does he need him? *Non*. He wants his brother's attention. But his jealousy, it eats him up. He does not love his brother; he wants to *be* him. Any attention his brother has, he must have. Anything his brother has, he must have. How much better if his brother is dead? Then there is no competition, no more the agony of keeping up. Now he can get the attention for himself and be the star brother. He probably did better in his life after his brother died. Doing his own thing, being himself. Until he met your husband. And it started all over again. You know of the work incident between your husband and St Priest?'

'Yes.'

'So St Priest is suddenly the bad guy at a job where he was excelling, rising fast in the company, doing the things he himself is good at. And your husband becomes the consultant. He is brilliant. People like him. People *trust* him, even though he has only been there a few months advising them on quality issues in the plant. He and St Priest, they were not in professional agreement most of the time. And St Priest, he is feeling those twinges. Watching your husband, feeling jealous like he did with his brother. And so it begins again. And then your husband, who is fired, becomes the hero. Everyone likes and admires your husband; people turn their backs on St Priest, and he is demoted and humiliated. So he *hates* your husband. But he wants to *be him*. Same exact dynamic. The jealousy becomes pathological, and St Priest is again a dangerous man.'

'How much longer will it be before you can arrest him? Surely you must be close. Surely the way he has been stalking me gives you more evidence.'

Brevard shook his head. 'There are things going on I cannot tell you. Please just trust and go with me on this.'

I looked at him. 'I find that request ridiculous.'

He smiled a little. 'I am telling you what I think you must know. So you will keep your guard up. And if you know anything I should know, you must tell me.'

'And do you believe what I told you yesterday? Did St Priest tell you that crazy story of walk-in souls when you questioned him yesterday?'

Brevard frowned. 'Not exactly.'

'But you believe me?'

'I believe you. But he did not admit to that – he wouldn't, do you think? He did talk of the connection between the two of you, and how the three of you – St Priest, you, Olivier – would go to dinner sometimes. How you would always order red wine, no matter what. How he once came with Olivier to Chez Eugene to hear you play guitar.'

I went very cold, though a part of me was distracted by the idea that it mattered so much what wine I ordered. 'That . . . that happened, but it was with Laurent. Me, Olivier, and Laurent, along with Eugene and Annette. I never met St Priest, I did not know him, and he and Olivier were most definitely not friends.'

Brevard considered this. 'This is what he does, I think. He hears the story . . . and puts himself in the middle.'

'Maybe it is Laurent who had better watch out, not me.'

'Perhaps so. I believe he was also meant to die in the crash. But with you, it goes to another level; with you, it is obsession. It was not Laurent who got a bouquet of flowers, who had a tracker on his car, who was followed through the woods, who was married to Olivier. You are the pattern. And now you are the connection to Olivier, and that makes you the target. Keep that close in your mind.'

'OK. St Priest's dangerous, specifically to me. And you have not arrested him because there is something else going on here – something that ties in with Olivier, Laurent and St Priest. All three. And it is more than this jealous pathology, or you'd have him locked up by now.'

Brevard watched me steadily. 'You would not be wrong to think such a thing. So I tell you again to be careful.'

'Maybe everybody else should be careful.' I reached out to give Leo a bite of my croissant. I was not as afraid as I should be. I had nothing to lose.

Brevard gave me a measured look and took my hands in his, leaning close across the table. 'I can see you are going to be trouble, Madame.'

I could not help the slow smile that spread across my face. 'Are we having a moment?'

'*Oui, Madame.*'

TWENTY

I heard them before I saw them: my brothers. My big brother Christopher and his husband, Redmond Koh.

My brother's voice was loud and lazy, just as he liked it, and he was slyly playing the role of *American Tourist* to the hilt. One of the best things about my brother was how subversive he was.

The two of them had met in Singapore, where Redmond ran a freelance financial consulting business and my brother was on vacation. Hooked up through a discreet dating app. The sex had been excellent, according to my brother, who often gave me too much information. Redmond had moved to the US, and they had married two days later. No serious issues with their prenup; Redmond had money and was careful. They were deeply in love and ridiculously compatible. Redmond liked the South.

Redmond was something of a hunk. He had a clean-cut look. Hair very black and soft, short on the sides and at the back, thick and luxurious on the top. He wore a tight gray tee shirt with a pocket. Skinny jeans. High-top red Converse. He fit in better in France than my brother who was in loose, old fart jeans, with his Ralph Lauren button-up shirt untucked and hanging loose, no socks, leather loafers. They were a handsome pair. They got second looks.

I used to get along with my brothers. I used to think we were close.

No one tells you about the collateral damage of grief. When someone you love dies, you often lose everyone else. You cannot explain how grief actually works in reality, you can't explain that your need for solitude is not a rejection, you can't fight the cultural expectations, and you can't go back to the person you used to be. They want the old you, who is lost to time.

Spending time with my brothers was agony now. There were

unspoken rules in the subtext, rules I had not agreed to. I got pained looks and discomfort when I said Olivier's name. Spoke of France. Spouted phrases in my unique Southern girl French. Cried over Leo, wondering and hoping he was somehow still alive.

My brothers, who had zero idea what I was going through, felt entitled and qualified to give me some gentle advice. I was not *moving on* or *letting go* as I should. Grieving for over a year was a sign of mental illness – did I know that? So I had three months left to go. They were not amused when I said that grief does not have a sell-by date. The word *martyr* had come up.

Chris saw me differently now. Less than. My opinions on politics, or the weather even, were now suspect, pounced upon, and I was clearly a person who needed to be schooled. I had somehow been demoted from the independent, opinionated sister that made him laugh into someone he could not respect. Chris seemed to expect me to step up and make amends – for what, I did not know. I was in the penalty box and continued to accrue demerits.

No doubt he resented being left behind. If you are surfing the waves of grief, you are also in the ocean, in the wind, seeing the world in a way you never thought of before. There is exhilaration in that. I was freer now than I had ever been, and the whole world was open to me. It was like someone had knocked the wall down and I could walk into a world I never knew existed. I was not the woman I used to be. I was better.

And so I stepped away. The best thing about France was not going home.

Brevard gave me a patient look. Long silences seemed not to bother him. 'Where did you go just now?'

'Yeah, sorry. Olivier used to call Leo my Awareness Support Dog. I tend to drift off.'

He nodded. 'It is a time for serious thoughts. But now that you are back, I must ask you, who are these noisy men who stare and walk toward us, waving their hands?'

'My brothers. Arriving without warning, all the way from the US of A.'

'They just show up?' He tilted his head to one side. 'You are not happy to see your brothers, are you, Madame?'

'I'm not.'

Brevard squeezed my hands, then let them go, but he was slow about it, under the sharp eyes of my brothers, which I admit I liked. He settled back in his chair, ever watchful, ever the cop, and I knew that this family dynamic interested him, and this curiosity made him a good detective. And he, after all, was not the one I wanted to leave.

Olivier had not gotten along all that well with Chris or Redmond. Which was starting to make sense.

TWENTY-ONE

L eo sat up with a huff when he caught sight of Chris, tail wagging madly. Chris hooted loud enough to get looks from people across the street, and rushed over to Leo, crouched low, getting kisses all over his face. Redmond was afraid of dogs, so he hung back and then settled tensely into a chair with a slightly worried smile.

'You *found* him?' Chris said. He was shaking his head, grinning from ear to ear.

'Yes.'

'Where was he?'

'Near Chamonix, in the forest, by *Le Parc Merlet.*'

'I don't know where that is. Oh, poor boy, poor guy. He – those are burns?'

'He's OK, Chris, and it's a long story. Capitaine Brevard, this is my brother-in-law, Redmond, and my brother, Chris.'

Chris looked up at Brevard and grinned. '*Hey.* I see you are keeping my sister company.'

Brevard nodded coldly. Chris was not going to get through that French reserve. 'Bonjour.'

'Did we interrupt an interrogation?' Chris said with a grin and a tone of amusement.

'Yes,' Brevard said with a snap. He spoke to the waiter, and more coffee and croissants were on the way. The waiter secured two more chairs, and we were four and a massive dog grouped around a table that was tight for two.

'Why are you here, Chris?' I said.

He lost his smile. 'Man, I saw that crazy video up on the Internet. You didn't answer the phone. I went by your house, and you were already gone. And I did try to call you last night, to let you know we were here.'

'Yes, I saw that a call came in around three a.m.'

'We landed in Geneva and had dinner and got into our hotel pretty late. The time thing, sorry. Brought you something.'

He looked at Redmond, who reached into his pack and pulled out an unsealed, crumpled letter, addressed to Olivier.

'I told him not to open it,' Redmond said.

I gave him a tight smile and looked over at Chris. 'You came all the way to France to give me this?'

'Well, that YouTube business – that was pretty disturbing – and I couldn't find you. You left in a pretty big hurry. And there are other things. About our business.'

The smile was gone from my brother's voice, and I felt a sick coldness in the pit of my stomach. 'You thought it was OK to open my letter?'

'I was picking up your mail. The letter was from France. It looked important.' He gave Brevard a look. 'My sister's husband – she's a widow now, I am sure you know. He evidently bought her a guitar at a store in Metz, and it's all paid for and needs to be picked up. *And*,' Chris said, 'my brilliant but absent-minded brother-in-law left his backpack there, so Junie can pick that up, too, when she gets the guitar. Which set my brother-in-law back a good nineteen thousand euros.' He gave me a frown. 'Quite the guitar, I'm thinking.'

I froze, my stomach tight and cold and . . . thrilled. Olivier had bought me a guitar? If it cost nineteen thousand euros, I knew exactly what guitar this was. It did not seem like a thing that was possible. He should have paid off the car. Something practical. Olivier was always practical, except on things like that. Things he wanted me to have.

Brevard leaned forward. 'A guitar store in Metz? The name of this store, please?'

Chris handed Brevard the letter. He frowned at my brother and handed it to me.

'Your mail, Madame.'

My hands were trembling. The letter was in French. There were parts I had to puzzle over. Olivier had purchased a guitar and paid in full, two days before he died. The inscription had been stenciled upon the guitar exactly as Olivier had requested, no plate attached anywhere to compromise the structure. How wonderful my engineer husband understood that kind of thing.

The news was astonishing to me, but also explained the

phone call he had made, telling me mischievously not to look into his business account until he had come home. And after he died, I saw that he had taken out that exact sum. Now I knew why.

The owner of the store was concerned. She had not been able to get in touch with Olivier: the phone had been disconnected, the email bounced back, the letter to the address in Annecy had been returned; she was trying the residence in the USA. Would Monsieur Lagarde please be so good as to let them know if he would pick up the guitar, or if they should arrange shipment. Please also be aware that they still had his backpack, confirmed by phone when he had called after he left, and could ship that as well if needed.

I had thought the backpack had burned up in the plane. I felt cold all over and strangely happy. His backpack. A new guitar. And not just any guitar. I got the feeling I had more and more often. That Olivier was somehow gone and somehow here. And then I wondered. Had he had a premonition? Had he known he was going to die?

I handed Brevard the letter. It was police business now, thanks to my big-mouthed brother. Brevard would want the backpack. He took a picture of the letter with his phone and handed it back to me. '*Merci*. I must go. I will be in touch.' He nodded at my brothers.

I gave him a worried look. 'I know you'll take the backpack. But the guitar?'

He put a hand on my shoulder and squeezed. 'The guitar is yours, of course. Do not worry about that, Madame.' And he was gone.

There was nothing I wanted more than to go to Metz to get my guitar, but first I had to get rid of my brothers. I felt the thrill of this magical gift from Olivier. It felt meant to be, a sign of his love, another moment that strengthened our connection. Olivier used to give me a matter-of-fact look and tell me we were a perfect circle. It took me all this time to understand.

My brothers had their heads together, talking intently. They were entirely self-absorbed – no questions about why I was talking to a cop, or how I had found my dog. A relief, actually. I did not want to get snarled up in explanations, and they just didn't care. Compassion fatigue, and I couldn't blame them.

And I was pretty sure I knew what was going on here, and I wanted to settle that now. Quickly.

I sat back in my chair and took the last croissant just as Chris was reaching for it. I fed it bit by bit to Leo. 'Let me guess why you are here. You want to split up the business. You take your half and I take mine.'

Off Beat Forensic Accounting. Chris had come up with the name for our business, and I admit I loved it. It attracted a rather wealthy Southern clientele. Quirky, lots of money, and that subtle sense of humor you find in the South. And I had not done one minute of work since I had arrived in France, and I had missed two rather major deadlines with clients I didn't much like. Clients who had enough money to know they didn't have to wait around for me to get on with things. I knew Chris was pissed. I knew he'd had enough. I didn't even blame him. In truth, I didn't much care. The things that used to matter to me just didn't anymore. I could see Chris's side of this. I was unpredictable these days.

Chris and Redmond exchanged looks, and Chris shifted in his chair. 'I actually want to buy you out.'

'What? Take all of it? Why?'

'I want to take things in a new direction.'

'Oh, right, Chris, don't talk around the point – you want to do business with that jerk, Jack Manton. We've talked about this. He's a down and dirty debt collector. I won't have anything to do with him.'

'He brings a lot of business to the table. A lot of money.'

'A lot of misery, too. It's pissant work. I won't do it.'

'Well, ain't that the point? You want to fuck around with that elder care shit—'

I held up a hand. 'Yeah. I guess it's time to split things up. So good of you to stop by and make it official without ever letting me know you were on the way.' I leaned across the table. 'Fine, then. Half of what is in our investment accounts goes to me. Take me off the lease, effective immediately. You keep the name of the company. I keep my clients, you keep yours.'

My brother nodded. 'What about Doctor Benton? She's been working with me since . . . Olivier died.'

'Millicent? Hell, yes, keep her. She didn't want to work with me after my husband died in case I was distracted. Even though I was doing my best work, and you know it. Which made my grief none of *her* business. I won't work with her again.'

'I'd like to keep her account, Junie – she's lucrative – but I won't lie to you. She's asking to have you back.'

'Tell her to fuck on off.'

'I won't quote you on it, Junie.' But he grinned a little. 'I'll have an attorney draw it all up and then you can let your attorney look at it. I don't want to cheat you, Junie-Bug.'

My heart was beating hard. I felt abandoned and thrilled. I no longer wanted to work with my brother. I had thought about it before. Crunched the numbers. I should be OK, especially without the overhead of the swanky office Chris insisted upon. Olivier had tried to talk me into doing this a long time ago. I wondered why I hadn't.

'Well, then, Junie, do you want to come to dinner with us tonight? We have reservations in Geneva.'

'Thanks, but no thanks, Chris. I'm going to Metz to see a woman about a guitar.'

Chris and Redmond stood up. Awkward hugs all around. 'I guess I'll see you at the holidays,' Chris said.

I had hated the holidays since Olivier died and no longer wanted to pretend. 'No, Chris, I won't see you at the holidays. I'll be in France.'

He nodded, smiled, gave me a little wave. Turned and headed away with Redmond, who gave me a serious look over one shoulder. Then Chris said something and laughed, and the two of them had their heads together, deep in conversation.

And just for a moment, I saw my brother. Really *saw* him. As if a strong wind had blown away my hurt feelings and my fury. And I saw the big brother who came to the edge of the swimming pool and pulled me out, standing up in a hell-fire fury to the swimming teacher who was of the toss-them-in-and-let-them-sink school of instruction.

He was seven then. I was all of four.

I saw the brother who lent me the money to buy my first guitar, from the money he got from doing work for the neighbors, because even then, my brother was born to make money.

The brother who was too dyslexic to get through college, who taught himself what he needed to know and built our business with me. A lucrative business that financed the endless stream of his beloved cars. Two years and time for a new one for Chris, whereas I would keep a car until it gave up and died, and then I would cry and let it go.

We had stuck together when our mother had died young, a lucky escape from our father. And Chris had stepped between Daddy and me more times than I could count – our father who remarried and remarried, always drifting further and further out of our lives. His death more of an afterthought for Chris and me. Maybe something of a relief.

But I have such memories of the four of us in a time that seems worlds and worlds away. How my mother always cooked the Thanksgiving turkey the day before, and we had a midnight feast that was as informal as it was fun. Then we would eat it again the next day at a giant meal with gravy and dressing and all the usual stuff. A house full of people, some of them I barely knew. Relatives, friends, someone my mom had met at the grocery store the week before.

I wish I could go back sometimes just to watch my beautiful, ordinary little family, when my mother held us together with the magic only she could weave.

So many things I missed. That young family who had no idea what was coming straight for them. My mother. Olivier. The days when my brother actually liked me, and when I felt that I was not completely alone in the world.

That connection with my brother was drifting away. But he was happy and in love at last. He had a future, and I had a past. We no longer lived in the same universe, my brother and me.

The collateral damage of grief. I wondered if we would ever find our way back. I felt very lost.

TWENTY-TWO

Grief is liberation. How strange and exhilarating it felt. The sense of freedom. The sense that I was remembering who I was.

The idea of ever going home again made my stomach hurt. Maybe I just wouldn't. I should have been afraid of St Priest, run home to be safe, but I didn't care if I lived or died, which is one of the most underrated beauties of grief. People talk about it as though it's a bad thing. It's not. It's glorious. And I wasn't backing down.

I would do exactly what I wanted to do. I would stay in France, to hear the rhythms of a language that was close to my heart. France was a good place for solitude. I liked the casual common sense of the French. The reserve. Polite and discreet. I was not required to smile when I walked down the street, and it was not considered odd to keep myself to myself. Nobody noticed, nobody cared.

Still. I was over that mocha pot coffee and would order the Technivorm Moccamaster pot I had at home. Also the Breville coffee grinder, because the grind is as important as the beans. Olivier and I used to argue about that, and he'd been right.

I no longer had to dread the holidays. Pretend that I was OK. I was an anonymous woman who currently resided in a tiny second-floor apartment in Annecy, over a small bistro, on a noisy street, with a window box where I would plant geraniums next spring. I had a very large dog who owned my heart, and soon I would have the guitar of my dreams. There was no requirement that I be happy. There was no requirement that I have hope.

But that was where the planning stopped. It was the future that haunted me, not the past. A future without Olivier was too bleak to contemplate, so I wouldn't make future plans. I had no future. I just had now.

The wind was in my hair. Leo was sitting up, alert, watching the road. I pulled over, got the wraparound sunglasses out of the glove compartment and put them on his head. He gave me a sloppy smile as if he had been waiting for me to figure that out.

I made a quick call to the music shop. Let them know I was on the way. The conversation turned awkward. There had been police from Metz, regarding the backpack. I reassured them that I was aware, and on my way for the guitar only. I had the letter they sent, and my passport for identification. They reassured me the guitar was there and ready to go, and there was palpable relief on both sides.

I pulled into traffic, and we were off.

I was driving to Metz with Leo, where I would fetch my beautiful new guitar. A last gift from the man I love.

TWENTY-THREE

B revard was waiting for me when I came out of the music store, the guitar tucked into a hard-shell case, held closely to my side. Standing across the street watching, straight posture, very tense. The look he gave me was quite serious.

'You're still here?' I asked as he trotted across the street. 'You got the backpack OK?'

'My colleague picked it up, and I have been through it, so yes, thank you, and I see you got the guitar. It is a very special thing? You are happy with the inscription?'

I opened the case and showed him. The inscription was stenciled in black on the neck of the guitar, inside a swirl with a tiny heart. *A Toi Pour L'éternité, Olivier.*

Brevard looked at it shyly, hands behind his back. 'Yours for eternity. That is very beautiful.'

I nodded. Tucked the guitar back into the case. 'One thing I wanted to ask you. Why were you so surprised that Olivier bought the guitar in Metz? Because there is a metallurgy lab down the street. Maybe he was here to drop off some kind of sample and just saw the guitar. Maybe he was investigating something that made him a target for the crash.'

Brevard shook his head. 'Your husband was in Metz to see me.'

Brevard knew Metz. He took the guitar and guided me down one street, and then another, and I lost track because I did not have the navigation gene, and I could get lost in my own backyard. He led me to a small place, catty-cornered on the end of a street, looking a bit the worse for wear, which is often the kind of place I like best.

The owner knew him. Nodded when we came in.

It was a quiet afternoon – only a couple of other people there – and Brevard guided me to the table across from the bar, that had a booth running along the back. He did not sit across from me but sat right beside me, thighs touching in the tight space. Leo made himself small beneath the table with a groan.

'So the food here is simple and good,' Brevard said. 'The best thing is the Margherita pizza. That would sound good to you?'

'It sounds like heaven, Capitaine Brevard.'

He shook his head at me. 'You must call me Philippe. And Leo, will he eat? Shall I order him a pizza, too?'

I smiled. 'He would love that. But he's on the baked chicken, yogurt and sweet potato diet right now. I'll give him a bite of my crust.'

Brevard settled the guitar alongside the table, tucked in very safe. He went to talk to the man behind the bar, and I fished in my purse for one of Leo's pain pills and a stick of string cheese. Three small balls of cheese, the first one with the pill tucked inside. Leo knew very well what I was up to, but he consented to eat the pill so long as it was followed by two more bites of cheese. Shepherds always negotiate.

Brevard made two trips, a bowl of water for Leo, mineral water for the two of us. He settled back in, close beside me. 'That is a pretty dress,' he said.

That surprised me, but I nodded and said thanks.

Brevard frowned. 'I do not understand your brother coming all this way with a letter. Did he worry about you because of the YouTube video? Did he come to see how you are? You will have a family dinner tonight?'

'No, he . . .' I felt my face grow red. It was embarrassing, how little I was loved now in the world, how alone. These things I did not like to admit. 'He came to buy me out of the business we run. A forensic accounting firm. He wants to take on clients I don't want to work with. He wants to renew the lease for an office I never go to.'

Brevard cocked his head to one side. 'And you are OK with this?'

'I've been thinking about it for a while. Olivier always thought I should. We'll split the business in half. We are very different; it does not make sense to work together. He does nine to five at the office and talks a lot on the phone. He is the rainmaker and brings in a lot of clients. Runs the numbers and the software for the routine kind of work. I do the tricky investigations, and those bring in the big bucks. Things you can't do with just the software. I work slower than he likes. Because for the really complicated stuff, it is about seeing something that feels off, like a wrong note of music. It's intuitive for me. Hard to explain. I have a routine for my days that annoys my brother.'

'What is your routine?'

'You can't possibly want to know that.'

He just smiled.

'*Ça va*. Every morning, for three hours, I play my guitar and think of nothing else. And then, for some reason, when I sit down to work, I can see it. Money trails and where they lead. I would find them anyway, I think. But somehow these parts of my life, the music and the trails, it is like art. The mind and the body and the creative side. All together, there is a sort of harmony. I can't explain this to my brother. I've tried. He tells me to get the work done first and play the guitar later. So I can get more hours in. Which just isn't up to him.'

Brevard nodded. 'It is better, then, that you split. You have extraordinary days. It makes me envious. Your work you can do anywhere, so now you can stay in France, which is a good place for you, I think. And I know what you mean because investigating is the same. Patterns and a feeling of something off. Like a little glow of light all around it.'

'*Yes*, exactly.'

'There is intuition in my work as well. I get you, Madame.' And he smiled at me. And the pizza came.

I felt oddly happy, but maybe it was the pizza. The smell of bread and cheese and basil, the man beside me who offered to order pizza for my dog. The strange sense I had that I had been here before in this exact moment, a feeling that had become familiar since Olivier died, the feeling that this was a future memory. Like a piece of the puzzle had snapped into place.

We ate happily, and Brevard looked down at Leo from time to time. 'I am not used to this, to have the dog always. It reminds me of when I was a little boy and went to a camp that was on a farm. We slept in a barn with cows.'

'Yeah, pretty much the same thing,' I said.

'Leo is having a hard time staying awake. Why does he not sleep?'

'Yes, poor baby. He is exhausted, and he had a pain pill that will make him want to sleep. But he won't.'

'Why not?'

'Because he is a Shepherd. He is on the job.'

'And he is guarding you?'

'At the moment, Philippe, he is guarding *us*. Leo has decided you are one of his people. I hope you are grateful and impressed.'

He peered under the table at Leo, who lifted his head and enjoyed that wrong way that Brevard always petted him. 'I have never been owned by such a dog.' He wiped his hands on a napkin and pushed his empty plate away.

'Now that we have eaten, and it was quite wonderful, Leo and I thank you. And now that you have become the property of my dog, I wonder if you would please tell me what you found in my husband's backpack that made you look so serious. And why you were meeting my husband in Metz.'

He took my hand and kissed it. 'There are times when I will talk to you as a man talks to a woman. And there are times I will talk to you as a cop. Right now, it must be as a cop.'

As a man talks to a woman? That put me somewhere between panic and intrigue. Part of me wanted the other guy, to talk to me as a woman. But most of me wanted the cop. I had a bad feeling about this. What had been going on with my husband that had him meeting with Capitaine Brevard?

TWENTY-FOUR

B revard took out a small worn notebook and a pen that had a fat nib and flowed with bold black ink. 'A request, Junie. You will write for me all of your husband's email addresses here, please? Work ones included.' He handed me the pen.

'Why?' I had them listed in a note app on my phone. Not all that secure, but welcome to real life.

'I need to make sure I have all of them, even if they have been deleted. I will double-check my list against yours, to make sure nothing was missed.' He put his hand over mine. 'There were issues with his work email – this one here.' He tapped the page. 'And this personal one here.'

'What kind of issues?'

He hesitated. 'Your husband asked to meet with me, as a friend of a friend. He wished to have my opinion but to be unofficial. I was clear with him that there is only so far un-official goes with a cop, but he still wanted to go forward, so I took his request seriously. He seemed worried.

'We agreed to meet in Metz, which is where I am stationed most of the time. He had an errand there – your guitar, I think?'

I could picture it. Olivier would have been quiet, with that gravitas he sometimes had when he was making a decision. I wondered if he drank coffee or was too tense. If he wore his black sweater. Small personal questions that I was too shy to ask. Important only to me.

'What exactly was worrying him, that the two of you had to meet in person? That you could not have discussed on the phone?'

'He wished to be private and to measure me, I think. See me face to face before he would say what he had on his mind.'

That sounded very much like my husband. My husband being careful. I gathered a handful of the silky dress in my fist.

'So we met in the market, outside at a table, drank coffee, he and I, and he talked around things just a bit. He did not seem like someone I should push. So I gave him some time. I liked him.'

I nodded.

'Two things were worrying him. One was with emails he had been getting. Three in total, I think. All payments through L'Argent Facile, so all he has to do is click and follow the links to deposit money into his bank account.'

'I've never heard of them.'

'It's new, mainly in Europe, like PayPal or Zelle. Someone can send you money that you access through email.'

'Who sent them? Do you know?'

'It seemed they came from LABAC. They are an eco-activist organization – have you heard of them? *La Bagnole Aux Chiottes*?'

I had to laugh a little. 'Does that mean what I think it means?'

'Yes, basically that cars should be flushed down the toilet. We French have to make a joke. They are peaceful in their protests, fairly new, but gathering a lot of momentum. They are not just against gasoline engines in cars, but electric, too. No cars at all.'

'You are *not* telling me that Olivier took those payments because—'

'No, no, Madame, he did not click the links or take payments – he was not stupid, your husband. He figured it was the usual kind of scam. But then his company let him know that his work email had been hacked. His specifically, which they found odd. And that the report he had sent to them with the Mont Blanc safety analysis had been targeted. He had sent it encrypted and secure – that is the normal business practice with his company. And in truth, he said, there was nothing in there that was particularly sensitive. And his company, Prometheus, had excellent security. But they wanted him to be aware that they closed down the old account and gave him a new one.'

'I don't have that email address.'

'Yes, but I do. And on the day before he died, there were

two more deposit attempts sent to him through L'Argent Facile, supposedly from LABAC. We traced them and found that they were not actually from LABAC; we have been in close touch with the organization. But the link to the money for the deposits has gone dead, so we can't trace the account numbers.'

'What was the second thing he wanted to discuss?'

'The Mont Blanc Tunnel analysis.' Brevard cocked his head to one side. 'What did he say to you about that?'

'Not much. I just know it was ready to go, but he delayed turning it in for a day or two. It was nothing he wanted to talk about on the phone. We were both tied up with work, and our calls were mainly personal. But he seemed worried about something.' I grabbed Leo's leash and twisted it in my hands. Leo raised his head, and I put the leash down. Smoothed out the folds of my dress.

Brevard gave me a serious look. 'You would know, I think, that part of his job was a risk analysis – not just for infrastructure, though he said that was most of it. That and maintenance, the integrity of the materials. But also the threat of sabotage and terrorist attack. Here in France . . . we keep a close eye on such things.

'And the Mont Blanc Tunnel, it has a massive amount of truck traffic – it's a crucial part of the supply chain in Europe. And the emissions from the tunnel traffic are significant. Your husband was worried it might be a target for terrorists, and he wanted me to tell him how likely it was to have a tunnel as a target, as part of his analysis. With his email hacked, and those weird emails, it made him wary. I was able to relieve his mind on that. As a terrorist attack, to target a tunnel is very rare.'

'But why? It seems like a no-brainer. Shuts down traffic, causes enormous damage, people die. The fires are hard to put out. The Mont Blanc Tunnel fire cost millions.'

'March twenty-fifth, 1999. Thirty-nine people died. It did not reopen until 2002, at a cost of two hundred and five million euro. Please know I remember this. Many of us do. But tunnel safety with Mont Blanc is state of the art. Traffic is funneled and tracked and under observation; there are emergency people on site at all times. So, frankly, it would make for a terrible target. Since it is assumed there will be fires, which is an ongoing issue for tunnels, there is a twenty-four-hour monitoring system, fire fighters are on site, exhaust systems set up, safety for people in tunnel shelters. A speaker system that tells people what to do, broadcasting on the car radio.' He smiled a little. 'That annoys people very much, the radio broadcasts.

'And there is constant monitoring by the French and Italian police, automated detectors all through the tunnel. Emergency stations every hundred meters. All of the traffic is carefully managed – you are not allowed to stop, overtake another vehicle, turn around, use high beams, even honk your horn. If you do, they will know about it.' He gave me a look. 'Your husband told me that women are more likely to survive a tunnel fire than men. Because it is disorienting, with all the smoke, the visibility is soon gone, it is dark, so men stay in the car, shut the windows and wait for help. Women get out of the car and look for help, find the shelters. So that is why there are systems in place now, to tell people what to do.'

I nodded. Olivier had told me all of this.

'Everything is in readiness and on high alert. So a sabotage attempt is going to fizzle, like a match you blow out. Remember, for a terrorist, it is all about the drama of the attack. And being unexpected. If the firefighters are already there, that takes the fun out of it. As a target for a protest, always possible. This is an everyday thing in France. As a target for a terrorist, too much trouble for a small effect.

'Still, I think your husband already knew all this and had thought it through. He wanted to get a professional law enforcement assessment to add to the report. And to put this on our radar. Curiously, he also wanted to know, if the tunnel became a target, who were the kind of people who would do such a thing, since I did not think LABAC was violent or dangerous.'

'And that got your attention? That maybe he had someone in mind?'

Brevard did not commit to yes or no. 'I told him that while

it would be rare to target a tunnel, the way things like this work is to think globally and look locally.'

'What does that mean?'

'The reasons are big ones – big politics where people feel helpless and hopeless and maybe even threatened . . . and this makes them angry. And if they are already angry, there are predators who will fund them and use them. There will be connections between large-scale operators and local malcontents, and they meet in dark-web chatrooms. Your husband wanted to know if I saw much funding by big business, rather than militant organizations, and, of course, the answer is yes – business, money laundering, militant groups, all snarled up in a coil. The terrorist act itself is most often done by local guys, or someone not local who hooks up with local guys. It makes sense to know the territory, and everyday ins and outs.

'I told your husband that if he had any suspicions of a certain person or persons, he should tell me. Timing is the key to this – these acts are often connected to a public event of some kind, and we could watch this person and stop them before anything happens, or even be on guard with extra security.'

'But why set up faux payments from a specific activist organization like LABAC?'

He smiled at me. 'This is very common these days, with the Internet, social media. People pretend to be part of the group; they join protests and are violent to make the world angry and turn them against the organization. Who are the protesters, who are the bad actors? This is rampant all over the world. Your husband thought this over and asked me about using this strategy to discredit specific NGOs. That has been very much in the news. In Europe—'

'Yes, yes, they are considered . . . civil society groups, and are protected. Laurent has been schooling me.'

'Exactly. And they can have enormous influence. And this tactic has been used by politicians and law enforcement. To accuse them of ties to terrorist groups and shut them down. Sometimes it is true; often it is not. And your husband was getting ready to begin work with Laurent Valiente's NGO.

So he was worried the NGO was being targeted for exactly that.'

'And?'

'And he thanked me for my help.'

'Come on. Get real. You've talked to Laurent, right? Olivier was going to work for the NGO; they were getting ready to ditch their blue hydrogen investors. It's all . . . a big mess of money and old grudges. And my husband's plane was sabotaged. If Laurent had been on that plane, it would have taken both of them out, which I think was the plan.'

'Yes. And this is under investigation. I can't tell you any more.'

'You don't have to. I know who's behind this and so do you.'

'I am not at liberty to comment on that.'

'Because you don't just want St Priest; you want the investors behind this, and maybe to confiscate their bank accounts. And maybe to see whatever else they might be up to.'

He tilted his head sideways and gave me a small smile. 'I am not at liberty to comment on that.'

'And if you arrest St Priest too soon, everybody else fades away, and all you have is . . . St Priest. That would be enough for me. He's the one I want you to go after. I don't care about those other guys.'

'But I do. Two people were murdered. Who will they go after next? This is sabotage for reasons that were personal as well as big. Small-time and vengeful for St Priest – a coward who sets things up and does not face his target. But with big money and high stakes, and major investors. You may not care about those other guys because you don't have a face for them. But I care very much.'

'So the investors are behind St Priest driving home a personal vendetta to take down the NGO. Cut the head off its influence and punish them for changing sides, and setting them up to be suspected of activism and maybe a terrorist plot. But surely you know this is all smoke and mirrors to make Olivier and Laurent look bad. Right? You don't really think there is a real terrorist plot snarled up in this?'

'What I can tell you is that the French government would look with great fury on such a thing.' Brevard looked at me steadily. He did not smile.

And I realized he thought exactly that. That there was a real terrorist plot tied up in this. And I wondered why.

I shut my eyes very tight, and Leo stirred and sat up, watching me. I was in over my head. I wanted to take Leo back home to our little apartment, crawl into bed and put a blanket over my head.

Brevard took my wrist. 'Please, Madame, do not be distressed. This is my job to handle, and not yours. But I must ask. Your husband, he told you about the fight?'

'Fight? What *fight*?'

'He arrived at our meeting with a bruised cheek and swollen knuckles on his right hand. A cut on the side of his head, cleaned and stitched.'

I went cold inside. 'Olivier did not get into fights. That's just . . . hard to believe. Someone attacked him.'

'No, Madame. He threw the first punch.'

'*Olivier?*'

'He admitted this to me. We discussed it in detail, as it involved St Priest and the NGO. I wish to know what he told you about it. We found a bloody white shirt inside the backpack that he left at the music store. Which I think he just stuffed in there when he changed his shirt after the fight, and there was also his small laptop notebook.'

'He used it to play online chess.'

'Yes. And on the laptop are three photos. One of your wedding. One of you playing the guitar with Leo looking up at you. And one of all three of you on a hike.'

'Yes. Tennessee. Smoky Mountains. We loved it there.'

'I see. The Smoky Mountains.' Brevard frowned at me. 'Did you and your husband spend a lot of time in Tennessee, in these Smoky Mountains?'

'Yes. He worked in that area, for a while. But we haven't been back in . . . years.'

'And he said nothing to you of this fight?'

I shook my head.

'Sometimes a man will not tell a thing like this to his wife.'

'I will tell you again, Capitaine. My husband . . . I have never known him to get physical, to fight or be aggressive.'

'So we will say whatever brought him to this was a big deal. And his state of mind? The last time he talked to you?'

I frowned. I had thought about this a lot, puzzled over it. 'It was pretty clear that there was a lot on his mind, but he wasn't going to talk about it in a quick phone call. He said we would discuss things later, share a glass of cognac, curl up together on the couch, sort things out. And that got my attention because he only drank cognac when he was really upset. So that, yes, that worried me. And then right before he got on that little plane, he sent a text.'

'Which said?'

'*Coming home as soon as I can. I love you.*' I chewed my fist. 'Clearly, you know more than I do. Clearly, he talked to you, he talked to Laurent – he pretty much talked to everybody *except* me.'

Brevard took my wrist and pulled my fist out of my mouth. 'I cannot understand you when you do that. I am sorry I have upset you. I know these things are hard to think about. Please know that I am after your husband's killers, and keeping an eye out for Laurent and the NGO, because there are some who would immediately shut it down – do you understand that? We have many new laws on terrorism, and it would be easy enough to do. If there *is* a terrorist plot . . . I cannot let that happen. And, in particular, Madame, I will be watching over you. I have people keeping watch on St Priest, and that is information you will keep to yourself. I have had you on my mind since the day I met you and took you to identify your husband's body, and told you all the details about what happened to your husband. You were so in shock, Madame. I have worried for you.'

And he leaned very close and kissed me. Pulling my bottom lip gently into his mouth, disengaging slowly.

I leaned into him because I wanted to. I wanted to put my head on his shoulder, I wanted him to put his arms around me, I wanted to cry. And then I pulled back. My experience with French men was they kissed you as soon as they liked you and ten seconds later you were in a relationship. And while he was investigating my husband's murder . . . he was also investigating my husband.

'To kiss you is OK?'

'You are a policeman investigating the death of my husband. This kind of thing is OK if you are French?'

He laughed. 'No, Madame, it is not OK, not even when you are French.'

TWENTY-FIVE

W*alk-in soul.* The very term puzzled me, I didn't know what it was, and St Priest's explanation – that he was somehow my husband come back to me – brought a wave of sick fury every time I thought about it, and I thought about it a lot.

I could not concentrate on the account I was analyzing. I set my work aside and made coffee, then sat at the kitchen table with my laptop, Leo's head on my bare feet. And began rambling around the Internet, which brought me cascades of information.

According to the definition, a walk-in could happen when the original soul of the body wanted out, due to trauma, illness, whatever might have happened in their life to make them want it to end. A soul who was intensely unhappy and worn out, looking for respite. Sanctuary. An end to the struggle. And once it was set in motion, there would be an accident, an illness, a trauma, making a two-way street. A way out for a soul weary of a life no longer wanted, and a way in for the soul who wanted another chance.

The walk-in soul, with its own purpose and goals, revived and inhabited the body. It didn't have to go through childhood. It didn't have to risk dicey parents. When a person died, their soul could go into another body and live on, with the permission of the original soul, who left. It had to be a matter of mutual consent. Supposedly, there were soul contracts. One soul wanted out, the other wanted in. Did they shake on it?

Sometimes in a soul shift, eye color changed.

The walk-in retained the memories but not the emotions; they brought their own consciousness, their purpose, their intentions, which could cause havoc if the original soul was married. Had children who loved them. Families imploded. Part of me thought this could be a nice little excuse for abandonment. *Sorry, love, but I'm not me anymore.* But if they weren't fitting into the old soul's life . . . well, who could blame them? They usually returned with purpose. With a plan. Things to do.

And it was starting to do my head in.

They've made movies about this. *Here Comes Mr Jordan*, made in 1941. *Heaven Can Wait*, in 1978. Both about walk-ins.

And what Charl St Priest was trying to sell me was that his soul had walked out and Olivier's had walked in.

I knew better. I knew he was not my husband. Still – the issue of the tiny lily of the valley hidden in the bouquet haunted me. How had St Priest known? There had to be some kind of explanation. He was not Olivier.

And the territory of walk-in souls was a dangerous place for the bereaved. It made sense that people would yearn for this. The mysterious and magical return of someone they loved.

I wanted Olivier to come back to me somehow, someway. And I knew that he was close, with that mysterious bittersweet presence that those of us who grieve know so well. We just don't tell you about it. We don't want you reframing this and backing us into corners. It is a private thing, and precious, and you are not needed here.

It all came down to belief. You know what you know. Gut intuition was the way I had lived since the moment Olivier died.

In truth, I did not think that I would ever let go of the expectation that somehow, someway, Olivier would walk through the door, with that end-of-the-day smile, with a kiss hello, and we could resume the steady and beautifully mundane happiness of our quiet nights together. That somehow and someway we would pick up where we left off. That somehow, someway we had actually never . . . left off. That we were still *us*. I know the brutal twisty culture of grief would tell me to let this go. The culture of cruelty that did not see the beauty of my grief. That did not heal trauma but made it so much worse. That pathologized the agony of loss, as if to be human was to be . . . wrong. But I knew that I was not the only one who looked to the door, wondering if one day it would open and the one I love would walk through. Did grief hold an intuitive knowledge we had forgotten?

I shut down my laptop, rubbed my eyes, picturing St Priest in my husband's coat, following me through the woods. St Priest, who had taken his appropriation of my husband to a sickening manipulative place, appropriating Olivier, appropriating me.

He would be back. He would come after me again. And I would be waiting for him. Because when you don't care if you live or die, you are always the most dangerous person in the room.

TWENTY-SIX

I spent the next two days working gently, steadily and happily with my Druzhinin guitar, which was so much better than I had ever imagined. The sensuous feel as I wrapped myself around it. The gentle vibrations of the music, how sensitive the guitar was to any change in pressure on the strings. The range and tones I was only just beginning to explore. I had been yearning for a guitar like this for so long. Refusing to spend the money. Until Olivier took that decision out of my hands.

And when I was not playing, I spent hours catching up on client work at the kitchen table and thinking about Laurent. I was still a little afraid of him, though I was not sure why. He had called once, and I had turned off my phone. But there was much Brevard would not tell me, circles within circles, and I knew it centered on Laurent, St Priest and Olivier. I wanted to ask Laurent about Olivier's fight. I wanted to know if he'd received emails promising payment from LABAC. I would call him first thing. Tonight, I had plans.

My time on the balcony had brought Eugene up to the apartment. Customers had heard me play, even though the balcony looked discreetly over a side street, on the right-hand side of the restaurant.

There had been assumptions. I had somehow become the resident guitar player at Chez Eugene; customers wanted to know what nights to come for dinner to hear me, and Eugene and Annette thought it made sense for me to play a bit, now and then, and afterwards sit with Leo at a discreet table and have dinner. They felt I was too much alone. I would do this, please. Just try and see.

It seemed to be accepted that I was not going back to Kentucky.

I never had any interest in performing. People seemed to find that strange. It was not an issue of stage fright. It was an issue of privacy. I always went deep into the music, to that place in my head that it took me, which felt an intimate thing. It was odd to be watched when you were doing that.

But I knew that Eugene and Annette were right; I was too much alone.

So this would be my first time since that night long ago when Olivier, Laurent and I had eaten dinner, and Laurent had called me Barbie with a Guitar, and I had decided I loathed him. Tonight, I would play music in Eugene's café and put Laurent out of my mind.

I wore jeans and my favorite black sweater, and the worn, comfortable half boots that would need to be replaced. I indulged the urge for red lipstick.

The café was crowded for a Tuesday night. Eugene looked at me with quite the smile and sparkle, and there was an expectant energy in the air. He led me to a small area in the back that was all set up. A comfortable chair, a bit of cleared-out space. No big tall stool, I had begged him. There was also a small table, on which there was a bouquet of flowers – hydrangea, three roses and a spray of lily of the valley – placed on a little yellow cloth, and a thick candle in a jar, the flame flickering.

'This is OK?' Eugene asked me. People were watching us. Looking at the guitar. The dog. Me.

'It's lovely. How kind you are.'

'Yes, but I appreciate this. When you are done, just go to that little table over there – see that?' He pointed. 'I reserved it for you. That way, you won't be having a dinner on display.' He patted my shoulder and headed to the front door, where a man walked in, looking around. A tall man. Laurent.

Eugene seated him at the table he had reserved for me, and they both turned and looked at me. Eugene gave me a little wave, and Laurent a nod.

I felt ambushed. My stomach went tight, and my hands started to shake. I took a deep breath, and Leo looked up at me and leaned close.

Laurent looked good. A brown leather jacket, loose jeans and a black sweater. Freshly shaved, a recent haircut, hair gelled back.

OK, then. I would ask him my questions tonight.

But first it would be me, Leo and the music.

It was a full house, which was not difficult; the café was a small place, fifteen tables close together, painted concrete floors, whitewashed walls. A huge rustic chandelier in the middle, candles on every table, the smell of shallots and garlic and roasting meat, and I was surprisingly happy to be there. Leo settled beside me, and I think it was Leo who brought the smiles and the good feelings I got from the crowd. You cannot go wrong with a dog.

I looked around the room. People were eating, some talking, most watching me. I smiled at them, then forgot them and began to play.

It was a good crowd. Kind. Applause, smiles, attention at the end when I finally looked up. It is a funny thing, that you can feel an audience. When they are just happy you are there. Cheering you on. I did not know if it was always like that, but it was like that tonight.

I gathered up my guitar – Leo sat up and looked at me. I offered the flat of my hand, and we did a high five. For this, Leo received a large round of applause, a whistle and a cheer.

Laurent was smiling when I got to the table where there were two bottles of champagne jammed together in the center. He stood up, and we exchanged two *bises*.

'Feeling festive?' I asked him, looking at the bottles.

He laughed. 'These are sent to the table for you. Well, one of them was sent to you; the other is for Leo. Do you give your dog champagne? He is very French after all.'

'He is too young to drink.'

Laurent pulled out my chair, and we sat.

'You need a new pair of boots, Junie.'

'I know.'

'It is OK that I am here?'

I nodded. 'I've been wanting to talk to you. But let's drink first.'

'Champagne is OK? Not red wine?'

'Champagne is better.'

He sighed. 'So you are sane after all.'

Annette brought us braised chicken in sauce, carrots, leeks, red lentils. A plate of roasted chicken and a bowl of water for Leo. I had to maneuver carefully not to knock Leo's bowl over – it was tight quarters here – but somehow I liked it. It was strange not to be alone. It actually felt good.

'Thank you for the dinner,' I told her.

She squeezed my shoulder. 'Thank you for the music, Junie.' She wore a loose silky dress and trailed a subtle scent. But her hair was coming out of the chignon, and she had an air of coiled stress. The restaurant life.

Laurent uncorked the champagne deftly and filled our glasses. 'Eugene called me. He did not want you to eat alone.'

'I might be glad to see you.'

He gave me a sideways smile. 'Let me know when you decide.'

The chicken was tender and piquant. The champagne cold and crisp. My guitar was tucked behind me, against the wall, and Leo was eating quietly, taking time over his meal, as he always did. He had impeccable manners. And there, just for a moment, I felt a small, warm joy. These moments felt extraordinary to me. These ordinary things.

By tacit agreement, Laurent and I stayed with small talk while we ate. Mostly about Leo.

'He is picking up a little weight, Junie, and his coat is looking shiny again. Soft.'

'Soft? His coat is like lamb's wool; it takes forever even to get it wet.'

He gave Leo a bite of his chicken in sauce and did not ask my permission. Leo was happy about it.

'He is eating well,' Laurent said.

'Yes, he is. Mainly chicken, rice and yogurt. Sweet potato mashed up with molasses. And apples.'

'Apples?'

'He will lie down on the floor, put an apple between his paws and eat every last bit, even the seeds and the core. I have a bowl of them on the kitchen table, but I can only leave them out one at a time, or he will eat them all at once.'

'He is allowed to jump up to the table?'

'*No*. It's just . . . *apples*.'

'He is very big. I do not think it would be much of a jump. He has only to lift his head.' Laurent looked across the table at me. 'You are not afraid of me now, Junie? You had that look when I was helping Brevard to find you in the forest. As if you did not even know me. That same look you had before.'

'What do you mean, *before*?'

He shook his head, shut his eyes and took a deep breath. 'Olivier's funeral. You might not even remember, Junie; you were just so . . . lost. How you came into that place, the funeral home. Eugene and I were waiting for you inside, right by the door.'

'I don't remember a lot.'

'That is a good thing, I think. People seem to fight with that, as if forgetting is a bad thing. But it is a gift, to forget. And you . . . that day, you were so strange. So wary. You looked at us and you did not know us, did you, Junie? I felt like you were looking at strangers that day, that everyone there was a stranger to you.'

I nodded. 'That I do remember. It was surreal. All the people, men in suits – and you are right; I did not know when I walked in who anybody was. I wondered if you were there for Olivier's funeral or for someone else. And everyone was staring at me, and I could not make myself take a step forward. I could not even come through the door. I could not breathe.'

He nodded.

'But I do remember the next thing. That you took my hand and led me in, and sat me in a chair, and crouched down beside me, and told me to breathe, with you, because somehow you knew what to do. How did you know?'

'I just knew.'

'I thought I was going to die.' I brushed tears out of my eyes. 'I didn't mind. I wanted to. People don't know that the death rate of spouses in the first few months of loss is almost seventy percent. I looked it up, later.'

'This is something I know.'

'And you made me breathe, and I have always thought . . . I have always *known* that you saved my life. I always knew I should have died that day.'

'I won't ask you to thank me. But I will ask you to forgive

me. Because I know how this is. And I worry now that you are afraid of me, and that you blame me for what happened to Olivier.'

'I don't have a poker face, do I? Everyone knows just by looking at me exactly how I feel. Look, I was shook up that day in the woods, and I thought you had told St Priest where I was. But there was a tracker on the car. Brevard showed it to me. But I also know there are things you haven't told me. For instance, that Olivier was getting email transactions supposedly from an activist group. Surely he told you about that. You know things you should have told me. And I don't even know how to find out, unless *you do* tell me.'

Laurent touched my hand. 'I will tell you what you want to know if you are sure you want to hear it.'

I sat forward. 'It's such an odd thing. Part of me really wants to know every last detail. Part of me is crushed that *Olivier* did not tell me. And part of me just wants to drift away.'

'Tell me your questions.'

And it struck me that in offering to tell me things and asking me what questions I had, he was really asking me what I already knew.

I picked up the unopened bottle of champagne and handed it to Laurent. 'This is a private conversation, so let's take the champagne upstairs and have a talk. Because Brevard has Olivier's missing backpack. Olivier left it at the guitar shop, by accident. With a bloody shirt stuffed inside. So I know about the fight.'

'Yes. Brevard and I discussed this. He told you everything?'

'That Olivier threw the first punch. Which I do not believe.'

'Oh, believe it, Junie. It is true.'

TWENTY-SEVEN

We settled into my homey little kitchen. I rounded up two glasses while Laurent opened the second bottle of champagne. Normally, I would be sleepy after a good dinner. And after three glasses of champagne? I have been known to sing at that point. But not now. Now I felt wide awake and tense.

Laurent settled back in his chair; he was tall, long-legged. 'Olivier was very happy, you know, after he decided to come to work with me. He wanted to come home each night to you. That was my lure, to tempt him. You could live in Annecy or Metz, or Chamonix. And already you have the apartment here.' He shook his head. 'We would have been so good together on this.'

I looked away, thinking about a future that was no longer possible.

'You know we were in the French army together, when we were young. Our year of duty. And Olivier, they would not even let him march in the parades. He would get the footwork off and throw everyone out of timing. They made him do paperwork in the office instead. Then one day, he called me in France, and he called Eugene, and he told us he had finally learned to dance. We laughed and said we didn't believe him.'

I smiled. 'He agreed to go to one private dance lesson. He knew I loved to dance, and he wanted to try, if only to show me how impossible it was. But then it came to him, halfway through the lesson, that the dance steps could be equated with chess moves. Once he figured that out, there was no stopping him. He could remember all the steps and map them out in his head.'

'It was impossible for me to beat him at chess, and I myself am very good.' Laurent was smiling. 'And I asked him, *Why, Olivier, would you even try to learn to dance?* And he said . . . *I have met Junie.*'

I put my hands over my face. 'Stop, please, Laurent, and tell me why Olivier got into a fight. Brevard told me about it, but he didn't give me any details. What the hell happened? He didn't hit *you*, did he?'

'Your husband was my friend. He would not hit me, even over blue hydrogen, though sometimes I thought he wanted to. No, it was not me. He punched St Priest. Downstairs, while the three of us were having dinner at Chez Eugene.'

I stared at him. 'Olivier would never have agreed to have dinner with St Priest.'

He waved a hand. 'I set it up for us to meet St Priest for a business dinner, and St Priest was very late. But Olivier knew St Priest was coming. I had already told St Priest in a formal email that Olivier had joined the NGO and we were going to take things in another direction, and no longer accept their funding, once the current contract ran out in twelve months. And that I would deliver the report they had funded as agreed. That this would not be unexpected, as it had been clear for some time that we were at odds over using blue hydrogen as a bridge to green. And St Priest knew I had changed my thinking on this; we had had many discussions over the previous six months. Once he got the email, St Priest called. He was very calm, very pleasant, and said he had a proposition for me and would like to meet over dinner. Olivier and I thought it best for him to be at the meeting, although . . . in hindsight—'

'Yeah. Hindsight.'

'And St Priest, he arrived so late we did not think he would show up. But then he arrived after we had eaten. We were finishing off our bottle of wine and having coffee. The place was almost empty, and Eugene was in the kitchen with Annette. It was late, almost midnight.

'Olivier had been tense all through dinner, waiting to get things settled with St Priest. And he had told me that he suspected St Priest would be bringing an offer to buy out the NGO. He said they would offer us both big salaries, but we would have to give up control. He thought this would be their plan for making a killer acquisition.'

'Which is what?'

'Buy us out and then terminate the NGO. This is a strategy used quite a lot in the US. For example, big pharmaceutical companies in America buy little companies who have a good product and are starting to get a reputation and cut into the market share just a bit. And when a small company is innovative, and maybe a future threat, the big companies, they buy it up, terminate the research and basically kill it off. And they do this when the companies are small, so they don't trigger any kind of antitrust laws or regulations. It is part of their way of doing business. Olivier felt there was a good chance this would be St Priest's next move, and I said he was being paranoid, but no. He was right. That is exactly what happened.

'Olivier knew, of course, that the work was all I had since Violette died, the only thing that kept me going, and I would not want to sell out and have it killed off when I had put so many years into it.' He sighed. 'So . . . St Priest arrived and everything went straight to hell.

'Olivier was very rude when St Priest got there, full of apologies, too late for dinner, but in time for us to talk. St Priest said he had come with a solid offer of what he called big funding, which came with just a few strings attached, and a very big salary for me, and for Olivier, too, if he wanted to be in on this. St Priest was smiling like he was *Père Noël* and Olivier just looked at me across the table, with a very mean little smile.

'And then Olivier, he said, *We turn your offer down*, and did not even give St Priest time to lay out the specific details. St Priest said, *What do you mean? This is a wonderful thing, building the NGO, doing good in the world. Read it over and give it a chance*. And he handed a copy of the paperwork to me and to Olivier. Olivier, he read it fast and handed the paperwork back to St Priest. And Eugene, he was watching us from the kitchen, looking worried and wondering what the hell was going on.

'And Olivier pointed to St Priest and said that the list of investors behind this offer work hand in hand with some of the dirtiest polluters in the business. He said their goal was to get hydrogen subsidies but use dirty hydrogen, not green, while promising to change over in the future. St Priest was calm and matter-of-fact, as if he was dealing with a child who was having a tantrum. *I am still an engineer*, he said. *And a very good one*. He pointed out that there were risks to green hydrogen, that the process was a threat to the water supply of the cities where the plants would be built, the tech was inefficient, and there were leaks and explosions that put people at risk. That we must take care not to advise people to go blindly into this new technology without assessing the risks. Which, of course, was true. St Priest held his temper. But Olivier, he did not.

'Olivier told St Priest that he was working in one direction only. To discredit the green hydrogen and green steel industry, and to acquire small companies and NGOs and kill the industry off. Because what he was calling an offer of funding was really a takeover. And in truth, when I looked the paperwork over in detail later, it was clear that was exactly what it was. They were setting up to take us over and kill us off, just like Olivier thought. And I also noticed a very interesting thing. That the offer was dated three months before, so this had been in the works before Olivier even came on board.

'And Olivier, he was so angry. He stood up and threw his hands in the air.'

I could picture that. There would have been no reasoning with him.

'And now Olivier was shouting, and Eugene was running out of the kitchen, and the men at the next table were staring. But Olivier, he did not stop. He said this was just business as usual with oil and gas companies, and he told St Priest what he could do with his offer, which, I promise you, was as imaginative as it was rude. And he told St Priest that he and I would now work together to advise companies how to change over to green hydrogen. That he would live in France, and he would go home every night to his beautiful wife. And that is when it happened. St Priest said, *Fine, go home to your little blonde bitch*. And Olivier punched him very hard, the table went over, and it took me, Eugene and the two men who were finishing their dinner to pull Olivier off St Priest.'

I sobbed and then I laughed. 'I wish I'd been there.'

Laurent grinned. 'It was a hell of a night. St Priest, he was in a fury when he left, and making threats. And Olivier and I apologized to Eugene, and tried to clean up, but Eugene waved us away and said Olivier should go and get his head looked at; he needed a couple of stitches. And Olivier, he was still a little drunk, and quite happy, and singing as I took him to the clinic, and he laughed and said he had been wanting to punch St Priest for a very long time and that night he would go to bed happy.'

Laurent rubbed a hand over his jaw. 'Olivier and I just didn't get it. How dangerous St Priest is. We had no idea what we were dealing with. St Priest has been plotting to bring down my NGO since I changed direction, and having Olivier involved was a bonus for him. And Junie . . . St Priest, he wants everything. The company, Olivier dead . . . and *you*. Everything Olivier had, he wants to be his. And that is my fault.'

'How is it your fault, Laurent?'

'Because I am the one who gave St Priest the idea, about walk-in souls. I am the reason he did all that with the wedding bouquet and the videos, and I must tell you the truth about that.'

'Brevard told me about St Priest. He told me this is a pattern he has. It has nothing to do with you, Laurent.'

He shook his head. 'You want it all, don't you? Everything I know? Just listen.'

TWENTY-EIGHT

L aurent took a breath, staring into the kitchen but not seeing it. 'When I saw you at Olivier's funeral, it came to me that you were so much like Violette. And I thought this is grief. Mine and yours all jumbled up. But then . . . when you came for Leo and you drove up to my house, and I saw you get out of the car, and you smiled at me, then *I knew* you were Violette. I could see it. It was like . . . like my soul cried out to you. And I had hoped for you and I to go forward and get a second chance. For love.'

And that was why he had looked at me like that. Standing on the porch of the cabin he had built when Violette died.

I took his hand. 'I am sorry, Laurent. I can't be your Violette. But I understand you. It is normal to see the person you love because you are looking for them. But I am not Violette and I am not . . . I am only your friend.'

He nodded. 'Yes, I get that now. I think that maybe I have been crazy with this.'

I felt a wave of grief sickness in the pit of my stomach. 'It's normal, isn't it? We see the ones we love. Somehow we see them. A glimpse out of the corner of the eye . . . someone in a crowd just walks by and looks so much like them that we hope and think that maybe it is them.'

He squeezed my hand. 'But do you ever wonder, Junie, if ever it could be more than that?'

I grimaced. 'You mean like that crazy talk from St Priest? About walk-in souls? Did he discuss that with you, too? Where did he even come up with that?'

Laurent looked away. 'He made of it a mockery, something disgusting, when he talked to you like that.'

I leaned back into the couch. 'I can see the lure of it. It's . . . intriguing. To think that somehow, someway, Violette or Olivier could come back. But it's dangerous, Laurent. For people like us.'

'Yes, I get that, I went off the deep end on this. And now we have St Priest who takes it and twists it all up. And I am afraid he got the idea from *me*. From one of the notebooks I have kept since Violette died, and very private. He saw it on my desk and took it. I did not know it was gone until he brought it up. Until he laughed at me and asked if I had found Violette.' He grimaced. '*Les vautours de deuil.*'

'Vultures of grief? Oh yeah, that resonates. Leave it to the French to have a name for this.'

'This happens. People who are hungry for the details of your grief. I find it very strange. But St Priest, he is in a category all on his own.'

'I think I need another glass of champagne.' I brought the last bottle over; we still had half. I skipped the glasses and took a swig, handing it over to Laurent, who smiled and took a long drink.

'You should know this, Junie. How happy Olivier was. That the two of us would work together, how it was going to be *trop bien*, and that he could not wait to go home and tell you it was time to move to Annecy for always.'

'Laurent, Olivier must have told you about those emails he got – fake ones from LABAC.'

'Yes, I got them, too. And I gave the links to Brevard, but there seems to be no way to connect them to St Priest. And if all this blows up and they shut my NGO down, that will be the end of me.'

I had the grace not to try to argue him out of it. I knew it was true. I knew that if I hadn't found Leo, it would have been the end of me.

'You said you are under contract for another three months. Are you still getting ongoing payments? Because if you are, and the NGO goes down, we can make sure they go down, too.'

'How?'

'If your NGO is shut down for being connected to terrorists, then they are connected, too. And if I follow their payment transactions to your bank to their server, then I can ramble through their transactions and find all kinds of dirt.'

'Such as?'

'Financing the account they used for L'Argent Facile. If I can get that, they're toast.'

'And you just need a copy of the payment transaction from their bank to the bank of my NGO?'

'No. I would need to know when a new transaction was going through from their bank to yours, and be there, online, with access to the account when it is actually going through. This is all about timing. So if they are making regular automated payments to your NGO, that would be the way to do it.'

'How does this help you? All you will have are the payments to my NGO, which are all legitimate no matter who is behind them.'

I nodded. 'So it works like this. I can mirror their server while the transaction is in progress.'

'What does this do, then?'

'Basically, it gives me a log of the transactions they've made. It's a process used for backing things up, and to connect a database between computers. It gets me into their database.'

'This is legal?'

'*God, no.* And neither is the software I'll be using.'

He gave me a slow smile. 'I can give you what you need.'

'So they're making good on the payments?'

'Junie, I have been putting together a report on the impact of green hydrogen on local water supplies. They have been financing this for two years. That contract is not up until I turn in the report, which will be three months from now. And they want it very much. They can use it to show the downside of green hydrogen.'

'Why would you give that to them?'

He sat forward. 'Because it is ethical. Because it is a contract between us, and they have been financing it. The information is essential to know, no matter which side you are on. The point is not to hide the problems but to deal with them. And that is included in the report as well.'

'That's the problem with guys like you and Olivier. Ethics. You should learn to play dirty. And just to be clear, what I am doing is completely illegal. I don't give a shit about the blowback for me – I'm from the South, and revenge is in my DNA. And I will deny, deny, deny your involvement. Once under pressure, I will tearfully confess that I got access from Olivier. That may or may not protect you. And whatever I find, I'm going to turn it over to Capitaine Brevard. So when they try to take down your NGO . . . we'll take them down, too.'

'I'm in, Junie. Get your phone; I'll send what you need right now. You have WhatsApp?'

I nodded. It was probably safer than anything else. I grabbed my phone off the table, disturbing Leo, who groaned and rolled over. Laurent pulled his own phone out of his pocket.

'And Laurent, is there a certain day of the week or the month when the account transactions go through? Anything on a regular, automated schedule? That's the way it usually works; it will be in their payroll system. Because this doesn't work if I am not there when it's going through.'

He nodded. 'Monday mornings, nine a.m.'

'That's the time it comes through or the time you check your account?'

'This is when the money comes to the account.'

I smiled at him. 'You sweetheart, you. I'm going to need your bank information, and passwords, and it will be a two-FA identification right?'

He frowned. 'Two-FA?

'Two-factor authentication. Do they text you or email a code?'

'No, it is a password and then a pin number. So I can give all of this to you.' He pulled out his phone. Typed in the information, and hit send. He did not hesitate. The benefits of making a request to a man who is on his third bottle of champagne.

He looked up from the screen. 'You have them now?'
'Got it.'

'So I am deleting this from my phone now. And turning it off for a while.'

'And we never had this conversation.'

He shook his head at me and gave me a quick kiss on the side of the cheek. 'It is late, and Leo is snoring. I should go.'

He tipped the champagne bottle back and finished it off, and handed it to me as I walked him to the door. We exchanged *bises*. 'I am here for you, if you need me. Be careful of St Priest. I am glad you found your very big dog.'

TWENTY-NINE

I knew Eugene and Annette would be working late, wrapping things up in the kitchen. I did not want them to hear. It was an instinctual thing, hiding grief.

I threw myself on the bed I had shared with Olivier, jammed my face into the pillow. Leo snuffling with distressed worry at my shoulder. Giving me doggie kisses.

The life we could have had. The life we almost had. If only I could go back. Catch hold of it. Keep it from slipping away.

And my mind was working fast. I believed everything Laurent was telling me. And I knew there was a missing piece. I was not getting the whole story from anyone – not Brevard, not Laurent and, of course, not St Priest and his dangerously unpredictable twisted fury with my husband. I wondered how closely Brevard's officers were keeping watch on him.

I lifted my head, told Leo everything was OK, sat up and petted him until he settled. I might not know the missing parts, but I knew I was part of the mix. Terrorism and sabotage and the Mont Blanc Tunnel. And an angry person giving a big fat *fuck you* to Olivier *and* to Laurent.

Greenwashing companies eating up big chunks of government money – that I got. That it was snarled up with St Priest, Laurent's NGO and Olivier – that I got. But the Mont Blanc Tunnel? Terrorists? Olivier worried about something to the point that he talked to a cop like Brevard? That was the missing bit that baffled me. Because Brevard was clearly convinced there was an actual terrorist plot.

And if I had to deal with any other people my husband pissed off, I would have to give them a number and send them to the back of the line.

'You really stepped in it this time, didn't you, Olivier?' I said out loud. 'Why didn't you just come home?'

Leo lifted his head and looked at me.

And I heard Olivier's voice strong in my head. *I tried.*

THIRTY

I had not slept. It was a reality shift . . . things I had not been aware of, things that had been happening all around me and Olivier. I knew my husband's heart. I knew he had done nothing wrong. But he had been in the depths of trouble.

And how much I resented that people would not leave us alone, to live our small and average life. And how much I resented being surrounded by people now who *knew things*. And did not tell me. Things I had a right to know.

I knew from experience that what always tripped people up were the routine money transactions.

And now I had the financial links to the NGO account where I could take a look at the transactions from St Priest's investors. And use those to track other transactions that might shed some light on what they were up to. I could use the log of transactions I got to get a look at other places their money went. There was a lot of information to be had.

I was upset and crazy with champagne last night. But I was stone-cold sober now. It was two thirty a.m., and I wanted to keep watch right away. Just in case something went through early. Or Laurent was off about the time. Minutes mattered.

I took Leo out. I fed him an early breakfast. I sat at the kitchen table, too nervous to drink my coffee, but wide awake, computer up and software running. Playing online back-gammon on my phone so I did not go insane. I put the phone down at eight thirty a.m. At eight forty-seven, the transaction went through, and the software captured it and nailed it. Copied the database. And then I got out.

I took a breath, made a fresh copy and began going through their transactions. And found the account number and balance for the L'Argent Facile transactions, and a deposit made the day that last payment email link was sent to Olivier. I had them.

I sat at the table, hands shaking. I copied the information

into a thumb drive. Hid the drive in a plastic bag, triple-wrapped, in Leo's huge bag of kibble. I picked up the phone to call Brevard, then hesitated. I had the leverage I needed. I would have to figure out the best way to use it.

THIRTY-ONE

I t was not possible for me to stay in the apartment.

Leo and I headed out in the Z4, with the top down, me bundled up as usual in one of Olivier's old sweaters. There were two places I wanted to go. I wanted to see the shed where St Priest had kept Leo. Not a smart thing to do. More like an irresistible compulsion. And I wanted to see the airfield where Olivier had taken that final flight, to see his beloved mountain. I wanted to walk the path that Olivier had walked, to see the things that Olivier had seen, just before he died.

I drove past Eugene's and glanced up at the bare balcony, thinking how it used to look, when I would hang flower baskets and have giant pots of tropical plants, which used to make Olivier roll his eyes because they would not survive the winter. Unless I forgot to water them and then they would barely make it to fall. Leo loved to stick his head into the plants and smell the flowers, and lie down happily with yellow pollen all over his nose and the top of his head. Then he would stretch out on the balcony and watch the street. Guard Dog TV.

What a little sanctuary it had been.

Now I haunted garden centers like a ghost and sometimes fell in love with a clay pot and brought it home, but I did not commit to anything living. I did not have the heart for that anymore.

The small airfield had been a pretty place in the picture on the website. I drove past a short, paved runway, surrounded by mountains. A little bit terrifying. And found Fournier's Flights – the office located in a low-slung building that had once been a café. A wide aluminum hangar attached. Madame Fournier had been a careful businesswoman, and a gifted mechanic, and had wanted to fly planes since the age of three. It said so in her obituary. Her business had been thriving and growing steadily.

The tiny office looked forlorn when I drove up. A man and a woman were gathering dead flowers and weather-stained teddy bears, wreaths with fading ribbons. Homage to the dead. This is what things looked like afterward. Dead flowers and rain-soaked ribbons.

I admired them. For tossing the dead flowers into the rolling garbage cart. Clearing things out and clearing things up. It seemed to me it would be more peaceful once things were squared away, a weight off the shoulders that came with a cost – what could be more lonely than to scour the person you loved away? I had a drawer full of Olivier's old socks.

I felt shy about catching them at such a time, and I felt out of place. Feeling out of place was my new norm. I had planned just to cruise through the parking lot for a quick in-person look and then head right back out. But now I was caught.

A little girl, maybe seven, with her arms full of teddy bears that I knew she would keep, turned, saw the car and pointed at Leo, who was sitting up beside me watching her, the family, a bird that circled, the breeze ruffling his fur. The little girl waved at him and shrieked something that made the man and woman look up. They smiled at me as if they knew me and I cruised to a stop.

'*Grand-mère*, it's the lady with the dog.'

I felt my face grow red and my stomach go tight. I did not want to intrude. I did not know this family of Madame Fournier who had died like my husband in the crash. It was an odd connection, but a strong one. The woman, mother to Monsieur Fournier and paternal *grand-mère* to this little girl who had lost her mother in the crash. Child and grandmother very blonde and blue-eyed – perhaps like the husband, the father? In the obituary picture, Madame Fournier had been dark. Straight red-brown hair cut short. Dark eyes. Serious with an air of gravitas.

'Sorry,' I said with a small wave. 'I did not mean to intrude.'

'You are Madame Lagarde?' the man asked. He was dark-haired, dark-eyed. The brother of Madame Fournier, the uncle of the little girl.

'Yes, I am sorry, I shouldn't have come. I just wanted . . . to see where.'

The woman nodded. 'I understand. You found your dog?' She smiled at me. 'We heard about him on the news and in the papers. I am so happy to see you found him. One good thing.'

They watched me with a stiff, kindly formality, and I wanted nothing more than to escape.

'These are Mama's bears,' the little girl said. 'I will take them home and my papa will run them through the washer, and then I will arrange them all on my bed and keep them safe. Uncle Fabrice says there are enough of them for my very own zoo. May I pet your dog?'

I looked to the uncle and the grandmother, and the woman smiled. 'Is this OK?'

'Yes.'

Leo stood up in the seat and leaned out of the car, and the little girl held her hand out for him to sniff. He lunged close and gave her kisses.

'He likes me,' she said. 'Can he come out of the car?'

'I don't think—' But Leo put his paws up on the door frame and jumped deftly out to the pavement. People who think service dogs work like canine robots are misinformed. Not mine, anyway.

'*Leo.*' I headed out to get him. 'I'm so sorry; he knows better than to do that.'

'It's because he likes me,' the little girl said. 'And he wants to see the bears.'

I kept an eye on Leo. He was definitely fond of teddy bears, and I would not put it past him to help himself to one or two.

'Down,' I told him, and he settled with a groan. The little girl sat cross-legged in front of him, stroking his very large left paw and introducing him to all of her bears, which was going to take some time.

A man came out of the hangar. Stocky, heavy glasses, thin blond hair. The husband of Madame Fournier.

'Monsieur Fournier, I am Junie Lagarde, Olivier Lagarde's wife. *Widow.*'

He gave me a half-smile as I fumbled, and I knew he had likely done exactly the same.

'Please forgive me for stopping by. I did not think anyone would be here. I just . . . wanted to see.'

He gave me a long look. 'I have actually wanted to be in touch with you; I did not realize you were in France.'

The little girl looked up. 'Papa, *regarde*, this is Leo the Lion like in the news, and I am showing him Mama's bears.'

He smiled at her.

The grandmother gave me a gentle smile. She had an endearing charisma that made me want to tell her all about Olivier and how I missed him, and I had the feeling she would understand exactly how I felt. She reminded me of my own mother, long gone.

She put a hand on the little girl's head and nodded at me. 'It is good that you and your Leo have stopped by. Marie has been very taken with Leo's adventures, and it is good for her to know he came home to you safe.'

Marie petted Leo on the head. 'Uncle Fabrice said that Leo had been herding ibex and guarding them from the wolves. Do you think he really did that?'

'Yes, that is what he told me,' I said. 'Leo is good at herding, and he is very protective.'

'It has helped her, the stories,' Fabrice said quietly.

'I drew pictures of Leo and put them on my wall.' She stroked Leo's head, and he had the satisfied look of a dog who has lived many adventures and liked having his picture drawn.

The grandmother waved a hand toward the office. 'Please, you will come in. I could use a break, and Fabrice has made coffee.'

The welcome felt genuine. And I was curious to see the inside. The office. The hangar. The places Olivier had been on that very last day. Leo led the way, my ambassador to the world, and no one seemed at all alarmed by his size or obvious kinship to a wolf. Fabrice helped Marie gather up the bears, and she handed one to Leo, who took it gently in his mouth. And we went through the empty hangar, where I took in the smells of oil and fuel, and mechanical things, a hangar that was wide and empty without a plane. The concrete floor was stained but swept clean. The shelves were empty, showing dust and the empty space left by things that had been recently packed away. A place in transition.

A pair of Madame Fournier's worn overalls hung from a hook by the door, and I turned my head away, wishing I had not seen them, knowing that somehow that image would stay with me. Like Olivier's sweater folded neatly and tucked beneath the pillow on my bed.

I had a moment where I wanted to turn around and run to the car, feeling an overwhelming shyness and that sense I had now of being Other, but I was well and truly caught and I followed Leo inside where it was warm. I smelled coffee, and there were croissants and madeleines on a small wobbly table, and there was a small commotion of drink and food passed around.

Monsieur Fournier watched me with a knowing look, motioned me to a plastic chair and brought me a plate with a croissant and a small cup of dark rich coffee. Leo settled at my feet, nosing the bear. I watched him, terrified he might decide to shred it, like his other stuffed animals, but for now he was content to nose it around and lick it. He gave my croissant a long look, then went back to the bear.

The office was almost empty. Just about packed up.

Clearly, the Fourniers were as curious about me as I was about them.

'How are you doing, Madame Lagarde?' the husband asked me. He studied me and did not look away. He likely knew exactly how I had been doing.

Marie looked up at me curiously, and I said yes when she asked if she could feed Leo part of a croissant.

They were leaving Chamonix, the husband told me. 'The lease on this place will be up in three weeks, and we've just about got everything out. Today is our day to wrap it up, and we are leaving for good tomorrow.'

'We are going to live in Brittany, where Papa and Mama were born. We have lots of family there and we are going to live near the sea.' Marie smiled at me. 'But you cannot ski there.'

The husband nodded. 'It will be . . . very hard to leave. This was the dream of my wife. And you? You are staying in France or going back to the US?'

I told them about our place in Annecy and how much I loved it there, and the husband watched me closely. We were very different. I held tight to the connection of place, and he wanted something new. Less painful.

But they knew Chez Eugene and had been there many times, which was a wonder to us all, how mysteriously our lives had been intertwined.

'What is this?' Marie said, looking up at me. She pointed to the burn scars that wove a tapestry through Leo's fur. Marie's heart-shaped face had gone very pale.

Everyone froze. This was going to be tricky.

'You see, Leo was hurt in the crash, but he is all better now, and those marks are like badges of courage that show what a brave dog he is.'

She nodded. 'He pulled Mama from the crash so she did not burn. So *she* would not have badges of courage.'

'Yes, that is true. Leo is very proud to have done this.'

Marie turned away and picked up one of the bears, showing Leo how it could dance.

'You feel safe to stay in France?' the husband asked suddenly, frowning hard.

And that caught me. I looked down at Marie who was whispering to Leo, who sat quietly with a benevolent calm, but the little girl was completely tuned in to the conversation of the adults and holding back tears. I wished I had not come.

'That is an interesting question,' I said.

There was an immediate flurry of silent communication.

Fabrice and his mother stood up, and Fabrice motioned to Marie. 'Come along, Marie, I will help you put the bears in the car. I will give you a piggyback ride and help you carry them. Tell Leo goodbye.'

She hesitated. 'Goodbye, Leo.' She looked up at me. 'He may keep the bear if that is OK with you.'

'If you are sure you can part with it, yes, Leo would be happy to keep the bear, and he says thank you.'

She kissed the bear and Leo goodbye, and Fabrice swept

her up and away. The grandmother looked from me to her son. 'The two of you should talk.' Then she smiled at me gravely and followed Fabrice and Marie out of the door.

It was clear that this husband of Madame Fournier had things he felt compelled to tell me. That he had been making up his mind. About what to say and how much.

Monsieur Fournier leaned back in his chair. 'Forgive me – you are up for a discussion on . . . hard things?'

'Very much so.'

He grimaced. 'You know that the plane was sabotaged?'

'Yes.'

'The police have arrested no one for the murder of your husband and my wife. A thing I find very strange. Because they know exactly who did it.'

I took a quick hard breath. Felt the slamming of my heart.

He opened the center desk drawer. 'I have something you need to see.'

THIRTY-TWO

How strange it was that this man and his wife had eaten dinners in Chez Eugene, and Olivier and I had an apartment just above. How strange it was that Madame Fournier and Olivier had died together in that crash. That Leo, who sat quietly at my feet, one possessive paw on the belly of a stuffed pink teddy bear, had pulled both of them out of the plane. Had been burned in that very same crash.

Madame Fournier had died upon impact. Olivier had been alive when Leo had pulled him away from the plane. I thought of my husband's last moments. The last things he had seen. The morning fog of Mont Blanc. The mountain, the rocks, the flames, the smoke and the wreckage. I wondered how bad the pain had been. How long it took him to die. I hung tight to the thought of Leo, right there beside him.

Monsieur Fournier cleaned his glasses on the tail of his shirt. 'It seems a strange thing that you came here this day of all days, when we are packing up to leave.'

I shrugged.

'I cannot wait to get out of here. To go home to Brittany and the sea. Just sitting in this chair makes me sick to my stomach. I hope never to come back.'

'I wish I had taken the time to find you, and speak to you, after it happened. To tell you how sorry I am about your wife.'

'But you did speak to me.'

'*Did I?*'

'At the morgue, I am afraid. We were both there at the same time.'

'I don't remember that. But there are a lot of things I don't remember.'

'It is the same for me. But you were very kind to Marie, who was outside with her Uncle Fabrice. You talked to her about Leo, and how he had given my wife doggie kisses for sure. That he was lost but you would find him and make sure he came home safe.'

I had no memory of meeting any of them.

'We were in shock, you know, all of us. Marie would wake up crying in the night, and she would ask about Leo, so we would make up stories about the adventures he had. How her own *maman* had been rescued from the plane by a brave heroic Shepherd. So that she could have a good picture in her mind of a hero dog, and not think of fires or a crashed plane. She kept wanting to go to the mountain and find him, but I told her that he might return to the airfield, and that since no one else was looking here, that is where we keep watch. I could almost not believe it, that you would drive up with your Leo on our very last day. I tell you, Madame, it is a great relief to me that you have found your dog and brought him here, because Marie has looked for him every time we came. And today she finds him. This will make it easier for my daughter to leave. I hope never to come back to this place, ever again.'

I knew that I would come back again. Following the trail of my husband, like a ghost haunting the past. 'So when did you find out about the sabotage, Monsieur Fournier? Capitaine Brevard called and told me several days ago, and I immediately caught a flight to France. He also told me that Leo had been sighted in the woods by the Parc de Merlet, and that is where I found him.'

'Yes, Brevard sent me a link to that very strange video from the Parc. And, of course, I recognized the man.'

I sat forward. 'You . . . you knew him?'

'Have you only just been told about the sabotage?'

'I only just found out.'

'*Merde*, that is cruel. I should have called you, but I was told to keep this quiet while they did the investigation, and I thought they would tell you all of this. And I did not think it would take so long, or that this man St Priest would still go free.'

'So it was St Priest who did it?'

'He was there. But the actual sabotage was done by a woman that Brevard recognized, but he would not tell me anything about her. But I heard him mutter *Mae* when he looked at the video and so am sure this is her name.'

'Did he tell you *anything* about her?'

He shook his head.

'How did *you* find out about St Priest and this mystery woman? How do you know all this?'

'The nanny cam in one of Marie's bears. You see we have security cameras all around the office and the hangar, and this Mae disabled all of them. But in the passenger's seat of the plane is one of Marie's bears, this one with a camera for when we had the au pair. My wife was always very . . . very careful of such things. We have it all on video, it was on my computer feed. Everything they did.'

'*Show it to me.*'

He reached in his drawer and handed me a thumb drive. 'The police took my computer, as I knew they would, so I made several copies, and this one is for you. I am so sorry. I thought they would have told you, and they would have maybe shown this to you. It is . . . terrible to watch.'

I took the drive and tucked it carefully into my purse. 'Just to be clear. Capitaine Brevard has the whole thing on video stream, the whole sabotage act, he knows exactly who did it, and no arrests have been made.'

'Precisely.'

I stood up. 'I have to leave.'

He nodded. 'I understand. Please, we will exchange email addresses and phone numbers, because I think we would be smart to stay in touch. Be careful, Madame. These two are still out in the world.'

Going to the shed where Leo was kept would not be possible today. I would go to the apartment in Annecy, I would set my computer on the kitchen table, I would watch the video.

I drove home carefully, hands trembling, that grief sickness in my stomach, Leo draped across the passenger's seat, his giant head in my lap, pink bear under his paw. The wind blew all around me, the snap of change in the air, and I got the strangest sense of my life like a deck of cards being shuffled, then laid out one by one. But I could not know what the cards were showing and how things would play out.

THIRTY-THREE

My laptop was hooked up and on the kitchen table, with the drive Monsieur Fournier had given me plugged in. I downloaded and opened the file, turned up the volume. And the face of my husband's killer filled the screen.

Leo stood beside me, and I wound my hands into the thickness of his fur.

She wore a very tight black tee shirt – some kind of North Face thing that you saw on every person walking down the sidewalks of Chamonix. Pants pretty much the same. Black, sleek, hugging her curves. She wore a balaclava, and a wisp of dark brown hair escaped from the back like a tail. She moved with an odd robotic quality, eyes empty, but movements sharp, tight. Whatever was going on with her, I did not think she was drugged. Totally focused, and in some world of her own.

Why, I wondered. *What kind of person does such a thing?*

The nanny cam picked up the sounds quite distinctly, and I heard a man's voice. 'There you go.' He handed her a tool, a tiny circular saw, and I heard the buzz and saw the cloud of metal filings as she crouched down and deftly cut into a bolt in the floor slide of the pilot's chair.

'Not all the way through,' the man said harshly. And I knew that voice. I knew it was St Priest. But I could not see him yet. Just a shadow, a flash of arm. But I knew the coat he was wearing. The black dress coat that belonged to Olivier.

She did not speak. He leaned into the cockpit, and there he was. And I watched as the two of them worked together.

It didn't take long. Slicing deep into two of the four bolts that held the pilot's seat in place.

'Fuck,' I said. '*Merde*, you fucking fuck fuckers.' I wanted to kill them. To grab hold of them and tear the flesh from their bones with my bare hands.

The woman stopped and focused on the bear, as if she sensed my presence and heard my thoughts. Something odd in her face. A flicker of grief – takes one to know one – and she touched the bear's head with a gloved hand, patted it twice and turned away.

Then all I could see was the inside of the plane, the bear sitting right where my husband sat in the last minutes of his life. And I heard St Priest muttering, but still the woman did not speak. Then the clatter of a sliding metal door, opening, closing, and the video cut off. And the woman? She looked familiar. I had seen her before, I knew it, but I could not remember where.

I used the private number that Philippe had given me. Sent him a text.

I know things.
You are safe? You are OK?
I am safe. I am not OK.
As soon as I can, I will come to you.
Tonight?
Tonight. You are very much on my mind.

THIRTY-FOUR

Nine p.m. and I was back at the kitchen table, trying to make myself watch the video again, but I couldn't. I couldn't. I shut the laptop and moved it into the pantry. Away and out of my sight.

Leo and I had gone out and walked the streets of Old Town Annecy. We had crossed the boulevard and walked alongside the lake. It was chilly out and looked like rain, and Leo kept close to my side, more protective than usual. He knew I was a hot mess.

Walking helped. I did not know what else to do with the frenzy of energy inside me. And the peaceful feeling I always had in Annecy began to return. The feeling that I was somehow in the right place, the occasional bout of homesickness, which was happening less and less often because, without Olivier, I had no home. No matter the snow, the mountains, the endless rain. I saw the water ripple on the lake, the evergreen trees like arrows into the sky, the people walking the twisty streets, the lights of the bistros, the mountain beyond the lake, Mont Blanc behind the smoky mist.

And then I realized that Leo was limping, and I needed to get him home. I tried to make him go slowly up the stairs, which he would not abide, and I took him inside, gave him a pain pill and fed him baked chicken, rice cooked in broth and yogurt – a gentle diet. He was healing, coming up and down the stairs with only a little bit of a limp. The blackened skin of his burns would always be there, but the flesh was more supple now, and healthy; the infection had cleared. He was steadily gaining weight.

Early yesterday, I had discovered a stack of worn dishtowels at the back of a drawer. They were on the kitchen table now, next to my half-filled wine glass, and I folded them neatly, over and over, a shrine to a happier past.

It stunned me now how I had taken that happiness for granted.

And then Leo gave a huff and ran to the balcony door, and I opened it and let him out, and I saw Philippe, moving quickly on the street outside the apartment, disappearing; then I could hear his footsteps as he ran up the stairs. Leo was at the door before I was.

Philippe wore jeans and a brown sweater, a jacket, his dark thick hair gelled back. He gave me such a look. His eyes were a muddy brownish hazel, his eyebrows thick and dark.

'Madame,' he said and put his arms around me. 'Bonsoir, *mon fiston*,' he said softly to Leo, who was trying to squeeze between us. Philippe lifted my chin and kissed me gently. I put a hand on his chest and pushed him away. He took that in stride and led me to the couch.

'I saw it. I saw the video. I saw the woman who sabotaged my husband's plane. And I know her. I don't know how, but I do. And St Priest was with her, and she's the one, isn't she? The one you're after.'

He took my hand. 'This is a terrible thing for you to see, and I am sorry. I have seen this video. I want to know how you got it. Please tell me everything. From the beginning.' He settled close to me and kept hold of my hand.

So I told him. Everything I knew, everything I thought.

He listened intently. Watching me always. Afterward, he sat for a long moment, thinking.

'Do you know who she is?' I asked him. 'Do you know why she did it? Why she . . . why Olivier?'

'I will tell you,' he said. 'Her name is Mae. She is from the American South. Like you. She lives near the Smoky Mountains. Where you and your husband used to hike.'

THIRTY-FIVE

Philippe filled me in, speaking quietly, steadily, very serious. She came from a family of affluence and education: Mae Yvonne McDermott. She had not rated highly on IQ tests as a very young child, but was considered dangerous, highly intelligent and formidably quirky, by the security and intelligence services of France. She was unpredictable in ways they had never seen before. She had been nonverbal as a child, so deeply enmeshed in anxiety that at school she was mute, at home a nonstop chatterbox.

I paced the apartment, frowning. 'I know I have seen her, and not too long ago, but I don't know when and I don't know where.'

He studied me. 'And you are sure she did not know your husband?'

'I don't think so. You have to understand – that area, it's full of people from all over the world. It's a big tourist draw: Dollywood and skiing in Gatlinburg and the Smoky Mountains. There's a strong international community of singers, musicians, dancers. And it's a rural low-wage part of the country. So big manufacturing companies, some of them French, like to build factories there, because labor is cheap.'

'She is one you would notice. The memory will come if you do not force it.'

'But why? Why is she doing this?'

'She lost her entire family in the Smoky Mountain National Park – the Gatlinburg wildfires of 2016. You know of this?'

'I remember it as well as you remember the Mont Blanc Tunnel fire.'

I curled up beside him on the couch, and he told me her terrible story.

Thanksgiving weekend, the family gathered together, Mae set to arrive the next day, working late in her little vet practice in Strawberry Plains, Tennessee.

Her big brother, her mom and dad, their ancient Standardbred bay mare, their Rottweiler/cattle dog mix – overtaken and consumed in a wall of fire while running on foot from their family home on a steep twisty road, in the Smoky Mountains, in Gatlinburg, Tennessee. No warning, no hope of rescue. I could see it in my mind's eye – all of them running together, all of them burning, three hundred yards from their house. Horse on a lead rope, dog on a leash, mom, dad and big brother, all heaped together in the middle of the road, unrecognizable after the fire. There was no chance of safety or sanctuary, no matter how fast they ran. Roads blocked by the carnage of fire, air thick with smoke that would have choked them as they ran, communications down, no advance warning so they could have evacuated in time. Thick plumes of smoke were their first indication that the mountains were on fire, and by then no rescue could get through the twisty mountain roads that were blocked with downed and burning trees, and fallen, sparking power lines, even if somehow someone knew you were there and needed help. The blackened bones of their two-story chalet showed the remains of a wraparound porch, a garden, all nestled in a thicket of trees that were now skeletal, stunted and dead.

I sat down on the couch and put my head in my hands. 'I remember that. Oh God, it was awful. It went on for days, smoldering and building, and nobody did anything to stop it; they just watched it. And then suddenly the fire got caught up in winds. And when I say winds, I mean those terrifying tornado-size winds that come down the mountains when it starts to get cold out and sweep through Gatlinburg, Pidgeon Forge and Sevierville. There's a name for them . . . *Mountain Waves*. Nobody was warned; you had tourists who didn't know how to get out – even if it had been possible, all those narrow mountain roads and all those wood chalets. People tried to call for help, but the phones didn't work, all the services went down, and nobody could get to them even if they got through. And then afterwards. I think that was even worse.'

'How was it worse after?' Philippe asked.

I turned sideways on the couch, sat cross-legged and pulled the blanket throw into my lap. 'The way they were treated.

Even during the fire while it was unfolding, the minute it hit the news. It was right after an election, when suddenly the whole country was divided into red states and blue states, and there was an onslaught of massive, vicious reactions in the national papers. And all through the comments sections, you have people saying that the people there deserved it, they were too stupid to come in out of the rain, they voted like idiots against their best interests, and it served them right. It was unreal, the things people said, and the things the newspapers printed. That's the way things are now – no matter where you live, no matter who you are, people vilify you. But if you live in the South, it's worse, and there is no mercy. They can print a picture of a sobbing mother who has lost her baby in a sudden flood, and people will say *tough shit*, they deserve it down there in the *taker states*. If people said things like that about Olivier, I think I'd . . .'

Philippe waited but I didn't finish the sentence. 'Yes. I see. It explains a lot.'

'It doesn't explain why she went after Olivier.'

'But he worked there once?'

'In Sevierville? Yes. And Olivier and I went to Gatlinburg once on New Year's Eve. But I don't think he knew her.'

'There is no evidence that he did. In fact, she was chosen for him. She left the US after the fires, lived off and on in France. She loved the Alps, the mountains; it was like home for her, without the bad memories. But she was very angry, and deep into the chatrooms on the dark web. We monitor, we have their conversations. She met St Priest there, where he was trolling and looking for someone just like her. St Priest tells her he has funding to do something about the climate change that caused the fires in the Smoky Mountains and the ones that were raging through France. And it is the fires that got her attention; he would know this. It was St Priest who targeted your husband and Laurent. He told her they were involved with an NGO funded by the gas and oil companies, and for Laurent this was true. So the plan was for Laurent, and then Laurent and Olivier, to go down in the plane crash, as punishment for pretending to work for the good. This had been in the works for several months. Pulling Olivier in was pure luck for St Priest. Who knew by then that Laurent was taking his NGO in a direction that infuriated him.'

'Why didn't they claim credit for it, then? The crash that killed Olivier? Since that's the whole point of a terrorist attack?'

'The plan was for this to be the first strike before they went after their real target.'

'Which was what?'

'The Mont Blanc Tunnel. It was supposed to happen one after the other. The crash and then the tunnel.'

I put my hands over my face. 'Why the Mont Blanc Tunnel?'

'That will get the attention of the world, more than a small plane crash which is quickly forgotten. Everyone will remember the fire there years ago, and the people who died a horrible death, but if they shut down the tunnel and the supply chain, and all the truck traffic, a lot of money is lost yet again, which means a lot of attention to the cause. The emissions of traffic going through the tunnel have got very bad, and what no one tells you is that there are alerts there all the time, because sometimes the air is so bad that the people who live there cannot even let their children go outside. And the little train in Chamonix that goes up the mountain so people can see the glacier . . . there is no more glacier. Even the permafrost is melting.'

'I thought you said tunnels are never a target.'

'I said *rarely*, Junie. And not all terrorists are logical. If she tries going after the tunnel, it's not going to work. But I must shut this down before she even tries.'

'Then why the long wait? It's been months since Olivier died. Why hasn't she done it yet?'

Philippe leaned back and sighed. 'We think she changed her mind.'

'What? *Why?*'

'Because of all the attention on the death of your husband, and Mae, she is not stupid. She figured it out that your husband was not the guy she thought he was. She saw you in the articles and your picture on that day you went to identify your husband's body. And that your dog was lost. She is a vet; she has a *petite* practice in Tennessee, and takes in homeless animals. She was furious with St Priest, and felt she was betrayed yet again. She went home and back to her animals. And she might have stayed there. But then the lawsuit against the National Park Service brought by the families of the victims of the fire – it had been going slowly through the courts and it looked like there would be justice, and acknowledgment that mistakes were made, that people should have been warned, and there would be big payouts. Then suddenly it was thrown out of court on a technicality that looked very much like collusion with your justice department and the park service. And that threw her back into the red zone. We know she is back in France, but we cannot find her. But we think she is focused on you.'

'Focused on me *why*?'

He sighed. 'She feels very badly about your husband, and your missing dog who is no longer missing. But she is mainly angry, and we think St Priest has convinced her that using you in her sabotage plan is too good an opportunity to pass up.'

'So, what, I'm a photo op? For publicity?'

He nodded. 'That's what I think St Priest will have told her. We both know he is just going after you because you are Olivier's wife. But remember that we are watching him. He will lead us to Mae, and we will get them both before it happens.'

'Sounds like I'm going to be collateral damage.'

'I've put in a request for a protection detail. If I arrest St Priest, then we lose our chance at finding Mae, and I think she is just as dangerous to you as he is. It's a risk, but I think it would be better to get them both. You could go back home to the US until this plays out.'

'Why would I be safe there? She knows Kentucky better than France. And it doesn't matter. I'm staying, and I'm not backing down. Happy to help, and be your bait, Philippe. But if something happens to me, will you make sure Leo is OK?'

'I will not let anything happen to you. Or Leo.'

'Good luck with that.'

THIRTY-SIX

Philippe stood up and put his hands on my shoulders. 'When did you last eat? Because I have had nothing since coffee this morning, and you and I are going to have dinner. Put your shoes back on and come with me.'

I hesitated, because I did not think I could ever eat again, but a glass of wine sounded good, and I wanted to get the hell out of the apartment and walk.

Philippe knew where he was going, and Leo, achy from the afternoon ramble, was left at home with a Kong full of chicken. We pattered softly down the stairs, and out on to the street, where it was just starting to rain. Annecy in the fall. Two streets down, he led me into Bistrot L'Atlas. Things were winding down there, but the kitchen was still open, and we were seated quickly at a table along the back wall. Philippe sat across from me. He ordered a bottle of the local red, the steak and frites, and I ordered the mussels in white wine, with frites as well. The wine came quickly along with bread in a dish, and Philippe filled my glass.

I settled back into my seat with a sigh. The shock was wearing off. I took a sip of wine and realized I was starving. Glad to be out of the apartment, and out into the night. Our knees touched under the table, and Philippe smiled at me.

'You have been here before?' Philippe asked.

I nodded. 'One of my favorite places.'

He told me about his son, who was in university. They had been estranged due to his divorce, but his son was beginning to thaw and had even come to his apartment in Metz to stay for a weekend and make fun of the divorced dad decor. And had I heard from my brothers? And, please forgive him, but did I not think the kitchen table in my apartment was ugly?

That made me laugh. I lifted my wine glass. 'Yes, actually, I do. I hate it.'

'There are markets close where we could pick something up you would like. I will take you. We will take my car; yours is way too small.'

'Really?'

'Really it is too small? Yes.'

'No, really you will take me.'

He smiled at me, and I knew that was not all he had on his mind. 'We will make a plan. I can take you late in the morning, tomorrow – it is Saturday. After we have coffee. Do you eat breakfast?'

I nodded. '*Café crème, jus d'orange*, yogurt.'

He shuddered. 'You must not have yogurt for breakfast.'

'What must I have?'

'You are a woman. You must have *la chocolatine*.'

'I would not turn that down.' I smiled at him. 'You are from the south of France?'

'How did you know?'

'Because you say *la chocolatine* and not *pain au chocolat*.'

'I cannot help it if the rest of the country says it wrong.'

I scooped mussels out of the shell and smiled at him, just a little bit smugly.

'And also, Madame, you must explain to me something. Am I in the way of something between you and this friend of your husband, Laurent Valiente?'

'And if I explain this, I get *la chocolatine*? There is nothing but friendship with me and Laurent.'

He shrugged. 'I ask because I hear things. That you went to his home for dinner the night before you found Leo in the Parc. That he had dinner with you at Chez Eugene. He lost his wife, you lost your husband. There would be a certain sense to this.'

'He knows things about what happened to Olivier. He was supposed to be on that plane. So we drank a bottle of champagne together to talk about the things he knows that *you* did not tell me. And, in truth . . . I bring Olivier with me to him, and he brings Olivier with him to me. That's the connection.'

'Then that is out of the way. I did not really think you

would go for that one if there is me, but I wanted to be sure.'
And he began to ask me about my guitar – did I like it, how
was it different from my other ones? – while he finished off
the steak and frites.

Olivier used to tease me for eating mussels with a fork, so
I used my fingers and managed to splatter Philippe with juice
and wine. He did not seem to mind and was happy to share
the giant pail of mussels, which were always more than I
could eat, and he ate them like Olivier did, using a mussel
shell, broken in half on one side.

And then he split the last of the wine between my glass
and his, and looked at me sideways.

I had just taken a bite of bread and swallowed hard. Took
a sip of wine. Did not look away from that steady gaze. He
put a hand lightly on my knee, under the table.

And we were looking at each other steadily, making promises that were silent but thrilling. I waited for that moment of
panic I so often felt, but it did not come.

Tonight?

Tonight.

THIRTY-SEVEN

We walked back to the apartment holding hands. Took Leo out for a late-night pee, then tucked him on to his mat in the kitchen. I had left music on for Leo; he loved Charo and Dolly Parton, bossa nova jazz and flamenco guitar.

'I like this music.' Philippe stood up and offered me a hand. 'We will dance.'

'You dance?'

'*Oui*, because once a girl I liked very much, she told me . . . *pour les femmes, danser c'est comme les pipes pour les hommes.*'

I burst out laughing.

He cocked his head sideways and smiled at me. Took my hand. 'Like this, Madame.'

Brevard began with a simple box step. One hand on my waist, then he took my left hand and placed it firmly on his shoulder, and I felt the heat of his skin and the hard steadiness of his muscles beneath his crisp white button-down shirt – cuffs rolled precisely back two times. Then he held my right hand in his and guided me across the tiled kitchen floor.

He swept me into an easy slow spin, pulled me close to his hip and held me there.

Brevard was a perfect partner. He led me gently, waiting a beat for me to react so I never felt rushed or a bit behind. With Brevard, I could relax. He'd wait for me to catch up. Because it was the partner that mattered more than the music.

'How is it the dancing didn't save your marriage? You are good at this.'

He shrugged. 'If it is not going to work, it is not going to work. She decided she too would learn to dance, but in truth she was a terrible dancer, and then I found her having sex with the dance instructor.' He frowned at me. 'You are amused?'

I sputtered. 'I'm sorry. It's just so horrible it's . . . really, I am sorry.'

'As you should be. You will have to make this up to me.' His look was severe, but I saw the flicker of a smile.

Another spin. Another box step. He swept me close, looking down at me, eyes narrowed. He leaned close and kissed me, and I lost my footing, but he kept me steady and upright. I leaned into him, feeling the softness of his lips, the warmth of his skin, and I rubbed my cheek along his chin, feeling the freshly shaven skin, feeling his hand warm and tightening on my hip.

He pulled me between his legs. This was the Samba now, almost better than actual sex.

And then he pulled me toward him, walking backward, watching me intently, heading to my princess bed.

'Isn't this . . . complicated?' I asked. The wine had gone to my head, and it was good that he kept hold of me so I did not fall down.

'Sex?'

'No, *you and me* having sex.'

'Ah.' He shrugged. 'I could lose my job.'

'Maybe we are moving too fast. Maybe we should wait till everything is resolved.'

'Maybe nothing. I do not care.'

'You're *good* at your job.'

'Yes. Very good. Good at my job, good at my marriage, a very good father, but that did not stop my wife and me from getting divorced, my son from stopping speaking to me, and my job was no good to me when I had a heart attack seven months ago. I came back from that different. I came back from that refreshed. A new man. I do not want the life I had, to work nonstop, to have no time to drink my coffee slowly, to cook my simple pasta, to make a lemon tart. I have let go of noisy things, and now I pay attention to what is important. And what is important, Madame, is you. And what I want is *you*, and what I want is *this. Now, not later.* Do we live as we wish or do we wait?'

He did not wait for an answer but leaned close to kiss my neck. 'And, Madame, I promise you, this will not be too fast.'

*   *   *

Philippe nudged me gently on to the bed, and I sat nervously on the edge. He put his hands on my shoulders, the pressure steady and soft until I was on my back, and he settled close beside me, a hand flat on my thigh. He ran his tongue along my bottom lip, then kissed me hard, and pushed my sweater up and out of the way. He did not stop there: the jeans were next, and then he was tugging my silky black panties down on one side, touching me with the softness of early exploration.

I caught my breath.

He put his mouth on me everywhere, and then took his time, and I shut my eyes tight and let him. The sweater became twisted and bunched and my hands were on the zipper of his pants, and then it was everything off for him, and the feel of his bare hot skin against mine.

I stroked his belly, his thigh, my hand moving where he urged with the thrust of his hips. He was hard, his muscles trembling, and I loved the look of him, dark hair on his thighs, muscular legs, the riveting beauty of a man.

'You see what you do to me?' he whispered, then made a noise deep in his throat. He slid inside me, on top of me, grinding tight and close at an angle that made me gasp.

'This is good for you? I will do it slowly, Madame. There are so many things I will do with you tonight.'

He was a relentless lover. We slept for an hour, tightly entwined, and then he was biting my shoulder. The bed shifted as he ran his hand down my back, massaging my shoulders with strong fingers, massaging my back, going lower, both hands on my thighs.

'This is pleasure for you, Madame?'

'This is . . . *pleasure*.' I bit the side of the sheet and shut my eyes tight.

'You cannot talk, Madame?'

I sighed, and he put his mouth over mine.

In the morning, he got a call and turned off his phone. Rolled over and smiled at me, quite sweetly. I liked the way he looked in the morning. Heavy dark beard, thick gray-black hair, mussed. He did not look nearly as tired as he ought to. I touched the skin on his chest. To sleep with him so close to me. These things I used to take for granted. How does one hold on to such moments?

'Work,' he said, with a grimace. 'For later. First you must have *la chocolatine*, *café crème* and *jus de l'orange* for your breakfast, and then, yes, I must go. But I will be back to you as soon as I can, because you are all I can think about. And I promise you, soon we will get rid of that ugly table which gives me a pain every time I see it.'

'And what did you use to do, Philippe? In your spare time? When you weren't having sex and sex and sex?'

'Work. *This is better.*' He pulled me on top of him.

'I demand *la chocolatine.*'

'You shall have it. But this first.'

THIRTY-EIGHT

One day after, I had woken up early thinking of Philippe, feeling happy, feeling peaceful, soft light coming in through the windows because I had forgotten to close the shutters the night before.

One day after, I had slipped into my red sweater, my favorite jeans and soft boots. The sky looked like early snow. I had taken Leo out and fed him, and had just picked up my guitar.

One day after. And I knew something was up when I heard the soft tap on my door.

It was early for a visit. Leo gave a warning huff and nudged my leg, and I gave him a treat from my pocket, and he came with me. He always does.

I opened the door cautiously, peering around the chain. I knew someone could kick the door open, but one has to live in the real world, and I had Leo right there. If someone kicked the door open, they'd likely take one look at Leo and run back down the stairs.

But it was Annette, and it was her day off, Monday, when Chez Eugene was shut, and she was there with a tall woman who hung back, arms folded tight, a dark-haired woman who looked sideways at me swiftly, curiously, then looked back down at the floor.

'Please, Junie, I am sorry to come to you so early and without warning, but I smelled the coffee and knew you were up. And I wanted . . . you need to meet my friend of a good friend, Béatrice.'

Béatrice. Her hands were shaking, and she looked back up at me, and I had the odd feeling she knew me, but I did not think I had ever seen her before.

'Please come in,' I said. Puzzled. Wary. I expected nothing but trouble these days.

'Béatrice wishes to say hello to Leo. She has heard all about him; you know he is famous here. Would that be OK?'

Annette's voice was high and nervous, not like her at all. She had dressed quickly, soft dark hair tied back in a lopsided ponytail; like me, she wore boots and jeans, and a thick oatmeal-colored sweater that hung past her wrists and looked warm.

I did not think Béatrice was here early in the morning to meet Leo in what looked like a hasty last-minute decision to knock on my door. And the look she gave him was wary.

'Of course,' I said, motioning them in, and we all exchanged *bises*, the three of us, and Leo watched calmly, leaning on my leg. He was still limping, still sore. It worried me, though I knew that this chronic psoas injury would take a while to heal. Especially since we lived at the top of steep stairs.

Annette glanced around the room, but Béatrice only had eyes for Leo. She held out her hand with great caution, and Leo gave her a wary sniff.

'Oh,' she said with a shocked laugh. 'He is so *very* big.'

'Let's go to the kitchen. I have a new coffee maker, so you must pass judgment. I won't lie to you. There's only so much mocha pot coffee I can drink; it is too thick for me.'

'You do not have to make it thick. And what is this thing?' Annette said, following me into the kitchen, which was a little more homey now – a nice way to say I'd added stuff. A big cracked blue bowl held Yukon Gold potatoes and aubergines. Leo had eaten all the apples. A net bag of lemons hung from one of the hooks on my overcrowded pot rack. A soft stack of worn cotton dishcloths were folded neatly to one side. And, of course, our ugly yellow Formica table, taking up half the kitchen space.

'It is pretty here,' Béatrice said. There was a sense of fragility about her. Her voice was soft. Too soft. Like a woman who is out of the habit of saying what is on her mind. Annette seemed worried about her. Even I, who did not know her at all, was feeling a bit worried about her.

'Sit please,' I said.

Annette was still staring at the coffee maker. She went over and gave it a long, serious look, then sat beside Béatrice, who was sitting up very straight in her chair.

Annette rolled her eyes at me. 'What one is this? It looks

very good, and you have a new coffee grinder too? Olivier would just get an old Mr Coffee and be done with it.'

'It's a Technivorm Moccamaster. Isn't it beautiful?' I had paid extra for the one in copper. 'I can't help myself. I seem to have developed a coffee maker obsession. I wonder if there's a support group for that.'

Béatrice laughed, a loud, oversized laugh, and she put a hand over her mouth. She had a certain physical presence, with her height, an ongoing buzz of nervous energy, but she was definitely damped down, definitely a woman who was trying to disappear.

Her hair was cut straight, just brushing her collar bone, bangs cut outrageously short, which showed a certain attitude, so there was hope for her still. It was pretty hair, dark almond and thick. Her white tailored shirt was buttoned tight to her throat, and she fidgeted with a necklace that she pulled out of her shirt, then tucked back in.

I made a fresh pot of coffee, and it was very good and very hot. Annette took hers black, but Béatrice watched me put heavy whipping cream into mine. I pushed the carton toward her, and she added a healthy amount to her coffee, watched it swirl and took a sip.

'*Bien,*' she said softly. 'What kind of beans are these?'

'Ethiopian, ground at thirty-eight.'

The silence was companionable, then heavy. Béatrice stared into her coffee cup.

I resisted the nervous urge for chit-chat. I would give Béatrice time. I would wait her out. She twisted her wedding ring around her finger. Looked at me.

Annette signed. 'Junie. Béatrice is here because she is the wife of St Priest. They are in the middle of the world's longest divorce, and, believe me, that is saying something in France.'

St Priest? I took a breath. I did not know what I had expected, but it sure as hell was not this. But if she was divorcing him . . . that could be interesting. Maybe she had things to tell me. Why else would she be here?

Still. I wondered why she wore her ring. It meant she was still connected to St Priest, in her heart. It meant she was having a hard time with the divorce. It made me wary. I wanted to ask her if she knew her husband was fucking nuts, but for once I stayed quiet. But just the name St Priest made me feel queasy, and I set my cup down, the coffee untouched.

Béatrice looked at me. 'For Americans, does the divorce go very fast?'

I shrugged. 'It goes until everyone runs out of money.'

Annette put a hand on my arm. 'Listen to her. She is on our side.'

Béatrice nodded.

I took a breath and leaned forward. '*I know your husband killed my husband*. Let's put that on the table.'

Annette put a hand to her mouth. '*Mon dieu.*'

Béatrice tilted her head to one side. 'Charl is a physical coward. He was afraid of your husband. So maybe he would have been involved, but he would not have the courage to do this alone. But I feel I must tell you that he is a danger to *you*. He hates your husband so much that it spills on to you. Because you are how he can still hurt him. It is not enough for him that your husband is dead. You are a part of his big revenge.'

I refilled the coffee cups. Trying to figure out what to say. I had a lot of questions. But what good would it do? If she knew the answers, would she tell me? If she knew the answers, would she lie? Why was she really here? Was this a woman-to-woman thing, or a manipulation?

'I want to know how St Priest got hold of Leo. How long he had him. How Leo got away. How Leo was . . . treated.'

Béatrice looked at Annette.

'Tell her,' Annette said.

'He wanted Leo to live; he had a purpose for him. But Charl, he does not like dogs. First, he wanted just to own the dog that belonged to your husband, as though it gave him some kind of secret power. But then it became tiresome for him, and he decided he would use Leo to lure you to Chamonix, to find your dog. And then on with the end game.'

'The end game?' I said. Annette was looking at Béatrice with a frown.

'The end game is you,' Béatrice said, looking at me. 'I do not know everything that he is up to, but there is going to be trouble. And I have told this to the police, but I am an ex-wife, so I do not know if they took me seriously. But you. You must take me seriously. And Charl – he has pictures of you. Pinned to a wall. He is prone to obsessions. He is *comportement dangereux et colérique*. Charl will look for a way to hurt you and make himself a hero. He must be the center of attention, always, and he is furious if the attention goes to anyone but him. And he is in a rage if someone has things he wants, because he thinks *he* should have them.

'And once he found out there were trail cams near the Parc, and the drones that were looking for wolves, he would take Leo there every day, so people would see them together. And one day, Leo tried to get away and bit him on the arm. Charl, he had had enough, and I think he was just going to leave Leo in the shed. But I was there to get my last box of things, and Charl, he was not there – that is our agreement. I heard Leo cry and I went to the shed and found him tied up to a wall, with a bowl of food and water just out of his reach. And then I knew that Charl was done with Leo, and things would not go well for him.'

I felt sick. I laced my fingers in Leo's fur. He seemed content though he was watching me now.

'I ran into the house for scissors, to cut the rope. And I was afraid all of a sudden of Leo – he was so wild and jumping and barking. I cut him loose and I could not hold on to the rope; he is very strong, your dog. He got away, and he ran off. And my hope was that you would find Leo. And I am sorry about what happened to your husband.

'But it is important that you understand that my husband is not *just* histrionic. He is also a sadist. He will make a big show, he will look for sympathy and admiration, and he will enjoy it more if you suffer while all of this goes on.'

'How long have you been married?' I asked.

'Twelve years together, eight years married. He stopped having sex with me the day we got married, but he has sex with everyone else.'

'Maybe for the best,' I said.

I leaned back in my chair, chewing my lip.

'He appropriates . . . that is the word you have? If there is something about you that others admire, he says he is that, too. If you have something he wants, he takes it.'

'He took her car,' Annette said, furious. 'An old classic Citroen 2CV? And he drove it rough and wrecked it because she loved it and wanted it back from him.'

'And the police, I told them that, too.'

'Why didn't they put him in jail?'

Annette folded her arms. 'What will they charge him with? Being a bad husband?'

'I was thinking more the murder of my husband.'

Leo nuzzled my leg. I stroked his ears. He closed his eyes, head on my knee. How often I had woken up, in the middle of the night, wondering if he was alive. And all that time he had been alone in the cold, trapped in the shed of Charl St Priest.

I looked at Béatrice who was keeping an eye on Leo. 'So tell me, Béatrice. You know what kind of man you married. You say you are getting a divorce. You know your husband killed my husband and the pilot of the plane, that he is involved in something creepy – and *shit*, he was mean to my dog. And yet you wear his wedding ring? This is something I don't understand.'

Béatrice held her hand out, looked at the ring, twisted it and put her hands in her lap. 'Because Charl, he said to me that I must wear it until the divorce is final.'

'And you do what he says?'

She gave me a steady look. 'I choose the times to go along or not go along. And for now, this is safer for me. I plot my escape one step at a time. If I wear the ring, he thinks he has control, and it goes easier for me. I will one day soon take it off and then I will invite you and Annette, and we will go to a café and drink wine and have a very good meal.'

Annette nodded.

I wondered if Béatrice would survive that long. I wondered if I would. I wanted to blame her; I did not want to plan future dinners. But I could see the pain and the stress etched in her face. In the slight downward slope of her shoulders, no matter how often she caught herself and straightened up.

'And now he has a target – you – and with his focus away

from me, this is the time for me to push the divorce; it will
not matter so much to him. I was just a goal – he needed to
be married because his brother was married – so now I can
get away. You are the prize, you see? He destroys you, he
destroys your husband, and even though your husband is dead,
he must take everything away.

'He tried, you know, to make a friend of your husband, to
be a part of his life.' She laughed. 'But your husband, he saw
Charl for who he is, and he did not hide his dislike for Charl.
He could be—'

'Quite blunt. I know.'

'So Charl, he knew Olivier was the one person who saw
right through him. And it drove him crazy. He began to watch
Olivier, to take little trophies from his office. Pictures. A note
from you. A beautiful black wool coat.'

I took a breath. 'Yes, I know he stole the coat. I've seen
him wearing it. I want it back.'

'He has these things at home; they are in the basement. I
have seen them. He has *showed* them to me. That is why he
was desperate to show the world he had your dog. He knew
that if he had your dog, he had you, Junie. He owned a part
of your family. He had destroyed Olivier, he would have
destroyed Leo, and he is most certainly coming after you.'

Annette leaned forward. 'Junie, you must take this to
Capitaine Brevard and let him deal with it.'

And that is where I hesitated. Philippe knew all of this and
had his own agenda. And this was *my* husband. I was not
going to sit around wishing someone would do something.

Annette gave me a suspicious look. 'What will you do?'

'I'll see it through.'

'How?' she asked, quite fierce.

'I am going to go and get the coat that I gave my husband
and see where my dog was kept.'

Annette shook her head. 'It is a crazy risk, Junie, *très fou.*'

I looked at Béatrice. 'I want my stuff back. My husband's
coat, the pictures, all the things that your husband took. And
I want to see the shed where he kept Leo.'

Béatrice put a hand to her chin, and there was a kind of
excitement that I sensed. 'There may be a way to do this and

stay safe. We can all go there together. Charl will be in Metz today. I have some things I want to pick up, and this will make it safe for me, all of us together, in case he comes home. And I will get the last of my things, and then I am gone, staying with my brother in Luxembourg.'

Annette raised an eyebrow. 'And then to Spain, Béatrice, with Bertrand?'

She smiled. 'And then to Spain. With Bertrand.'

'She has a lover there,' Annette said, which I had already figured out. 'But Béatrice. We should not do this. He'll know it was you who took all of Olivier's things, and Junie, you should not take this risk. This is only *stuff*.'

'Would you want this man to be looking at pictures of you and Eugene? Touching a picture of you and Eugene? Thinking the kind of thoughts he thinks? Touching Eugene's favorite coat?'

'*Wearing it*,' Béatrice said.

Annette folded her arms. 'I think it is a ridiculous risk. Eugene would tell you not to do this.'

'I'm not asking Eugene.'

Béatrice shrugged. 'But I like this plan. All three of us together, me getting the last of my things – I will feel braver if we are all together. And Junie will get all of the things that Charl stole from her husband, and me . . . me, I will leave my wedding ring in a champagne glass on the cabinet where Charl will see it when he walks in the door.'

'And then finally you will get away?' Annette tried not to smile. 'That part I like.' She threw up her hands. 'OK, then, I will go with you. *Va te faire foutre*, Charl St Priest.'

'*Oui*.' Béatrice smiled and her eyes were shiny.

THIRTY-NINE

We were quiet on the drive over, the three of us. Annette drove a worn but well-maintained black BMW diesel, and I sat in the back seat, listening to Béatrice and Annette talk in rapid French that I did not even try to understand.

I had left Leo in the kitchen happily settled with a Kong filled with peanut butter. He was achy today, and I wanted to save him the stairs. And in truth, while I would have felt safer with him there, I would not bring him back to the place where he had been held captive, even though, to Leo, St Priest would be prey. My dog had had trauma enough.

It was not what I expected, this chalet of Béatrice and St Priest. Béatrice was tense. We all were. The place felt dark to me, perhaps because of what I knew.

Annette parked the car gently, babying it as she always did. It was twelve years old, with cream leather upholstery that was worn, soft and stained in places, and it had an eight-cylinder engine that purred, and she handled it with ease, driving it like a slow-moving yacht.

Annette shut off the engine on the BMW. It tinked over and was silent.

In truth, the chalet was rather pretty. That annoyed me. Two stories, with a stone foundation, the typical look of the mountain chalets that were everywhere in Chamonix and around the Parc de Merlet.

It was crisp out and chilly. And the chalet was out of the way of the other places nearby, at the end of a rutted dirt road. It was very green here. Soon enough, it would be covered in snow. The mountains rose behind the chalet, the tall grasses and the forest surrounded us, and there was a wide dirt path that narrowed and veered off the road.

I checked the nav app on my phone. The chalet was 1.7 kilometers from the Parc de Merlet.

Béatrice dug in her purse for the keys.

Annette opened the car door, glancing at Béatrice. 'You are sure Charl is not here?'

'I am sure. He is in Metz at some business meeting he will not talk about.' She glanced over her shoulder. 'You don't see his car, do you?'

There were no other cars in sight.

'What does he drive?' I asked.

Béatrice paused, stared away from us and at the house. 'His family's old Land Rover. He took it when his brother died. His parents let him have it. His *belle soeur* was *trop fâchée*.'

The sister-in-law. The murdered brother's wife. I would be *trop fâchée*, too.

Béatrice headed for the house. 'Today I will finally cut loose. I will show you Olivier's things inside before we go to the shed where Charl kept Leo. And I will pick up that carton of things I want.'

'So you've already moved out, then?' Annette asked.

'Yes, mostly. But I left behind my grandmother's pan for the gateau and my pressure cooker, both of them things I want back.'

Annette frowned. 'You came back for a cake pan and a pressure cooker?'

Béatrice nodded and looked at us over her shoulder. 'Yes, Charl would not let me take them, because he knows that I love them. He hid them from me. To put in his collection of things he takes when he knows it is something you want.'

The steps were built sideways to the front of the house, and I held the rail, trailing behind Béatrice and Annette. It was cold, and I was chilled from the inside out. I wished I had my old barn coat that I had bought at a feed store in Kentucky.

Béatrice unlocked the door, and we followed her in.

It was wide open, with wood beams, wood floors, a shiny polished yellowish hue and there were lots of windows. All of the furniture was beige and worn. There was an electric stove on the side, glowing with simulated fire, and a large television screen on the wall. The wide wood coffee table had hinges so that it could rise and make a table, there in front of the TV.

It was dusty.

And had the lost look of a place where someone had moved out. Carpet indentions to show missing furniture. Uneven paint on the wall where pictures had been removed. An air of abandonment.

Annette glanced around the room. 'All the good stuff is gone.'

'All the good stuff was my stuff,' Béatrice said. 'I don't want anything he and I bought together.' She opened a narrow door at the back of the kitchen. 'This takes us to the basement downstairs. This is where he has your husband's things. I think maybe mine will be down there, too.' She headed down concrete steps, feet slapping softly, and I heard the creak of the railing as she held it tight.

The word *lair* came to mind as Annette and I followed her down.

It was a narrow space, but long. Dark and cluttered, and the light Béatrice switched on did little more than throw shadows. Bars of sunlight filtered through a tiny boarded-up window at the top of the wall.

This place felt like hell to me. A dark space of bad smells and malevolent intent.

Béatrice pointed to a dresser, a soccer ball and a jersey, all clumped together. 'Those belonged to his brother.'

'Victim one,' I muttered.

Annette narrowed her eyes. 'As far as we know.'

There was a wide old woodwork table, thick with grime, and old car parts and rusting tools. Sagging cardboard boxes bulging with things I wanted nothing to do with. Stacks of old files and magazines. I felt sick to my stomach, hoping Leo had spent no time down in this hell hole.

Béatrice frowned, looking at the wall. 'It is gone.'

'What is gone?'

'He had a board up. The pictures of Junie. Articles about the plane crash. About Olivier. About you. Both of you were in the news a lot after it happened.'

A clothesline sagged beneath the weight of wire hangers

that held sweatshirts, dress shirts, sweat pants, a soccer jersey . . . and a dress coat I knew very well. The one I had bought for Olivier for his birthday the first year we were married. Stolen out of his office by Charl St Priest.

Béatrice took the jacket off the hanger and handed it to me. 'I am sure you recognize this. Charl, he wears it all the time. He made a point of wearing it when he walked Leo near the Parc. He took it from Olivier's office. He took a scarf, too, and some pictures from your husband's desk. I know where they are.' She went to the dresser and rummaged in the second drawer.

I held the coat close. I wanted to put it on, but the memory of St Priest wearing it, seeing him wearing it in that YouTube video, made me ill. I hunted through the pockets. They were empty, except for a tiny folded-up card that was stashed in a small inner pocket. The note I had written to Olivier to tell him *Happy Birthday* and *I love you*. Someone had folded it carefully, tucked it into the jacket, and kept it close. St Priest? Olivier?

Béatrice handed me a wrinkled scarf, one of the charcoal-gray ones Olivier used to wear – he had three that I knew of. And the frame of pictures Olivier had kept on his desk. Wedding photos. Me playing the guitar and Leo looking up at me. A picture I had taken of Olivier and Leo, sitting on a downed tree, on a hike we'd done in the Tennessee mountains.

There were thumbprints on the wedding photos.

'You will be safe, Béatrice, if I take these things?'

'I will be far away in Luxembourg by tonight. I will never come back. Let me find my things, and then we can go.'

We found the pressure cooker in a box that looked new, as well as the cake pan, and a pair of panties that made Béatrice mutter. She stuffed them into her pocket, and we headed up the stairs. I felt nervous and I knew Annette and Béatrice were nervous, too. Charl was one and we were three, but there was no predicting crazy, and I felt the urge to get out and away.

'Here,' Béatrice said to Annette, who took the pressure cooker and the pan out of the box.

'It will be easier to fit in the trunk this way,' Annette said.

Béatrice reached into a cabinet over the sink and took down a fluted champagne glass. She took a breath, twisted off her wedding ring; it clinked when it fell to the bottom of the glass. She set the glass on the kitchen island.

'You are sure?' Annette said. 'We can put everything back if you'd feel safer.'

'No. I want my things, and Junie wants the things that Charl took from her husband. I have the ring off and I can already breathe easier.'

We piled into the car, and Annette fired up the engine, gravel and dirt spewing as she pulled away.

I held Olivier's coat very tight. I would have it dry-cleaned and it would be ours again.

A mile or two down the road, we all began to breathe. Just a little.

'The shed is over that way,' Béatrice said. 'It is some way from the house. To the left, Annette – you see it?'

'I see it,' Annette said.

I saw it, too.

FORTY

The shed was a good distance from the house. From any house. It backed up to thick woods, separated by a sagging wire fence that Leo would have gone over, under or through with ease.

Escape. Freedom.

The shed was really an old barn, aging wood slats weathered a silvery gray. There were wide gaps between the wood planks. It would have been cold inside. But sheltered.

Wide and tall, an uneven hard-packed dirt floor, some rusty farm machinery in one corner, two large stalls. Someone had kept animals here for years. Decades. But not for some time. Not till Leo.

The smell of old dog urine and dried feces wafted in on the breeze.

Béatrice was on tiptoe, Annette arms folded, frowning.

'See,' Béatrice said. 'He was there.'

Leo's stall. His prison. Annette and Béatrice hung back in the dark hollow of the entrance, but I went forward, taking it all in.

A new metal ring had been hammered into the wood, and a length of rope dangled to the ground. I went over, picked it up. Cut through with scissors, like Béatrice said.

The wood plank with the ring attached was bowed inward and showed fresh splinters and cracks. I found a tuft of Leo's fur, caught in a split in the wood. I pictured him jumping wildly, barking, pulling hard against the rope, hard enough to start the wood splintering around that metal ring. He would have eventually got free on his own.

The Shepherd has the loudest bark of any dog. People must have heard him. Barking. Crying. In distress. Why hadn't anyone come?

The water and food bowls were both out of reach. Fairly new. I picked them both up – bowls dirty and dusty and dry.

I walked out of the shed and tossed them hard over the wire fence.

Béatrice and Annette watched me but did not ask me why I did what I did. It would have been impossible to explain.

And in the car, as we drove home, I texted Philippe.

I went to St Priest's house with his wife when he wasn't there. He had Olivier's coat hidden in his basement, and I have it now. I saw the shed where he had Leo tied up and starving. You already know all about this, right? This isn't news to you?

The answer came quickly.

Mon dieu, Junie. I know you were there. I have just had a call. I have an officer watching St Priest. You are safe?

I am safe. He wasn't there.

I will come to you tomorrow, probably very late. But as soon as I can. You will please stay out of trouble until tomorrow night.

You don't have to come.

I will come no matter what. And Junie – St Priest was there.

FORTY-ONE

I had been to Carrefour Market to pick up some things, a rainy fall night, dark and chill. As soon as I turned in the alley where I garaged the Z, I was blinded by headlights. An old Land Rover, a classic, parked sideways blocking my garage, with the emergency blinkers on. It was damned annoying. I slammed on my brakes, I was going too fast, and Leo slid sideways into the floor and scrambled back into his seat. And then I remembered that St Priest had an old Land Rover that he had taken from his brother.

A man approached my car, and Leo set up a loud bark. I had tingly dread all through my body. The man bent close. 'You do not know me?'

It was St Priest. It was dark out, and I had the window half open. It took me a moment, but it was him. Unshaven, raindrops glistening on his cheeks and in his hair. I hit the button to roll up the window. He said something else that I did not catch over Leo's barking, which was becoming hysterical. I gave Leo the *silence* command which he overrode. This was feeling almost like a farce, St Priest trying to threaten me over the noise of my dog. But it was trouble, and I was sick to my stomach.

St Priest put a hand on the handle of the door. Which was locked, though I hit the button anyway to make sure.

'Junie,' he said, making a hand motion for me to roll the window back down, 'I cannot hear you with the bark of the dog. Please will you get out just to let me talk to you? Just for a minute away from the dog – he is so loud. Then I will move my car. You came to my house, after all. You wish to see me? I know you have been there. My things are gone. And my wife, she left the wedding ring on the counter.' He shrugged. 'This is for the best, I think. She knows I am not her husband now. I have been honest with her, and she knows I am for you now, Junie.'

Such a reasonable tone, the shrug of the shoulders, a sweet little smile. The star of his very own reality show. *I am for you now, Junie – The Charl Channel.*

'It is OK for you to take the coat, as much as I love it. But please give back to me the little note you wrote – the one in the inside pocket of the jacket where you say you love me. That I must have back. It is precious to me.'

I put the car in reverse as he talked, backing up slowly. It was tight quarters, and it was dark. My hands were shaking so hard I had trouble steering. The angle was awkward. Impossible unless I hit him.

St Priest slapped the window hard. 'Get out of this car.'

Leo lunged to the window with a snarl and a frenzied bark, getting between me and the steering wheel, and St Priest moved to the front of the car, illuminated in the headlights. He wore heavy boots and a gray sweater that was so much like the one Olivier used to wear, the one that I knew was tucked under my pillow, the one that I slept with every night as though it was a stuffed animal. France was full of men in gray sweaters, maybe a million and seventy-five of them somewhere in the country at any given time of the day or night.

I kept my foot on the brake, but I thought about it. Hitting the accelerator, running him down. Backing up and doing it again to make sure he was dead.

'I came back for you, Junie. I could not leave you. Please give me the note. Please just get out and talk to me, and for just one moment let me hold your hand. Let me kiss you, just once, very softly on the lips. And then who knows what may happen between us?'

He smiled sweetly, but his eyes were dead, cold, watchful. For a moment, I wondered why the hell he thought I would fall for this nonsense, and then I understood. My look of horror, my revulsion . . . that was what he wanted. That would give him a nice little meal to feed upon. My reaction was the point of the game. Béatrice had explained this to me, and it wasn't rocket science, after all. If you want to hurt Olivier, go after his wife. If you want attention, block a woman in her car and *make* her talk to you.

But the way he looked at me . . . even if I didn't believe he was Olivier, I was starting to think maybe St Priest did.

I shoved Leo out of my lap just at the moment St Priest slapped the hood of the car once again, this time hard enough to leave a dent. 'I know you went to the shed and threw the bowls away. You will never know how close I came to killing your stupid noisy dog. How can you stand to have this dirty animal in your house?'

'*Did you* . . . did you call Leo a *dirty animal?*'

He smiled at me. 'It is an easy thing to kill a dog. Get out of the car and come talk to me, and that keeps Leo safe. If you don't, I can find both of you any time I want. And if you don't want me to go to the police and tell them about the things you took from my basement, you will get out of this car right now.'

Leo was paws on the dashboard, biting at the front window, trying to get to St Priest, who came back to the driver's window, slamming it with a fist, and I wondered how long it would be till he broke the glass. Well, stupid to sit here and wait.

I revved the engine, foot on the brake, and he cursed and moved to stand behind my car, trapping me between his car and his body.

I did not snap. I made a conscious choice. I slammed the car into reverse and hit the accelerator, and was surprised when St Priest managed to get out of the way just in time. I was more disappointed than relieved. And then I was free, and on the road with Leo, driving a bit too fast in the traffic, and having the kind of random thoughts you have when you are in shock. Like how I was never ever going back to that garage, and it would be good to save the money it cost for the rent. I was trembling and my knees felt weak, and Leo was giving me kisses kisses and crowding close, and *I would kill St Priest before I let him touch my dog*. But I won't lie to you. I was scared.

FORTY-TWO

Two hours later, I sat huddled over my guitar at the kitchen table. Normally, I would be out on the balcony, wrapped in Olivier's heavy green sweater, wearing thick white socks, shoes kicked off. It was soft out now, not too cold. The rain had stopped, and it was dark and quiet, and I liked playing outside on nights like this.

I was still shaking. I could only hold the guitar for comfort, not play it. The balcony door was locked, front door locked and bolted, shutters closed tight, and I was cocooned inside with Leo, wanting Olivier there, wishing for Philippe. It was an odd thing how I suddenly did not know where Olivier ended and Philippe began.

But first I was going to have to think my way through and make a plan. I had tried to hit St Priest with my car, and my only regret was missing him. Was I going to admit to Philippe that I had tried to run St Priest down on purpose? I think I was. It was an interesting system of ethics. That I would try to kill a man, but not lie about it to my lover. The older you get, the more you understand what is really important in life.

I picked up the phone yet again. Set it back down yet again. The thought of talking to Philippe brought a surge of anger that I did not expect. Perhaps I had been angry for a while now, and only just figured it out. I was flooded with a suppressed fury that I had been ignoring, but it was boiling up now because I had been shaken and I had been threatened, and now I really saw it, now it felt very real. That I was collateral damage in an investigation that cut me loose and used me as bait to pull in Mae. And if St Priest was under surveillance, then where were they tonight when I needed them?

The only thing I knew for sure was that I was lost. And I didn't know how to find my way back. Or forward.

It was such a feeling. The aloneness of me. Like a hollow

emptiness that somehow fueled relief. I was untethered. Which brought . . . exhilaration. Nothing mattered. Not even me.

And I had missed my chance to run St Priest down, but in truth that was not a light decision to make.

I was not a killer. All of the rage I felt toward Mae and St Priest had nowhere to go, and it churned me. Who *they* were did not dictate who I was.

But when it came down to survival, it became a cold and simple equation. A cost–benefit analysis. It was not a matter of *would I live* or *would I die.*

Who would be the predator? Who would be the prey?

So I *would* kill him, Charl St Priest, somehow, someway. And I *would* kill Mae. The compassion I felt for the bereaved daughter and sister did not extend to the woman in the video who sabotaged my husband's plane.

It was just the *how* of it that stumped me. Logistics. But I would figure it out. I would give it my best shot.

I looked at Leo, at his bronze-brown eyes. I saw his fierceness. I saw his vulnerability. It was just the two of us; he got a vote, and I knew what it would be. Predators. We'd go down fighting.

I saw the blue flashing lights of a police car playing across the slats of the shutters and making stripes on Leo's fur. He was up on his feet trying to see through the slats. He huffed, and I gave him a treat. I opened the balcony door and saw the patrol car parked beneath on the street below. I recognized the man who got out. *Not Philippe.* Michel, in uniform. He saw me and waved.

'*Bonsoir, Junie.* And Leo. You are OK. *Bon dieu*, what a night. I am coming up; the Capitaine, he has sent me. *And* he wishes to know why you did not call for help.'

'He can ask me himself.'

'Oh, Madame, he is in a fury. He is *très fâché* but not at you. He is giving St Priest all kinds of hell, and it is quite a show, but I had to leave and come and find you . . . and your Z4. You have parked it illegally, Madame.'

'Are you here to give me a ticket?'

He laughed. Slammed his car door and gave me a salute,

and two minutes later I heard his feet as he thundered up the narrow staircase to my front door. I ran to let him in. I could breathe again.

As soon as Michel was in the door, Leo squirmed past me and did the leap of affection, putting his paws on Michel's shoulders and giving him a kiss. No matter how hard I tried, I could not convince Leo that this was not OK.

But Michel was a Shepherd guy and gave Leo a vigorous buffeting of petting that made Leo turn in circles of delight. 'I am to make you coffee and stay here with you, until the Capitaine arrives.'

'He's coming?'

Michel gave me a serious look. 'Oh, yes, Madame, he will come. It is a terrible thing, St Priest lying in wait for you, and the Capitaine becomes the storm when St Priest said you attacked *him*.'

'Well. I did try to run him over.'

Michel gave me a look. 'Because he would not move out of the way, yes? And you were afraid and you were threatened, yes?'

'I don't think St Priest told you that.'

'He did not have to. Our officer lost him and came just as you were driving away, but the Capitaine, he has made St Priest say it. The team, we have a nickname for you now.' He headed into the kitchen and made himself at home, finding the coffee maker and the coffee beans as if he had lived there all his life. He curled his lip at the mocha pot and went to the Technivorm. 'Please, you must sit down.' He grabbed my shoulders gently and led me to a chair. 'You are trembling, Madame. For you a terrible night. Also, I must report in.' He clicked on his radio. His French was rapid, and his voice down low, so I could not understand a word he said. But he nodded and said *oui* and *comprende* and started shaking beans into the grinder.

'What is my nickname, by the way?'

He laughed and gave me a look over his shoulder. '*Princess Rambo*. It is the Capitaine himself who named you.'

*   *   *

The minute Philippe walked into my apartment, the world fell into place. I felt safe even though I knew I wasn't. His look to me was stern, his cheeks were flushed, and he had a suppressed energy, muscles wound tight.

'Michel tells me you are OK.' He sounded formal. Distant. Leo danced around his legs, and he petted him absently. '*Oui, mon fiston*, I am here, and you are happy. You are protecting your mama, I hear. *Bien, mon garçon. Tu es sage.*'

I liked that Philippe thought that Leo's behavior tonight was excellent.

Michel stood up straight. 'Capitaine? There is coffee.'

Philippe nodded, spoke rapidly in French. Michel asked a question, and it seemed there were more orders for him, and it was going to be a long night. Michel was clearly delighted.

He looked at me with a certain gravitas, though I could sense, underneath, an energy. 'As you see, I must go. I am glad you are safe.'

I nodded at him. 'Thank you.'

Philippe waited for him to leave. He was frowning.

As soon as Michel was out of the door, I gave Philippe a sideways look. 'Are you here to arrest me for attacking St Priest?'

'No, I am here to ask you why you did not back up and try again, but it was dark and you were shaken up. Still, it is a shame your aim is so bad.'

'I did my best.'

He laughed suddenly, crossed the room and took me in his arms. 'I am on the hunt. Madame. We will keep St Priest busy with paperwork, and let him sit and harass him and shake him up. Then I will let him go, though I urge you to make a complaint. In truth, I have him off balance, and am holding him until we can get our people in place, so we can maybe get a hand on Mae. Everything is escalating.' He rubbed his cheek against mine. He needed a shave. I loved the rasp of his beard on my skin, and I traced a finger across his chin and wondered where all my anger had gone.

'Has anyone seen her?'

He shook his head. 'Do not pull away from me. At this point, she has to be close, and we will get her now or we won't. I am going forward, against orders. I am in command of my unit, and they can fire me later.'

'Who is they?'

He made a rude noise. 'Who isn't they? This is a joint task effort, full of snarls, and no one in charge but everyone with an opinion, and by the time they try to stop me, it will be too late. Please, sit; there is something I must show you.'

He led me to the couch and sat so close that we seemed just to flow together. He took my chin in his hand and kissed me while fishing the phone out of his pocket.

'Why did you not call me?' he asked, voice low.

I shrugged. 'Not sure. Maybe I am tired of asking for help. Maybe I am ready to take care of things myself.'

'This is nothing new.' He looked up at me. 'Do you really think you are all alone?'

'Aren't I?'

'I am your guy, you understand that? This is OK with you?'

I hesitated, and he looked at me and squeezed my hand tight.

'How can you say that to me, with all you have known and not told me?'

'Yes, you make a good point: you have your side of this, and these things are hard to navigate. But you and I must do our best. No more thinking you are alone with this.'

'And the officer you had watching him? Tonight?'

'Lost him, yes, that is true. It is dark and rainy, and it is difficult sometimes with only one officer to watch.'

'Fine, Philippe, but in the interest of total disclosure, I am going to kill St Priest. He called Leo *a dirty animal*. And I am going to kill Mae.'

'This is not a surprise to me, Madame.'

The charm of this man who believed me and took it in stride.

He pulled me into his chest, a hand wound tight in my hair. 'It is you and me now, Madame. And I am not letting you out of my sight.'

He scrolled his phone. 'Ah, OK, I have it.'

'What is it?'

'It is Mae. She has launched her *manifesto* on YouTube for

everyone to see, so they will go after the tunnel any time now.'
Philippe handed me the phone. 'This will upset you. I will
hold your hand.'

I settled deeper into the couch with Leo at my feet and
hit play.

She was not the kind of woman you forgot, Mae Yvonne
McDermott. Over six feet. Broad-shouldered, a weightlifter,
with tats on her arms and neck, a buzz cut, a gold stud in her
nose. My hands began to shake.

She wore camo and a flak vest, over a sleeveless tee shirt,
thick and muscular arms. Stood with feet planted, arms folded,
intent, frowning, sunburned, and you could only just see the
smattering of freckles across her nose. She wore heavy boots,
safe behind the persona of *Terrorist, American South*.

She looked angry, but the aura of despair was palpable. This
was a woman with her back to the wall, a woman who had
given up, a woman who was more than ready to die.

Her voice was hard. It was fierce. It was strong.

'In November of 2016, my entire family died in a wall of
fire that started in the Smoky Mountain National Park. It burned
slowly for five days before it swept through the small towns
of Gatlinburg, Pidgeon Forge and Sevierville, Tennessee. Five
days is plenty of time to warn people, yet nobody *was* warned,
and *nobody cared*. Don't take my word for it. Go look at the
national newspaper articles published at the time. You will
find no sympathy for the people who died, except in the local
coverage in Tennessee. In the national newspapers, you will
find derision, snark and utterly vile comments, blaming my
family for living in the American South.

'I have cut loose from the United States, where the politicians and corporate citizens and one-percenters look at the
average citizen as prey. You are mistaken if you think what
happened to my family was unusual. If you think the reaction
to their deaths was an outlier. Because in the United States of
America, we are *for-profit* citizens. *Citizen prey*. Our healthcare
system runs like organized crime, except it's legal. Student
loans to young adults who can't afford the high price of an
education have created a debtor's prison. Kids who don't come

from rich families are now skipping college, because they don't want to fall into a financial abyss, and yet . . . you will find national articles written in major newspapers by bewildered journalists who profess to find themselves confused by the dropping university enrollments.

'Thousands of our citizens are incarcerated every year in for-profit prisons. Some of them under the age of ten. Our maternal and newborn death rate gets higher every year, and our life expectancy is plummeting.

'This is the country I have left behind.

'For the past few years, I have been made welcome in France. I have roamed through the European Union, I have been skiing in the Alps, and lived near the beautiful mountain of Mont Blanc, where the glaciers are melting and global warming is causing havoc.

'In my country, people have gotten used to following smoke tracking aps, and the levels of particulate matter called PM 2.5, which is a scientific term for wildfire smoke. Smoke that can kill if you inhale it. Smoke that increases the risk of a list of diseases so bad and so long you're going to have to look it up yourself. In the past ten years, smoke exposure has tripled across the American West. And even on the American East Coast, thousands of miles away, particulate matter from wildfires is dense enough to produce air-quality warnings. We're talking about New York, Boston, Philadelphia. *High-value people*, by the standards of the US.

'And all of this summer, France has been burning. Global warming is out of hand.

'Nobody is immune. And for once the effects do not just follow marginalized people. In the US, even the wealthy are at risk, and a three-million-dollar house won't keep you safe. PM 2.5 is an equal opportunity danger.

'In the US, climate change legislation is business as usual, and monies are going into the pockets of the very corporations that pollute but promise to do better, to finance new technology that does not exist. The lobbyists and scammers who are always there will be sucking up most if not all of the government funds. There is no longer any hope for my country.

'But here in France, and in the EU, there is still hope. I know things are not perfect here. I know there is the Brussels Bubble of entitled influence that is either unaware of or uncaring about the average citizen of the EU.

'I believe in the people who brought the world the French Revolution, whose country is based on *Liberté*, *Égalité* and *Fraternité*, even if you don't always get it right. Where healthcare is a right, education is for everyone, and when things get out of hand for the average person . . . everybody goes on strike.

'I bring to your attention the Mont Blanc Tunnel. You already know the horrors of a fire there. There will be another one. One that shuts the tunnel down. And leaves the children who live in the valley beneath the mountain with clean air to breathe. Think of it as a step forward.

'Don't let your world go up in smoke.'

And I think of Olivier as I watch this, and how Mae sabotaged his plane and murdered the one man who would have understood.

Philippe took the phone out of my hand, then gave me a sharp second look. 'You remember now where you have seen her?'

'Yes. But not here, in France. At home. In Kentucky. Two weeks before you called me about Leo. I was at a garden center, trying to put a really heavy pot into the back of my car, and she came over to help me. She picked it up by herself – and believe me, it was heavy. And I thanked her, and she just looked at me a moment, then walked away. It was weird. So . . . so she was watching me then? Before I came to France?'

'Yes, very possible. She is complicated and not predictable. She is truly one who acts from conscience and trauma, and enormous anger.' He didn't like it; I could see that in the set of his jaw. I didn't like it either. She had been watching me for a very long time.

'You will come with me tonight to my apartment in Metz?'

'I . . . yes.'

'Good. And also tomorrow morning there is someone I need you to meet. You will not like her, but she is crucial.'

'Who is she?'

'Ah, she is the head of an organization that is officially called Global Eco. She runs what is euphemistically called an NGO – a sort of Eco Watchdog – with a mission to gather information and hold EU countries accountable for all their climate change obligations, things that have been funded and agreed to.'

'She sounds like a spy.'

'It is an NGO. They are all spies. But you are right. She is ruthless and smart and she gets a lot done that nobody else seems able to do, and she holds a lot of power behind the scenes politically and with the French intelligence community and politicians all the way to the top.'

He touched my cheek. 'This has been a hard night for you, and I am sorry. I see how exhausted you are. Please get a small bag packed for you and Leo, and we will go to Metz. And please hurry. We need to head out, Madame.'

FORTY-THREE

Philippe settled me into his Volvo sedan, giving me a quick, efficient kiss on the cheek. Leo luxuriated in the back seat on the soft beige leather, my quickly packed bag, guitar and Leo's bed, toys and dog food tucked into an impressively large trunk.

He smiled at me as we made our way out of Annecy and on to the A40. 'I have been wanting to take you home with me,' he said with a bit of mischief in his smile. Leo gave a groan of pleasure as he rested his massive bucket head on the seat. 'That one, he likes my car. There will be dog hair everywhere.'

'There always is.'

Philippe grimaced but held my hand, driving with expert calm and precision, left hand on the wheel, and I did not once feel the need to hide my face and scream. So different from Olivier. How strange it was to feel so close to both of these men.

'Did you mean what you said? You and me together now, navigating things *together* now. And you are my guy?'

He nodded.

I thought about that. In truth, it was past time to make a decision. 'Because I have something that will help you.'

He gave me a glance, then looked back to the road.

And I told him about the digging I had done. And when I told him I had gotten access to the computer servers of the investors who financed Laurent's NGO, and tracked one of the email payments from LABAC to their account, he gripped the steering wheel of the car. 'And there are a lot of other transactions I downloaded that you might have fun rooting through.'

'This is true? You really have this? And you did not tell me? Do you know how crucial this is?'

'Yes, it is true, yes, I really have it, and, yes, I know how crucial this is.'

'I *must* have it. Where is it?'

'First, I have to know what you will do with this. Mainly, I am worried about two things. One, that you will sit on this like you sit on everything else, and still wait to get going on St Priest and Mae.'

He threw his hands up, then grabbed the steering wheel. 'That is unfair, Madame, but I can see why you feel that way. It is a problem no longer; I am moving on this – that I promise. You saw the manifesto. This is happening now.'

'Yes, I saw it, and I found Mae terrifying and . . . the manifesto was kind of long, don't you think?'

He glanced over at me and laughed. 'They always are, Madame.'

I felt the thrill of impending revenge. I took a minute to savor it. He would get St Priest. He would get Mae.

'OK, the second thing is that what I did was illegal. I would prefer not to be prosecuted on this, but I did it all on my own.'

'I will not allow you to be prosecuted, Madame; I promise you that.'

'I don't see how you can make this promise.'

'Then you underestimate me. Where is this information?'

'Stored on an external drive, in my apartment.'

'Where exactly?'

I hesitated. 'Hidden.'

He squeezed my hand and did not push me, which was a relief. 'This is perfect, then. We will use it tomorrow, because with this person, it is always a negotiation. And this will give me everything I need.' Then he glanced at me. 'It will give *us* everything *we* need.'

I laid my head against the window, watching the stream of headlights in the dark. I had about a million and seven questions for Philippe, but they faded as I nestled into the corner of the door. I slept all the way to Metz.

FORTY-FOUR

t was the slowing of the car that woke me. The lights of the city, as we wove our way through the streets. It had been raining, and the pavement was drenched and dark. I heard the hiss of tires on wet asphalt as we turned into the square of Old Town, and I saw the floodlit Cathedral of Metz.

'You live here? In Old Town?'

'This is OK with you?'

'I love it here,' I said softly.

Philippe lived in one of the tall old stone buildings on the left side of the cathedral. I remembered being here at the Christmas market with Olivier three years ago, looking at these beautiful old buildings, envying the people who lived inside. Olivier and I had talked about it. Moving to Metz.

Philippe parked and grabbed my bag and guitar, and Leo and I followed him into the building, through tall heavy red doors that opened when Philippe keyed in a code. The doors echoed as they shut behind us, and Leo and I followed Philippe up stairs and more stairs to the third floor.

The door to the apartment was a freshly painted baby-blue. Inside, it was warm, dry, spartan. Wood floors, and heat from an old register along the wall, like an iron accordion painted white. Ribbed wood planks across the ceiling.

One black leather couch. A television, and a heavy coffee table, that held a coffee mug, stained but dry. A wall of electronics. A tiny galley kitchen along the back.

In the single bedroom, low to the ground, a platform bed with a chocolate brown bedspread. One wall had pictures. Everything nailed to the wall in a random order, as if getting things up was quite enough.

Pictures of Philippe's son, who looked very like him. Dark-eyed and shy. Taller than his father. Philippe's parents, young and smiling, on their wedding day. Text superimposed over a roiling river – *La vie n'est pas un long fleuve tranquille.* Life is not a river of tranquility.

I didn't have inspirational wisdom framed up at home in Kentucky, because I could not find one that said *Quit reading the fucking stuff on my walls.*

There were tall windows that started waist high, went to the ceiling and opened inwards. A marble fireplace, boarded up. A tiny bathroom, spectacularly clean. With new white towels in a stack on a shelf. A true French bathroom, with new fixtures, everything small, compact, perfect for the space. Which was closet-sized. And practical.

I ran to one of the windows, followed by Leo, who went up on his front paws to look, and I stroked his head as the two of us looked out on to the square.

'How beautiful this is,' I said, gazing out at the cathedral. 'I have always wanted to live right here in Metz. This is magical.' I looked over my shoulder at Philippe and saw the flush of pleasure on his face.

'My son says it looks like classic divorced male in here.'

'It's that wall of electronics. Which actually just says . . . wall of electronics.'

Philippe smiled and took my suitcase into the bedroom, and suddenly our two lives were running together, as he made room in his dresser, giving me two drawers and a wide segment of his closet.

'I don't need this much space.'

'You must have room to grow your things.'

'Can I get Leo set up?'

'I'll help you.'

I rolled out Leo's lambswool pad on the floor in the bedroom, knowing he would not actually sleep there, but he could line his toys up there when they were not strewn in every direction. I laid out Camille the Camel, his favorite, and Barkley Bear, and a chicken-flavored chew toy for dogs with steel-trap jaws. Three rubber Chuck-It balls in a row. I had forgotten to bring his new pink teddy bear and left it on the couch in Annecy.

'He has more stuff than you do,' Philippe said.

Leo immediately took possession of one of the balls. He followed us into the kitchen.

Philippe filled Leo's water bowl, and I gave him a second dinner, since he had not eaten the first one, and he sniffed both bowls amiably and headed for the front door, putting his paw on the doorknob.

'I will take him out for you,' Philippe said, attaching Leo's leash.

The two of them headed out and I went to the window, then the kitchen, then sat my guitar in a corner and tried to catch my breath.

I had not packed much. But I tucked a pair of jeans, some socks and two sweaters into one of the empty drawers. Along with a small soft stack of panties and a bra. How odd that felt. In the bathroom, I put my cosmetics in a corner of the small countertop, next to the razor in a stand. Philippe's soap was dark green and smelled like evergreen, masculine. Should I put my toothbrush next to his? I did not know. I tucked it into my cosmetics bag.

I went into the bedroom and curled up into a little ball on the bed and shut my eyes very tight. I took deep breaths and waited for the panic to hit.

It did not come.

When the front door opened, I jumped out of the bed, smoothed the bedspread, and walked into the small living room, to Philippe's broad smile. He saw my empty suitcase, peered into the drawer at my things, checked the bathroom.

Leo settled into the middle of the bed.

'He will sleep there?' Philippe asked.

I nodded.

'Perhaps he might like to watch television sometimes, on the couch, if we want to . . . shut the bedroom door?'

I laughed. 'He's used to that.'

'*Bien.*' Philippe got a soft white towel from the bathroom. Bent to wipe each of Leo's paws and laughed when Leo stood patiently, lifting them one at a time.

'I feel like his valet,' Philippe said.

'It's part of being owned by a dog. Welcome to the pack.'

Philippe slept pressed close against my back, arms wrapped around me, almost too tight, which I welcomed. He was here, alive, breathing softly, and I was acutely aware of him, his skin against mine, a room without history or memories. Sleep for me would not come.

I missed Olivier. And I welcomed Philippe. But I wasn't sure how I was supposed to feel. And I knew the world was full of people who had so little experience with grief that they would be happy to tell me exactly how I *should* feel, to tie me up in knots as they framed my feelings into their lack of experience.

I did not think that I would ever let go of the depth of love and connection I had with Olivier, but did I have to? And couldn't I have the same thing with Philippe? Could I not have both?

I knew the smug and all-knowing vultures of grief would tell me to let Olivier go and move on, but it was not possible to let it go, this connection I had with Olivier; it was too precious. Even to ask such a thing to make the rest of the world feel better was an invitation to yet another layer of trauma. I had no problem refusing. And sometimes, when Philippe looked at me a certain way, it felt as if I had Olivier in the room. Dangerous thinking, I had told Laurent. I needed to take my own advice.

Philippe's voice was a soft whisper in my ear. 'You don't sleep, Junie?'

'It's OK, Philippe. I like being here, curled up in your bed.'

'It is our bed now,' Philippe said. 'And I understand more than you think. My mother, she died when I was thirteen, and I watched my father go through this. It was an unbearable thing to see. But as I grew up, I became proud of him. When people told him to clean out the things of my mother, he told them to mind their own business. He never took her pictures down. This was a comfort to me, growing up. He always had her hairbrush and a bottle of her perfume on his dresser. Some of her pretty things in his closet, a pair of her shoes side by side with his. He never worried about what people said. Sometimes he would begin to see a woman, and sometimes it would last for a while, but for him it never quite took. I think he has not found the right person. I still have hope that he will. Another right person, like my mother. We did not talk about this when I was growing up, you understand, but during my divorce, when I was so devastated. He sat down with me, and we shared a bottle of wine, and he told me things, about how he got through it. How he learned to live with it. And he told me that he would miss my mother forever, and you did not get over such a thing, because love did not go away, and those that said move on were ignorant and also cruel. But that finding someone else was a separate thing and one really had nothing to do with the other. So I understand you, Junie, more than you think. I know that you can miss Olivier and love also me.'

'And you? Do you miss your ex-wife?'

He laughed. '*Non.* I admit to you, I had a very hard time at first. But that is like a different lifetime for me, and I have no feelings of going back. You will meet him, my father, and my son. We will have a Sunday lunch very soon. My son visited here a week ago when I had not seen him for five months. It is a long time, not to see him; we have always been close. He has been angry with me over the divorce, which is not fair, but the sex life of my wife and me is not his business, so I will not explain or tell him bad things about his mother, though there are many bad things to tell. He will have to work this out on his own. I am just glad he will now come to my home.'

He pulled me closer and propped up on one arm, putting a hand on my cheek, looking at me intently.

His touch was warm, his fingers strong, and this made me think of Olivier, who was always gentle with me, stern and unyielding when he was on the job, full of a shy schoolboy mischief and a quick smile with his friends.

I had that feeling of being anchored, being seen . . . being safe.

He smiled at me, a hint of something like recognition. And if he saw me, I saw him, too. You know them when you see them. The people of your heart.

'I see you, Monsieur.'

'I see *you*, Madame.' Philippe touched the wedding bands on my left hand. 'I was thinking we might get on with things. I like living with you. You feel the same way?'

'I won't lie to you. The last six hours have been pretty great.'

He laughed. *'Nous sommes bien d'accord.* Let's make it a permanent thing. I would like to get married even. Is it too soon for you? Do you want to be married again?'

I caught my breath. I had told Laurent I did not believe in walk-in souls. But maybe. Maybe I did. Or maybe I just *wanted* to. I just knew that Philippe felt right. That something inside me said yes. My gut instinct said run with this. Don't wait, don't drag your feet, don't fuck it up. Because life could go sideways pretty fast. And because it gave me . . . hope. That somehow I would be all right again, when I never thought I would. That I was not alone.

'Tell me what is in your head, Junie.'

'That being with you feels exactly right. Do you always move this fast?'

He laughed. 'With my ex-wife, we were back and forth for three years. This is different with you. With you, I just know. You do not have to decide until you are ready. I will be here. I am not going away.'

'I like being married. To the right guy.'

He nodded his head. 'And I am the right guy.'

It wasn't a question, but I said yes anyway.

He held up my hand. *'Regarde*, Madame. You can wear his wedding ring on your left hand and mine on the right, or you can stack them all in a row.'

'I'll experiment and see what looks best. This is OK with you? I love you and there is always going to be Olivier. This grief thing I have.'

He held my hand very tight. 'You see, Leo, he has already invited me into the family. I am his personal valet, and one of the pack, you told me that, *d'accord*?'

'D'accord.'

'So that settles it. And Junie' – he looked at me with that seriousness he so often had – 'I know you will always love and miss the life you had with Olivier; it is like the beat of your heart. We both have people of the past. We are not children in the world. But together we are the next chapter, yes?'

I nodded my head and studied his serious, beautiful face.
'Yes.'

He kissed my hand. 'How soon?'

'Let's start the paperwork.' Because no matter how fiery
the romance, this was France, after all, and there would be a
tangle of bureaucracy.

Philippe sighed and eased down on the pillow, keeping hold
of my hand. He chuckled. 'I forgot to say the most important
thing. *Je t'aime aussi.*' He pulled me closer and was almost
instantly asleep.

And me, I did not sleep, but I was almost OK. The French
have a quiet word for happy. *Contente.*

FORTY-FIVE

The next morning after coffee, Philippe kissed me smugly and told me we could be married in ten days if we got the paperwork together, and then he looked at me with a frown.

'I admit I am wary of taking you to meet Madame Reynard, but I really don't have a choice if I am to get what I want. Please be careful with her. She is dangerous.'

I did not tell him that I generally considered myself the most dangerous person in the room. When you are detached and do not care if you live or die, you are formidable. I was very curious about Madame Reynard and the behind-the-scenes powers she seemed to wield.

I did not think she would be curious about me. I was somebody's widow. Nobody much.

And I took an instant dislike to her the moment I met her. She gave me a little smile, as if I was exactly what she expected and she had not expected much, which would surely work in my favor. Being underestimated was always a plus. She tossed her head and turned on a radiant charm that was lost on me. I was more interested in the river of steel underneath. She was perfect for her job, running her spy network in plain sight, with a clear and articulate agenda. Philippe said people were openly afraid of her influence, which ran the gamut from blackmail to making things go your way, perhaps in government policy or securing a loan at excellent terms. She could provide information you might find useful, or understand there might be incidents you would like kept discreetly confidential. Always the carrot and stick. She was also very good at putting people together and introducing you to exactly the right person who you had not even realized you needed to know. She could certainly be useful. The general consensus was that it was wise to stay on her good side – pissing her off led to a dread

of what she would do in the future – and the universal agreement was that she got things done no one else could. For the
greater good, of course. And Philippe said that she liked him,
but that it would only take us so far.

Her office was in a large official building with seven stories
and two flights of stairs to the front door. Parking nearby was
impossible. Inside, her space was a hot mess, but none of it
was paper. Mysterious electronic boxes, some unhooked and
dusty, wires everywhere, a lot of blinking blue and orange
lights. A large computer screen on her left, an open laptop on
the desk, an electronic notepad turned on its face. Clearly a
woman who compartmentalized. Against the far wall was
a big-screen television, muted, with ongoing news a constant
stream. A tall stack of used paper coffee cups in one corner
caught my attention. No doubt she recycled.

Philippe became watchful, contained, wary. I had seen this
side of him before. He let her do most of the talking. I felt
that was on purpose. She liked to talk; her hands were in
perpetual motion, and her voice rose and fell. And she told us
all about the terrorist, Mae. Most of it I knew, but maybe was
not supposed to.

But I grew impatient and interrupted. 'If you know so much
about her, why hasn't she been picked up?'

She pulled her head back as if she had not realized I could
talk. Leo stayed quiet and watchful, stretched out by my feet.
She had not petted him. Or looked at him once. I thought she
might be afraid of big dogs. A lot of people are.

'It is not my job to pick her up. I gather information.' She
raised an eyebrow at Philippe. 'And as I understand it, she has
been rather hard to find.'

Her voice was high-pitched, all sharp angles and elbows.
She wore square sky-blue reading glasses that hung from a
turquoise chain. Her hair was thick and wavy, a rather beautiful
blend of dark blonde and white blonde, but she had pulled it
all into a black clip like a woman who takes perfect hair for
granted. She tilted her head and studied me. 'But it is true, I
have my sources; Philippe will have told you that. But I also
remind you that the man in charge is right next to you, sitting
so close and watching you in such a way that makes me wonder

what has been going on between the two of you. I know this
is a terrifying time for you. I know you must be very afraid
and worried.'

'I appreciate that you are trying to engage with me. But
you don't know me, and whether or not I am scared, or even
if I live or die, is nothing that is going to keep you up at night.
Philippe said you wanted to talk to me – and here I am. I'm
just going to get right to the point and tell you that I might,
hypothetically speaking, have some hardcore information on
bank account transactions linking the investment group represented by Charl St Priest to an account set up to look like it
is coming from an eco-activist group called LABAC. That's
why Philippe brought me here – that and he said you wanted
to meet me. And I don't want to waste your time, so can we
just get on with it?'

I felt Philippe squeeze my hand and knew he was happy
with me and that so far everything was going according to
plan. But he had been right to tell me this woman was
dangerous.

She gave him a look. As if he should have warned her. She
got up and closed her office door, looking at me over one
shoulder with a fierce little smile. 'I do not want us to
be overheard, and you are rather loud, Madame Lagarde.
No doubt you are upset.'

'You are also the noise police? And no, I've just always been
loud.' When you have a hearing loss, there is always someone
who wants to take you down a peg because you are *loud*.
You'd be surprised how often that happens. It's a dog up, dog
down world. I never let it bother me.

She blinked. I caught a little smile from Philippe.

She clattered on kitten heels back behind her desk and settled
into her rolling chair, which squeaked. I hated rolling chairs.
I didn't mind if other people sat in them.

'I do not wish to offend you, Madame Lagarde, but you are
an accountant from that place in the US.'

'*Forensic* accountant. Kentucky.'

'Yes. Kentucky.'

'We're actually on Google maps.'

She did not smile. Just opened her hands at me with a look

of apology. 'We have our team of forensic accountants here, you see, and I do not wish to be unkind, but I do not think you would have information on the level of sophistication that we need. One person, without the kind of training my people have, can only gather so much.'

Which showed how little she knew. Forensic accounting was not about teams of accountants slaving over reams of information, unless you had a decade or two to figure things out. Most people don't. Good forensic accounting was about going right to the heart of what you needed really fast and doing as little work as possible to get there. Being lucky helped.

'And, of course, there is the delicate question of access.' She gave me a gentle smile.

She had me on that one. My access was illegal. I did not look away and I most certainly did not look at Philippe.

I nodded and folded my arms.

'On the other hand. You do seem to have exactly what I need. Is it just the one transaction?' She gave me a sweet smile.

'I am sure you already know that when you are able to mirror a server, you get a copy of database and transaction log files.'

She actually laughed. 'May I say that I am delighted to hear this? And there are many new laws to help law enforcement deal with terrorists. So if Philippe is comfortable with how this information was acquired . . . I can have it now?'

'I have it, locked away in my office,' Philippe said sharply. Which was a lie. The location was information he did not want her to have. He didn't trust her. I should have told him last night where it was. When we could have turned back and gotten it.

'I want this immediately.' She folded her hands on the desk and looked at Philippe. 'What is it you want?'

I leaned back in my chair. My part was done.

'I am preparing to arrest Mae Yvonne McDermott and Charl St Priest. You will immediately take the obstructions out of the way of my judge and facilitate this,' Philippe said.

'No, Philippe, you must not go off on your own with your

team, not when we are so close. Now that we have this information, I can move fast with this. And, Philippe' – she raised an eyebrow – 'you know very well that these are decisions made at the highest level. You must not jeopardize our chance to take down those who fund Mae. I want the big guys, Philippe.'

'Why? People like that never go to jail,' I said.

She gave me a look of deep satisfaction. 'I do not want them in jail. I want to have them right where I want them. I want them crushed under my heel. There is much to be accomplished that way.'

'So they get away with it?' I said.

'In truth, Madame Lagarde, the world of climate change is *comme ci comme ça*. Big plans and promises are made, to show *the people* something *must* be done and *will* be done, and great sums are set aside for funding. Then the money goes into the hands of the usual players. Very little of it goes where it should. That's where I come in. To see that it actually does. You could say that Mae and I have similar goals.

'And I am in a unique position, Madame Lagarde. Law enforcement moves slowly, for good reasons, but frankly there are people with too much wealth and power who cannot be reached that way. Greedy corporate criminals, wealthy people snarled up in terrorist factions, government plots. It is my job to come at them from a different direction. If they have a thick snake of money and power wrapped around the throat of the average person in France, I can use their methods against them. Just because you don't know the details of what I am doing does not mean I am not doing anything.'

Philippe snorted. 'Many of them would prefer jail, after dealing with Madame Reynard. Believe me, her way is better. For some things, and people I cannot reach. But I will get Mae and I will get St Priest, and I will get them now, Madame Reynard; they are on the move. So no more lectures, please, on how you are the spider in the web. There will be *no more* collateral damage. And you know very well what I mean. This is hardly the first time this has played out bad.'

She tapped a finger on her desk. 'OK. Go forward. I take your word on this, Philippe, that I will be happy with the

information you have. I will take care of things at my end.'
She gave me a glance. 'Know also that I will keep your
husband's reputation safe.'

I took a deep breath. I believed her. And I admit that in
her office I didn't feel like the most dangerous person in
the room.

That was when Philippe's phone pinged wildly, followed
by alerts on Madame's computer.

Philippe looked up. The lines in his face looked deeper,
but he had an energy, wound up and ready to explode, the
way he was when he'd come to my apartment last night.
'Stolen Torvex,' he said, looking at this phone. 'An avalanche
management company, near Chamonix, Dominate the
Mountain, had a break-in the night before last. You are getting
this message, Madame Reynard?'

'What is Torvex?' I asked.

'Explosives.' Madame Reynard looked up from her computer
screen. 'And yes, I agree, they are on the move. Be careful,
Philippe. You, your people, emergency services . . . they are
often targets in a plot like this. But I will take care of the
issue with the judge—'

'*Trop tard*, Madame. This is just the mess I did not want.'
He grabbed my hand. 'Junie, we must go.' Then he stopped
and looked back at her. 'You do good work, Madame Reynard,
but I am beginning to think our goals are backwards. All the
efforts for the big-problem people with the money and
the power. Those people will always be there. The job should
be taking care of the small ones at risk.'

'You have your job, Philippe, and I have mine.'

'*Bonne journée*, Madame Reynard.'

'*Bonne chance*, Philippe.'

Philippe kept a tight hold on me. He was on the move, and I
could barely keep up. There would be no time for elevators,
and Leo and I followed Philippe as he thundered down the
stairs.

'Madame, where is this external drive of yours?'

'It's a thumb drive, hidden in Leo's big bag of kibble in
my flat.'

Philippe snorted. 'You think this is a good hiding place?'

'It is if no one but me knows it exists.'

'And now Le Reynard knows—'

'But you told her *you* had it.'

'She will go after it, Junie; she will send someone, and they will cover all the bases. They will first go to my office, then my apartment here, and then to your place in Annecy. We will get there first. And you will please drive, Madame, I have calls to make.'

Leo trotted happily beside us. Something was up, and he was all in.

FORTY-SIX

Philippe stayed long enough at the apartment in Annecy to retrieve the thumb drive. He told me to pack a few more things if I wanted; he would stay in close touch, and I was not to worry, but he had to go. He stationed a young officer outside to keep watch – L'agent Bernice Durand. It was cold out, and she wore a blue parka which looked new. Philippe had spoken to her quite firmly about the risks, and she was alert, serious and very much thrilled. I had waved at her from the balcony, taken her a cup of coffee, and Leo had huffed at me, paws up on the railing, for leaving him upstairs. This had made her laugh for the last time in her life.

I had instructions to be quick – no more than one hour to pack – then I would be sent back to Metz under the supervision of Durand, who had instructions to stay with me there. We thought that we were taking extreme precautions. We thought that Leo and I and L'agent Bérénice Durand would be safe.

But things had been set in motion the moment the Torvex was stolen, and by the time Philippe and I left Metz, Operation Mont Blanc Sabotage had been live for twenty-eight hours.

The avalanche ordinance had been stolen in the last twenty-six hours. Philippe was in a frenzy. Today the tunnel shut down for routine maintenance and would be closed to traffic for the next week and a half. After a phone huddle with Madame Reynard, he was sure that Mae and St Priest would wait until the tunnel opened again, offering a broad range of targets from one end of the tunnel to the other, for maximum impact and carnage. Philippe would get the paperwork through the judge, gather his forces and arrest them before they hit. He wanted everyone ready to strike in six hours, and he was quick on his feet, distracted, with a buzz of energy and concentration that impressed me.

'Please take care,' I told him, as he headed out the door.

He came back and gave me a hard kiss. 'You will not lose me again.'

I did a double take, but he was already gone, and I heard him running down the stairs. And I needed to get moving, get packed and get out.

But we miscalculated. Because, in truth, we still did not understand Mae. Philippe and Madame Reynard predicted her plan on models of behavior that had been proven over and over again, but did not take into account the individual woman, the darkness that consumed her, the way she stayed as true as she could to the woman she used to be and her personal code of ethics. She would not wait until the tunnel opened. The tunnel closed was the whole point.

Profiling was limited in predicting a woman like Mae. A woman who had killed my husband and Madame Fournier so coldly, so brutally, and then was tortured by regrets. A woman who was so angry that she felt the world had given her no choice.

I was as tense as Philippe and looking forward to Mae and St Priest being rounded up, the tunnel safe, going on with my life. I was deep in thought; there was too much too fast to process in my head. My packing was haphazard. My other guitar was set by the door, more sweaters and jeans rounded up, the old dishtowels thrown in for good measure, and my new coffee pot. I looked sadly at the spinach and the small brown cabernet tomatoes and the completely perfect eggplant and decided to take them to Philippe's kitchen in Metz. We would leave my car in the garage. No point signaling that I had upped and run. An abundance of caution until the paperwork went through and he got Mae and St Priest rounded up. He had no doubt that St Priest would twist and turn and lead him right to Mae if he could not track her down immediately. She was hard to find, though she'd been sighted once at St Priest's chalet near the Parc de Merlet, and Philippe was hoping he'd get them both at once. If not, St Priest must be persuaded to rat her out. She would be close. She'd come too far, was too invested and past the point of no return. A terrorist attack was like a wedding. Things always went wrong. You went through with it anyway.

The timing had been hard to predict until the ordinance was stolen. Now it was game on. Mae was close.

The knock on the apartment door was so tentative, so soft, that I would never have known Béatrice was there if Leo had not given the alert – a nudge to my leg and a huff. I thought it was Officer Durand returning my coffee cup.

But it was Béatrice, leaning against the wall when I looked through the spy hole, and I unlocked the new deadbolt and opened the door. Barely on her feet, blouse ripped at the shoulder. Bottom lip puffy and smeared with blood, eyes dark with shock. And she would know better than anyone where St Priest was right now.

'God. *Béatrice.*'

'I am so, so sorry to come here like this.' She swayed sideways.

I grabbed hold of her and shored her up.

She cried out, barely able to put weight on her left foot. 'I think it is broken.' She wiped her chin, smearing blood from her lip across her face.

'I thought you were safe in Spain.'

She laughed, caught her breath and held her side. 'He found me first, my husband.'

'I'll call Philippe. But let's get you to the couch.'

She nodded, and just as it occurred to me to wonder why Durand had not stopped Béatrice on her way up, Leo growled, snarled and stormed the door.

Things began to happen very fast.

Mae crowded the doorway, and behind her, St Priest. Instinctively, I stood in front of Béatrice. Saw Mae look over my shoulder with a knowing little smile. And a knife was at my throat, Béatrice pulling one arm hard behind my back – *merde*, she was strong. The knife was sticky and thick with blood – not mine. Leo leaped and Mae raised an arm and shot him. He yelped and wobbled, then dropped, and I slammed my head backward into Béatrice, felt a trickle of blood down the side of my neck, and slammed my right elbow into her stomach, felt her wobble. She screamed curses, and I felt her spittle on my cheek. But her hand went slack. Mae grabbed me and held me hard.

'Your annoying dog is OK, my darling girl,' St Priest said, giving me a loving smile, as if he still thought he was my husband. 'It is a tranquilizer dart. You see, we are going to need you both. The two of you have a way of stirring up the media, so we will make the most of that.'

I bit Mae hard on the arm, and she slammed a fist into my temple that rocked me with pain and made me go limp. I was suddenly sick to my stomach and only on my feet because Mae held me there.

'Not so much drama, Junie.' St Priest took me gently from Mae, pulling me so close I could smell the soap he used. 'I have you.' He kissed the top of my head, starring in his personal surreal fantasy life. 'I will take care of you, I promise.'

Béatrice laughed out loud.

Mae brought up the rear as we headed down the narrow staircase. She cradled Leo like a baby, stopping to go back into the apartment to get his new pink bear off the couch, kicking the door shut behind her.

St Priest hustled me down the stairs, one arm around my ribs, keeping me close and on my feet.

Once we were out on to the dark, rain-drenched street, Mae peeled off without a backward look, heading around the corner away from us, and Béatrice went to the driver's side of the battered old green Land Rover. A couple across the street stopped walking and stared at us. And I saw a blood trail, illuminated by a streetlight, pooling at the corner of the building, and no sign of L'agent Bérénice Durand, aged twenty-three, whose body was later found dragged behind a trash bin. She might still have been alive then, ravaged by multiple stab wounds, but had likely bled out by the time Béatrice started the car.

St Priest opened the door to the back seat of the Land Rover, squeezed my hand gently. 'Be careful of your head.'

I preferred Mae, even if she hit me. My knees buckled, and I threw up, vomit spattering his shoe. He kept me on my feet, patted my shoulder kindly and tucked me half sitting, half sideways, into the back of the Rover. I realized I was not alone in the backseat of the car.

Out of the corner of my eye, I saw the couple running toward us, and I had a small flare of hope, but Béatrice had the engine running, and we tore away from the curb, tires squealing, Béatrice laughing like a hyena, driving fast.

The man was tall, with a familiar presence, beaten so badly it took me a few seconds to realize that it was Laurent stretched across the seat, rousing enough to sit up and pull me close. Face bloodied, swelling below his left eye which was open only a slit. A trickle of dried blood down his temple, caking the hair over his left ear.

'Junie,' he whispered, putting his arms tight around me, chin on the top of my head. 'I tried to stop them. But you are still alive.'

'I think not for long.'

He laughed, but there was something feral about the way it sounded. 'I think we should kill them – all three of them. Béatrice, St Priest and Mae.'

'I am so up for that.'

Béatrice was driving fast, and the traffic noise muffled what we said. St Priest and Béatrice were squabbling like an old married couple, which, after all, they were.

'*Slow down*,' St Priest told her in the tone of a long-suffering husband. 'You want to get pulled over so close to the end?'

'Mae is driving too close behind us. All of that in the trunk of the car? If it goes off, do you want to be so close that we go up, too?'

He gave her a look. 'Always a step ahead of me, my wife.' His voice was a caress, and she gave him a sassy smile.

Béatrice put a CD in the slot on the dash, and Penny Dreadful's 'Mark of Cain' from the *Deadwood* album blared with hard guitars and the beat of drums, and I felt a moment of shock that we both loved the same alternative, gritty rock band from Athens, Greece. Before I realized the obvious: that she had taken the CD from my car. And when I looked backwards out of the rear-view window, I recognized the profile and headlights behind us. Mae was driving the Z4. No doubt she had Leo riding shotgun, sleeping off the tranquilizer dart.

St Priest turned to look at us over the back of the seat. 'Have you figured out where we are going, *guys*? We are on our way to the Mont Blanc Tunnel, Junie, with a sabotage plan your own husband has laid out step by step, so brilliant as always. We have avalanche ordinance, which is lovely little packets of Torvex with a fuse – this looks so much like *la saucisse à l'orange*. So easy to use, so available in the Alps – you light it and you get the hell out. They drop them from helicopters in the snow, to cause the avalanche. That was Olivier's idea, by the way, I believe he said "things to hand locally." And all packed into the trunk of your beautiful car, which becomes an IED. Have you seen a car blow, Junie? It is thrilling. A Z4 will go up in the air and the fire will be magnificent and very hard to put out. You and Laurent – and Leo, of course – are going to cause an explosion in the Mont Blanc Tunnel, following the terrorist plan your husband laid out in his analysis for his company. Please do not be worried; I think you will die very fast, much faster than Olivier did, burning in the crash of the plane. What do you call this in the US? The Fourth of July? And you will finish the job your husband started – a terrorist act to force the world to pay attention to global warming. The emissions from the tunnel are immense. All those cars and trucks going through for an EU supply chain – striking a blow for the change to electric cars.'

I swallowed. 'Olivier didn't like electric cars; he thought they were a fire hazard.'

St Priest laughed. 'Believe me, I know. That was just like your husband – nothing was ever good enough for him. But the world will not know that. The world will see you and Olivier and Laurent, planning an eco-terrorist plot that went sideways when he crashed. You could not let him die in vain, could you, Junie?'

'Ever the trailing spouse. And this time you get to pretend to be the hero?'

He shook his head. 'This time I *am* the hero.'

'And Béatrice is in it for the money,' I said.

Béatrice twisted her head to give me a look. 'You have something against money? It is an elegant thing, to get paid by both sides. There are no good guys here. It is all *merde*, no matter who does what.'

I didn't exactly disagree. 'But Mae. She's the real deal.'

'There must always be one who is the real deal. They drive the plot, they take the risks, they are like a tool in the hands. We could never have done this without Mae. She is very sad, you know. The money is not going to make her OK, however much she gets. I am fond of Mae. She is very alone in the world, and I am proud to be her friend.'

'And she is also very useful when something heavy needs to be carried.' St Priest looked at Béatrice and grinned, but she waved him off.

The rain turned to snow, the car slid sideways, and Béatrice corrected, then accelerated. St Priest looked at Béatrice and shrugged. 'She is always beyond reason, that one.'

But behind us, the headlights faded.

Laurent shifted and pulled me close to his chest. He smelled of blood, sweat and pain. He touched my temple, which was agony. 'They have hit you. It looks bad; even in the dark, I can see this.'

'Yes, I let Béatrice in when she came to the door. I thought she was St Priest's sad victim wife, so I opened the door and let her right in.'

St Priest glanced back at us. The music was loud; I did not think he could hear, but I lowered my voice. 'And Mae was right behind her and, boy, she can hit. My jaw hurts so bad I can barely open my mouth.'

He grabbed my hand. 'And your Leo?'

'They shot him with a tranquilizer dart before he could rip them to shreds. That's when Mae punched me.'

'She is dangerous, that one.'

'And you?'

He bent close to whisper right in my ear. 'They were waiting down the road when I left my house. They smashed into my car and knocked me sideways, and the airbags went off, and that is how I got hurt the most, but they also hit me when I fought them. St Priest had a gun and said let's go to pick up your fuckbuddy—'

'*Fuckbuddy?*'

'He is jealous, he is crude. Because you know, in his fantasy, he is a mix of Olivier and himself.'

'If I wasn't already nauseous—'

He chuckled. 'You threw up on him already. Also, if you think this might happen again—'

'Don't worry; I'll lean over the front seat.'

'Béatrice, she is the *patron*. Mae is the face of the operation, and St Priest – he is just out of his mind. None of this would have happened without Béatrice making the plan.'

'She seems to enjoy it.'

'They got the ordinance from my friend, Pierre Chandon, who owns Dominate the Mountain. He manages the snow and the avalanches. It is a crazy job. He lights the fuse and drops the bombs out of a helicopter. I do not know when they did this theft; I hope he is OK.'

'He is OK. They took the Torvex the day before yesterday, very early, and he reported it immediately. Philippe got the report and is after them. When Durand does not check in, he'll be looking for me. He'll find us.'

'Who is Durand?'

'A new cop. Philippe left her with me to keep me safe, and they . . . I think they stabbed her. I saw blood.'

He pulled me closer. 'I am sorry. But I do not think Capitaine Brevard will get here soon enough. Béatrice and St Priest and Mae, they were moving very fast to get me and then you.'

'Philippe thought they would wait till the tunnel was open again, but he knows they have the Torvex, and when Durand does not report in, he'll figure it out. He'll come.'

'Yes, this is part of the plan, to do this when the tunnel is closed. I heard them arguing. Mae said there will be more sympathy if they do not kill innocent people, and anyway it is so very guarded that going when it is open . . . too much could go wrong. Mae insisted and Béatrice went along, because there is going to be a big payment from St Priest's investment group once this is done. She said *something* must blow up. And she wants a Porsche. She has already picked it out. They have travel plans, but I do not know exactly where they will go.'

'Somewhere warm with a beach, no doubt.'

'It is somewhere on the Black Sea. Béatrice has already written the media announcements, and the articles are set to go out as soon as this is done. And Mae, she is a strange one. She is very crushed over the death of Olivier and seems very sad, but it does not seem to slow her down, and she appears to have forgotten she also killed Madame Fournier, who was my friend also. So she is the one I can't figure out.'

'We'll ask her about it before we kill her.'

'You are serious about this?'

'Very.'

'Junie—'

'No. Let's just say it. Philippe will be on his way to the tunnel, but that won't keep either of us alive, not likely. And neither one of us cares if we live or die. That is never going to go away. It's our advantage. We go down fighting, kill them if we can, but if nothing else, we make them sorry.'

'They plan to put me in the front passenger seat with Leo, and you go in the trunk with the bombs while Mae drives us to the middle of the tunnel. Then she runs and the car goes up.'

'Shit. I have claustrophobia. Why do I have to go in the trunk?'

'Because you are smaller.'

'Then we have to kill them *before* they put me in the trunk.'

'I am thinking we do this right as we get to the tunnel. That way is more dangerous, because we will have to deal with Mae—'

'No, no, no, we *want* Mae. She has to die, and I have to get Leo out of that car.'

'Yes. OK. And also maybe Philippe will be there, with police and emergency guys.'

'Philippe will be there. He'll have people there. He will put this together; he is probably on his way now.'

'But as you say, we cannot count on this.'

'Fuck, no. We have to do this; we can't just hope it works out. And I am *not* going in that trunk.'

'Yes, Madame, I think you are right.'

A truck passed, throwing up slushy snowy water, and I moved closer to Laurent so he could hear.

'So when we get close to the tunnel, and they are distracted looking for Mae and watching their backs, we attack. I take St Priest, and you get Béatrice.'

'Madame, be practical, St Priest is stronger and has the gun.'

'Yeah, but I am right behind him, and you are behind Béatrice, and if you think they aren't going to notice the two of us playing musical chairs—'

'*Quoi?*'

'Changing sides in the back seat.'

He nodded. 'But tell the truth, Junie. It is St Priest you want to kill.'

'He called Leo a dirty animal.'

'Then, of course, he must die.' Laurent studied Béatrice, and I could hear the murmur of her conversation with St Priest, but I couldn't make out the words. 'I can snap her neck pretty fast, which will cause an accident, but St Priest has the gun, so—'

'Yes, and he'll be aiming it toward you because you are the biggest and most dangerous, though I hate like hell to admit that.'

He chuckled softly. 'I know, so, Junie, you will have to be fast. What are you doing?'

I was digging in the crack at the back of the seats. 'Looking for a weapon, a paperclip, a pen, a pencil—'

'What have you got?'

'A candy wrapper.'

'What kind?'

'Reese's Cup . . . *does it matter*? Oh, wait. I have Leo's training clicker in my pocket.'

Laurent sighed. 'You will annoy him with this noise until he gives up and hands you the gun?'

'That would take too long; he looks like he might hold out. But it has a stretchy plastic loop, and if I can get it around his neck—'

'Yes, yes, but you must be fast; he will be distracted when

I go for Béatrice, so when it is around his neck you twist it and—'

'I have an idea on starting the distraction.' I whispered it to him, and he laughed out loud. I cocked my head to one side. 'Why is this so fun?'

'Relief, Madame. We have nothing to lose, and soon it will all be over, and before the sun comes up again—'

'We are going to be dead. Pinky swear, widow to widower.'

'*D'accord.*' He sighed happily. 'Look, Madame, at the stars with the snow falling. It is all so very beautiful, in the dark of the night.'

'So are you, Laurent. So very beautiful. In ways I cannot describe.'

'Oh, no, Madame, I insist that you describe them.'

So I did. It made him laugh, softly, as we tried to be quiet like children in the dark.

And then we saw them. The lights of the Mont Blanc Tunnel, arched and beckoning in the dark. The car climbing up the incline of the road that was wet with snow, and steep.

Laurent put a hand on my thigh. 'You are ready, Junie? I think it is time. *Bien d'accord?* We must do this before they stop the car.'

'I am ready.'

FORTY-SEVEN

The car swerved sideways, deep in a skid, just as I got the clicker out of my pocket and looped it around my wrist.

'I am going to be sick,' I wailed, leaping up and hanging over the front seat. Béatrice cursed and smacked me hard, and St Priest cringed and moved closer to the door.

Then Laurent had his hands around Béatrice's neck, and the car surged forward as she kicked out and hit the accelerator. She slumped but was held in place by Laurent's big-handed grip. I grabbed the head rest for balance and looped the clicker around St Priest's neck. He was supposed to grab at his throat like they did in the movies, but the plastic snapped, the gun came up, and he shot Laurent in the face, drenching me in the splatter of Laurent's blood and brains. Laurent was slumped half in and half out of the seat, and it did not seem possible to me that he was no longer alive, and I had once again been left behind.

The car began to spin. It lurched forward into the side of the slope, throwing me back in the seat. The driver's side airbag went off; it took one-twentieth of a second, slamming Béatrice with a 200-mile-per-hour impact, her head sideways and vulnerable, fragile neckbones pulped by the force. If Laurent had not already broken her neck, the airbags did.

St Priest's airbag did not go off. I scrambled back up, took the shoulder harness and pulled it up and around his neck. It was locked tight, but I did not need much play, just a quick adjustment to slide it tight around his throat and cut off his air. I pulled it tighter and harder and held it, feet braced against the back seat, leaning backward with all of my weight. St Priest was choking, flailing and making noises of absolute fury, but he was a long way from dead when the passenger's side airbag finally went off. And suddenly my right arm was burning from the release of sodium azide and the exothermic action of the airbag explosion, with the chemicals burrowing into my flesh, a searing second-degree burn that stretched from the back of my hand to my elbow, and my cotton sweater flaring over my skin. St Priest had blood running down his face, and there was white powder everywhere. I saw the gun on the side of the seat next to Béatrice. St Priest was slumped sideways but moving. I scrambled half over and grabbed the gun.

St Priest and I locked eyes. 'Junie,' he said. '*Mon amour.*'

I shot St Priest at a weird catty-corner angle through the side of the head, but it killed him just fine. Béatrice already looked dead, eyes wide, head awkward, hand outstretched on the seat, but I shot her in the throat to make sure and also because I wanted to. The airbag shards smoldered and caught fire, a row of three tiny flames igniting right next to Béatrice's fingers. And I noticed that she had put her wedding ring back on.

The flame on my sweater went out.

I looked at Laurent, his face destroyed, the inside of the car a slaughterhouse, and I was drenched with their blood, their fluids, their flesh. I touched Laurent's hand, which was still warm, and told him goodbye, and I felt a wave of pure envy. He was free. I would be too, very soon.

It would go like this. Save Leo. Kill Mae.

The back seat door of the car jerked open, and there she was. Mae, in a blind panic, moving fast. She grabbed me and dragged me out, shaking her head, eyes wide. She shoved me into the BMW, driver's side, engine running, the keys still in the ignition. This was my chance. I'd hit the accelerator and run her down.

But she was fast, and I was dazed, and she scrambled into the passenger's side, lifting Leo on to her lap. He was limp, eyes fluttering, paws twitching, as he tried to wake up. Mae had one foot over a backpack that rested at her feet. And I knew what was in that bag.

Mae was motioning me forward, so frantic and freaked that I knew, suddenly, exactly why. Mae had not planned for Béatrice and St Priest to survive. Mine wasn't the only car full of Torvex.

I hit the accelerator and the car leaped forward, and we headed toward the top of the steep incline to the brightly lit Mont Blanc Tunnel. I could see the Land Rover in my rear-view mirror, fire spreading to the engine, smoke beginning to billow, and I floored it on the slippery road. The BMW steering was tight; the car held to the road like a lover. And then, when I decided it wasn't going to happen, the Land Rover blew, with a bone-shattering explosion that was like nothing you can possibly imagine. Lights flared, and the Land Rover was airborne, then crashed back down, landing in flame and smoking metal. There would be nothing left to bury at the funerals.

And then we were there at the tunnel, the huge, rounded arch that seemed smaller in real life than it did in pictures. It was lit like a sports arena for a night-time game, men and women in uniform running towards us, cop cars everywhere, two firetrucks and pandemonium. I hit the brake and the car skidded to a halt. Mae put Leo in my lap, blew me a kiss and rummaged in the bag. She had two bombs left. She lit the fuses and held them up, and she screamed, '*Arrêtez-vous!*'

Everybody froze.

I heard shouting and thought I heard Philippe's voice. Mae held the bombs up as she got out of the car. If they took her down, Leo and I were toast. And I knew that Philippe would not allow it.

Mae skittered backward, away from the cop cars, the emergency vehicles, the army of men and women with guns. Then she turned and ran like hell into the tunnel.

For the longest time nothing happened. It was Philippe who called the shot that took her down, focused, watching, coolly calculating the distance until she was a good hundred meters out, a football field away. Saving everyone, all of us, from the shockwave that would have gutted our insides, collapsed our lungs, broken our bones and slammed our brains.

Mae Yvonne McDermott, born and raised in Gatlinburg, Tennessee, 13.4 miles from Sevierville, where Olivier and I had met when he was doing a consultation for an automotive supplier. Where Olivier said he wanted to be my forever guy, where we had decided to get married six weeks after we met while watching the fireworks in Gatlinburg on a rainy New Year's Eve. Mae Yvonne McDermott was taken down by a sniper at fifty-seven meters into the tunnel entrance, and then the Torvex blew. It is hard to be accurate with a moving target, and the bullet brought her down but did not kill her. I heard her scream. I saw her flail, the flames racing up her arms and legs. Then Mae was consumed by a wall of fire, and she was crying and calling out for someone, and it took her longer to die than I thought possible. They got to her pretty quickly but not soon enough, and Mae died in the flames, just as she wanted, just as she planned. And I envied her that.

FORTY-EIGHT

I watched Mae burn and thought of the ravaged flesh on my husband's body, thought of him choking in the smoke. I felt the fiery pain of the chemical burn on my arm and knew that, until now, I had not even come close to imagining how terrible his death had been.

Everyone was dead, and I was alive. Why was I here? *Why was I here?*

Leo was making grumbling noises and snuggling weakly to my lap, and I saw Philippe running toward me, officers swarming in every direction, and he was there so fast, ripping the door of the car open wide.

'Ah, Junie, *mon dieu.*'

I felt his hands on my shoulder, gripping hard, as he crouched down in front of me, looking at me with such an intensity.

He pushed hair out of my eyes. 'You are so hurt.'

'Not my blood.'

He took a ragged breath. 'Some of it is yours.' He took a folded scarf and wiped my face and my neck and grimaced. 'We must get you out, there may be more explosives.' He looked over my shoulder. 'Michel.'

And Michel was there, taking Leo over his shoulders as he always did, and I began to cry with deep shuddering sobs. Philippe pulled me out of the car, and lifted me into his arms, whispering things that would no doubt have been thrilling if only I could hear. If only my head did not ache so hard. If only I could catch my breath.

His car was close, and he took me there and tucked me into the passenger's seat. Michel was already there, settling Leo into the back. Philippe took his sweater off, the tee shirt underneath blindingly white. He pulled my sweater up, off and over my head, grimaced and handed it to Michel who bagged it for evidence. I shivered, but he slipped his sweater over me quickly, the wool still warm from his body.

He held tight to my hands and spoke in a low tone. 'What happened back there? Who was in the car? Before everything blew up?'

'Béatrice, St Priest.' I looked up at him. '*Laurent.* They're dead.'

'Tell me what happened,' he said gently.

'I don't . . . I don't remember.' But I did remember. I remembered every last detail and I always would. 'They're all dead, Philippe. St Priest, Béatrice – she was part of it—'

'I know.'

'And Laurent. Oh God, *Laurent.*' Then I looked up. 'L'agent Durand, she—'

He shook his head. 'We found her when she did not report in. Ah, Junie, I thought I had lost you.'

'I wish you had. I'm sorry, I wish you had. I don't want to be in the world anymore. I can't stand to be in the world anymore. I can't stand to feel like this anymore.'

I sobbed into his shoulder, and he held me very close. 'Listen to me now, Junie. It is the shock talking. I promise you will be OK.'

'You can't promise me that.'

'I can and I do. You will have me, and you will have Leo. And we will be enough. You feel me holding your hand? I will always be here to hold your hand.' Then he stroked Leo and called him *mon fiston.*

I was aware of more voices. More sirens. More flashing lights. Philippe talking and giving orders over the top of my head. I didn't want to know what he was saying. I didn't want to know or see anything else. Anything ever again.

'It's not my blood,' I whispered. 'It's not my blood. Everyone is dead. Laurent, Béatrice, St Priest. They all blew up in the car.'

There wasn't anyone else to rescue so the EMTs came running to me. I knew Philippe was talking to them: they were swarming, telling him that my heart rate was up, oxygen levels low. I didn't care. I was cold and it was hard to catch my breath, and Leo had somehow struggled out of the back seat and into my lap and was anchoring me in the car.

The EMT was muttering something about airbags and emptying bags of saline solution over the burn on my arm, which hurt but made it feel better.

She looked up and studied me. 'Any burning in your eyes?'

I shook my head.

'Don't touch them, OK?' She poured solution over both of my hands, and then more over my fingers. She looked at Philippe. 'She will be OK with this. But that temple swelling looks bad, I want to get her in—'

'No.' I looked at the back of the EMT truck, imagined the doors closing and trapping me inside. I grabbed Philippe's arm. *'They were going to put me in the trunk.'*

'I will take care of her,' I heard Philippe say, then he turned away from her, speaking rapid-fire in swift, incomprehensible French, and I knew he was giving orders and doing his job, but he did not let them take me, and he did not let me go.

And then . . . it was as if the last nine months never happened. I was back in that dark abyss. Just like the day of Olivier's funeral. Laurent had been there. Laurent had brought me back. He had made me breathe. And now he was gone in a blaze of headlights and a mist of blood.

It was happening again, that surreal feeling of being in a world I did not recognize, where nothing made sense. Philippe was asking me questions again, and it was not possible for me to answer. It was not possible for me to talk. The world was a hurricane all around me, noisy and full of burning, flashing lights and so many people talking, and I was hungry for air; I was drowning and no one could see it, and I could not ask for help. But it was OK. It was OK. Philippe would take care of Leo. I could drift away. Laurent was not here to understand and bring me back. This time, I would escape.

And then somehow I was out of the car and on my feet and running, running, and I heard a shout, and then Philippe grabbed me, holding me so tight and so close that it hurt and I was glad for it.

I glanced toward the tunnel and Mae, and Philippe gently turned my head away. But it was too late for that. It would only be one more terrible thing.

'*Take me home. I want to go home.*'

'Just stay close to me, Madame. I am your home.'

FORTY-NINE

One hour after her death, Mae's manifesto appeared on YouTube, and two days later it went viral under the title *TERRORIST: AMERICAN SOUTH – Mae Yvonne McDermott*. It was not *quite* ignored in the US, covered only by *The Huffington Post*, *Slate*, *The Knoxville Sentinel* and *The LA Times*. But it caused a ripple of shockwaves throughout the EU, most particularly in France, and got massive exposure in *Le Monde*, *The Guardian*, Reuters, the BBC and all major news outlets in the European Union. There were jokes about Americans who show their love for the EU by blowing up France. And a great deal of buzz about the *citizen prey* issue, with much-discussed shock that the home of Memphis, Nashville and the Big Apple had become such a bleak, dystopian place.

Some believed it. Some did not.

But the main focus was on the funding behind Mae. The dark presence of subverted climate change monies was a media tsunami when it was revealed that the funding came from a major oil and gas company headquartered in the US. So Madame Reynard and Mae Yvonne McDermott both got what they wanted. And left the rest of us to deal with the mess.

One week later, in Bulgaria, a twenty-something woman sat in a restaurant called Mr Baba, in the city of Varna, tucked neatly by the Black Sea. She looked out at the water, midnight blue in the darkness, lights rippling the surface, but what she was seeing . . . was *Mae*. The woman was a musician, she had a band, her biggest influence was the punk rock music of Pussy Riot, and she had been enthralled since she was eleven by their Russian feminist performance art. In press interviews eighteen months later, she would say that she could not get Mae out of her head. She ignored her dinner of fish soup and fresh bread, furiously writing lyrics on a napkin, a song called 'Citizen Prey' which six months later would launch her career.

And Mae was gone now, Mae was free.

And I rounded up the video of Mae sabotaging Olivier's plane, and the manifesto that I had downloaded, and all of the information I had put together in my illegal access to the accounts of St Priest's investment group that had been passed on to Madame Reynard, and I wiped it all from the memory of my computer.

Resilience is a curse.

FIFTY

T wo weeks later, Philippe was put on a mandatory leave of absence, pending the outcome of an official investigation into his decision to hold fire while Mae ran into the tunnel with two lit explosive bombs of Torvex. Although, publicly, the event was now called *Triomphe dans le Tunnel du Mont Blanc*, showcasing the state-of-the-art safety features, there were conflicting opinions, and the consensus was that Capitaine Philippe Brevard should have ordered the sniper to take the shot sooner, and that his misjudgment resulted in several million euros of damage to the Mont Blanc Tunnel. It had also been noted that he was in a relationship with the widow of Olivier Lagarde, a victim of the American terrorist, Mae Yvonne McDermott.

Philippe was still on salary, and the actual firing would take months. He had been offered the opportunity to resign with grace and had laughed and said *non*.

Also, two weeks later, the paperwork for our marriage was complete. And because Philippe was now out of a job, our little honeymoon plan of three days together morphed immediately into three weeks.

We told no one of our wedding; it was a private thing. We got married in Metz, late in the afternoon, running up the steps to the annex to the Mayor's office, Philippe, me and Leo, with two office workers as witnesses. We took a drive between Metz and Luxembourg – I admit I was lost – and stopped at a small restaurant for a late dinner, pommes frites, steak and champagne.

The next morning, we bundled up in sweaters, top down on the Z4, with the heat up full blast. I held tight to Leo, and he kept me warm. It was an impromptu road trip. I wanted to see Provence. Philippe managed to drive with expert precision and hold my hand very tight. He knew of a place we could stay in a very small town, that *yes, Madame, had lavender fields, but this is not the time of the year for them to bloom.* I didn't mind.

'A hotel? A B&B?'

But he would only smile at my questions.

It was a beautiful place, Philippe assured me; he had been there before. A perfect location, in the middle of town; we could walk wherever we wanted. And – amazing, this – a black baby grand piano in the main room, many windows with green shutters, a big farm table in the kitchen – much better than that ugly one in Annecy – and a tiny courtyard with an iron table, a big tree and a stone fireplace. *En vérité*, I must know that the plumbing was a little bit iffy.

As soon as we were several hours south and just a mile from the small town where we would spend our honeymoon, I began to feel easy in my heart. I looked at the road, the grass, the trees, the little hills a mile or so away, a gentle height that did not scare me, rocky and grassy; I could climb something like that and not be afraid.

We passed a lavender field, and Philippe promised to bring me back next summer to see the blooms, and then it began to rain so we had to put the top up on the car.

The town was tiny, population under two thousand, and Philippe, whose sense of direction was better than mine, took an easy turn left, then to the right, the road climbing high to the old town, away from anything modern, past a glorious bookstore, and a café and a market, and then to a narrow alley, stopping in front of a house on the corner, ochre plaster walls, pale green shutters. One side was two stories, and facing the street was a one-story wing, with empty windows and a sad, abandoned look, forlorn but beautiful. The shutters had been freshly painted.

'This way,' Philippe said.

A woman and a teenage boy walked past on the other side of the narrow street, giving Leo and the car a second look.

Philippe led me around to the back, through a sagging gate in a high stone wall. The garden was small. Grassy and weedy, and there was a big tree in the corner, and a weed-choked patio at the back of the house, with a stone fireplace that was worn, well used and thrilling.

'We will sit, the three of us, in front of that fireplace. And drink a bottle of wine. Leo will be happy out here.' Philippe looked at me over his shoulder and smiled when he saw my face. 'Really, Madame, you will love this.' He removed a key from a ceramic green frog that sat on the window ledge beside a heavy wood back door.

Philippe turned the key in the lock, struggling a bit with the door, which had to be shoved to open all the way, and Leo and I followed him in.

The kitchen had worn reddish tile floors, and a huge old wooden table that looked too heavy to move and needed to be cleaned. Someone had left behind a stack of old blue dishcloths, neatly folded and covered with dust. The stained white ceramic farmhouse sink had cobwebs in the corner. An old white two-burner gas stove made me happy. No convection stovetop, no garbage disposal, no microwave. Which also made me happy. An empty wall with scars on the tiles, where a washer and dryer could be set up – an inset in the wall with heavy-duty faucets, though they looked grimy and possibly worrisome. I tried not to think about plumbing.

I followed Philippe down a small dark hall, past a dreary bathroom, into a high-ceilinged open room with floor-to-ceiling transom windows and the piano. And what a piano, this black baby grand, set at an angle in the corner, tucked between the windows, deeply caked with dust and no doubt desperately in need of being tuned.

I loved it on sight.

Philippe played one painful note and looked at me, and we smiled.

The front door was heavy with black hinges. I veered to the right, looking from the doorway into a bedroom that was on the left, four sets of narrow French doors on the front wall that faced the side street. And a high ceiling. And more worn tile floors.

'What do you think,' Philippe asked me with a proud smile.

'I . . . I think . . . *how much are we paying for this place*?'

He grinned. 'Nothing, Madame. I bought it last year with the money from the house my ex and I sold after our divorce.

We own it. And yes, it needs cleaning up. The plumbing . . .'
He trailed off. Shrugged.

Yeah. The plumbing.

Leo ran to the French doors and huffed, giving me the alert.
Philippe looked out and nodded. 'There seems to be a white
cat taking a nap.' He tilted his head to one side and looked at
me. 'Do you like it as much as I do?'

'I love it very much. Bathroom be damned.'

'You are sure?'

'I am sure.'

I sat beside him at the piano. 'This is yours, then? You
play?'

Philippe laughed. 'No, Madame, it comes with the place,
and I know it takes up a great deal of space, but you must
love it like I do. You cannot fool me; I can see that you do.'

Leo had his nose to the window, whimpering and glaring
at the white cat who sat watching him from across the street,
which for some reason made Philippe sigh with happiness.
'And you will play the guitar, and I will make a lemon tart
with lavender . . . this is something I have been wanting
to try.'

I thought about the pasta he'd made for dinner in Metz,
which had been quite terrible. He grinned at me over his
shoulder. 'Some things I do very well. One of them is the
lemon tart. Me, I am a dessert guy. And I will clean up that
fireplace and we will sit outside and have the wine and
the tart.'

I smiled. How badly could he screw up a lemon tart?

'Madame,' he said, taking my hand. '*Vivons heureux, vivons
cachés. D'accord?*'

Let's live happy, let's live hidden? That resonated with me.
'*D'accord.*'

FIFTY-ONE

We stopped at a bakery and bought *les chocolatines* and goat cheese with honey. It was cool out, but the rain had stopped and the sun was bright. The owner of the bakery welcomed Philippe back, asked if he had gotten in touch with Monsieur Lombard for the plumping, which was bad enough to be well known in the village, and gave me a curious look.

Philippe smiled. 'Not yet. My wife, she loves the place, and the thing she loves most is the grand piano. And the little backyard garden for our dog.'

My wife. Our dog. The world tilted. And settled straight again.

Leo looked up. He knew he was *dog*.

Later, we rustled up three mismatched chairs from the kitchen. We cleaned the metal table, which would seat six comfortably, rinsing out the dusty dishcloths and using some cleaner we found under the sink.

We made our plans for the courtyard. Over there, the *muguet*. Day lilies, perhaps, a rose garden in the back. We were of two minds on the idea of wisteria along the fence.

The fence was crumbling in places, and the repairs would be expensive – maybe plant hydrangea there for a border.

'We will go out to dinner tonight, but tomorrow I will cook.' Philippe put his hand on mine. 'And if you hear sometimes the piano play, you must not be afraid. The owner, he has died; I bought this from his family. He was a jazz musician and composer, and he died quite young, and it seems from what they say in the town that you can sometimes still hear him play. Usually at dusk, so at least he will not wake us up.'

'Like . . . a *ghost*?'

'Yes, exactly.'

'He plays well?' I asked.

Philippe laughed and gave me a kiss.

'Between us, now, we have four places to live, and me without a job. We must downsize, Madame. But we will worry about this later.'

Three weeks turned into six. Philippe and I rambled around the countryside with Leo, top up on the Z because there was endless rain. We went to the sea, we walked the dusty paths in the hillside, we had olives, saw fields of saffron and blue crocus everywhere. We worked on the house, we hired the plumber, and a stonemason to work on the fence.

Philippe cooked terrible dinners while I played guitar. I played beside the piano, where I could look out of the front and side window, and I wrapped myself around my guitar like a lover. And sometimes I played out in the courtyard at night, with a fire going.

The kitchen only flooded twice, which Philippe swore was a serious improvement, and the plumber would get to that once the issues in the bathroom were resolved.

And somehow I loved every minute.

And one night, at dusk, when Philippe and I were drinking a glass of wine in front of the fire in the back courtyard, we heard the piano play. The exact Paganini Sonata that I had been practicing just that morning.

FIFTY-TWO

The night before we got the call, while we were still in the glow of our honeymoon and the newness of our little family of three, we curled up as we did each evening after dinner, a routine that we fell into so naturally you'd have thought we'd been doing it all our lives. All of us together in the front room with the piano, and the long windows with wavy old glass and the darkness pressing in. The mistrals were coming, and the air felt charged, and I was lost with my guitar in that place where I feel thrilled, where I feel content.

And then I was done. I always knew when it was time to stop. I had exhausted that well of magic, but it would come back to me; I could summon it so easily now, and I smiled because I knew that the music tonight was good, maybe my best ever. And yes, the bad thoughts and the bad feelings would come, and maybe somehow, someday, that would stop, but I would play again tomorrow morning and play again tomorrow night, and there would be sanctuary for me.

I set my guitar down beside the piano. Leo was deeply asleep, eyes shut tight, breathing softly. Philippe had laid out his chess pieces and was leaning over the board intently. His white shirt untucked, a trace of pasta sauce on one rolled-up sleeve, barefooted. Beard stubble rough on his face. He made notations on a pad of paper, the hieroglyphics of a chess strategy that he wrote like notes of music, then played them on the board. His sanctuary. Just like Olivier.

I knew better than to disturb him.

I moved softly toward the kitchen, but he caught my hand as I went by, eyes still on the chess board, and then he looked up.

'I have to tell you this,' he said. 'That I have never been so happy as I am when you play your guitar, *mon fiston* sleeps in the corner, and I settle into the chess.'

I smiled at him. And I loved that he called Leo his old son, and Leo loved it, too. The music was not my only sanctuary now. I had Philippe. I grabbed the front of his shirt and pulled him to me.

'You will manhandle me tonight, Madame?'

'That's my plan.'

He sighed happily and followed me into the bedroom.

He slept well, my Philippe, like men always do when you wear them out, one leg over mine, both of us in a tangle of sheets. His arm holding me close, his breath upon my shoulder.

But I would not sleep. Maybe later. Maybe not at all. Because now the haunting would come.

The things I had done. That I felt no guilt. Just a terrible sick sensation of wondering why it had to happen, struggling to accept that I could not undo it. I could never fix it. It would never go away.

A deep, dark secret memory embedded inside of me because these were words I could not say. But I thought about it. All night, every night, reliving it over and over again, one second to the next second, so deeply ingrained in my memory, and I could not fight these thoughts – they would not go away – and there was no sleep until I went through every last moment in my head at least three times. Sometimes more. Endless.

Different scenarios. Different outcomes. Laurent alive, me dead, both of us dead, both of us alive; the way the gun kicked in my hand, the coating of blood dripping down my neck. Nothing changed the outcome. And yet I was compelled to go over it again and again as if I thought it would.

And always the memory, so strong in my head, of St Priest, looking at me with such love, saying, *Junie, mon amour.* So softly. The gun in my hand. The sound of the shot.

FIFTY-THREE

But there are ghosts . . . and there are ghosts. Some of them still alive. It is hard to know which is worse. The living who won't let you go. Or the dead who won't go away.

As soon as Philippe's phone went off, I had a very bad feeling. We were having breakfast at the old kitchen table. The mistrals were supposed to be coming, and we were tucked safely inside. I had been gathering up the coffee cups, and I stopped, sat down, watching Philippe who had gone very tense.

He frowned, rubbed the back of his neck, said *pardon* and headed to the front of the house, sitting at the piano, which had been cleaned and tuned. Leo looked out of the back door, watching through the screen as the wind blew through the branches of the big tree in the little garden. One of the shutters was banging.

I watched Philippe from the hallway. I had not realized how much the last few weeks had changed him, had erased the lines in his face, how quickly he smiled these days, until I saw the weight settle back around him and I knew he was talking to Madame Reynard. I could not bear to watch this transformation. To see him lose that ease in the set of his shoulders, that air of mischief that I had been seeing more and more.

I went into the bedroom, shut the door and began to pack a small bag. A few minutes later, Philippe came in with Leo.

'You are going somewhere, Madame?' He smiled, but it was forced. He wanted to tell me, but he was not quite ready.

'I'm going wherever you're going.'

He nodded. Cupped my face in his hands and kissed me. 'You missed me, Madame? You have been five minutes without me, after all.'

'Missed you? What was your name again, Monsieur?'

He sighed and sat down on the bed. 'I have to tell you a thing.'

I nodded. 'I thought you might. What was the phone call about?'

I settled down beside him on the bed, and Leo jumped up behind us, sitting up tall, and I leaned against him.

'I hate this,' Philippe said. 'This intrusion in our life that is new.'

'You're here. Leo's here. So long as the Z4 is OK, we'll be fine.'

He frowned. 'They have received a video, Madame. Sent by Mae and addressed to you. Le Reynard has intercepted this from your email, which, of course, you never got. They have been into your emails for quite some time.'

'And you are only just telling me now?'

'They will let you watch this video from Mae, if we care to meet Madame Reynard in her office in Metz.'

I stood up. 'I don't want to go to Metz. Can't she just send it?'

'Security, Madame. Also, she wishes to speak with us personally.'

'I just bet.'

'Do we go or do we stay?'

'I don't know, Philippe. I don't want to go back, and I never want to see Madame Reynard again.' I bit my lip. 'But I will go crazy if I don't see that video.'

'Let us go to Annecy, Madame, spend the night, have dinner at Brasserie des Européens, and we can decide about Le Reynard along the way.'

Which meant we were going, and he was just easing me along.

FIFTY-FOUR

Twenty-three minutes into the drive home to the apartment in Annecy, where I had been so happy and I had been so sad, I began to hyperventilate. Tears began to stream. I started to scream, and I could not stop.

Philippe gave me a quick intense look and pulled over fast to the side of the road.

We were on a two-lane highway that led past the tiny village of Banon. Philippe drove through deep grass, then settled the car on to a dirt track under a tree. I could suddenly breathe again, and I cried softly, looking wistfully at the path that led through the tree line and into the fields. I wondered where it went. I wanted to follow that path and never come back.

Philippe, bless him, did not tell me to calm down. I admired how pragmatic he was, as if he had been expecting exactly this. And maybe he had. He got out of the car, took Leo with him on the leash, came round to my side and opened the door. The two of them peered in at me. Leo seemed to come to a conclusion and settled into the grass. Philippe put a finger under my chin and studied my tear-stained face. He seemed very calm, taking this in stride. Leo got back up to his feet with a groan, put both paws in my lap and gave me a kiss.

'*Avec moi,*' Philippe said firmly. He took my hand, kept hold of Leo's leash, and we walked away from the road. Stopped at the tree by the dirt path. 'We will sit,' he said.

I curled up beside him and cried softly into his shoulder, and he put his arms around me. Leo sat attentively beside me, a paw on my shoulder. Philippe rummaged through my purse and found a wad of tissues and handed them to me. No one seemed to be in a hurry. Philippe held me calmly and stroked my hair until at last I stopped crying.

'Can you talk to me now?' Philippe asked.

'Yes.' I wiped my face and blew my nose and told him every last detail about what happened in that Land Rover, on that terrible night. How Laurent had died breaking Béatrice's neck. How I had killed St Priest and shot Béatrice in the throat to make sure that she was dead. About all of the blood. And the brains. And the bits of flesh. And the smell. The only thing I did not tell him was how St Priest had looked at me before I killed him. How he had said, *Junie, mon amour*, with such love in his eyes.

'This is deep trauma inside you, Madame, and I am sorry for that. The body remembers and triggers a reaction. I have seen this a lot in my work. But I will tell you that everything you have said to me – it was perfectly done, as best as can be in such moments, where nothing can be predicted, and you must think and move fast. But . . . we will keep this between *us*, and tell no one else about it, most particularly not Madame Reynard. Knowledge is power, and we will give her none. If she asks you, Madame, you remember nothing.'

Which was exactly what I needed to hear.

And then all I wanted to do was sleep.

FIFTY-FIVE

We did not stop in Annecy but went instead straight to Metz. Madame Reynard was expecting us at nine a.m., but she did not look the least concerned when we arrived just after eleven. She looked from Philippe to me and smiled smugly. 'I understand I may wish you happiness in your new marriage. I wonder, though, that you would take such a long time off when—'

'Madame Reynard, please do not pretend you do not know I am soon to be fired.'

'You can take the job I offered you.'

I looked at Philippe – he had not told me this. But at least he had turned her down, so I could breathe again. He stared at Madame Reynard.

'We are here to see the video that you intercepted from the private email of my wife.'

She waved a hand. 'You *know* how these things work, Philippe; spare me the outrage and have a seat.' She bent over her computer, then looked at me over her glasses. 'Have you remembered, perhaps, anything about that night when you were kidnapped by Mae, Béatrice and Charl St Priest?'

'No.'

'Not even a detail? A small one? Perhaps—'

'Nothing. It is all a blank. I have no memory of anything that happened. Philippe says that is trauma.'

'Why don't you walk me through everything up to the point where it all goes . . . blank.' She smiled sweetly.

Philippe put a hand on my shoulder. '*Arrête ça tout de suite.* You have asked, she has answered, she does not remember, and you will not put her through this again.'

Madame glared up at Philippe, with a look that ought to have caused him pain.

'I'd like to see the video now, please.' I sat down in a chair. Philippe stayed on his feet.

Madame Reynard tilted her head to one side, focused, chewing her bottom lip. Pulled something up on her computer and turned it across her desk. I leaned forward, elbows on my knees, focused on Madame Reynard's computer screen, and then, like magic, Mae came to life.

She wore a white linen shirt, untucked from her blue jeans, tiny silver hoops in her ears, hair shaved on one side and chin length on the other. The color of mahogany, and it looked thick. It looked soft. She had big hands and broad shoulders, a round face, and she ducked her head shyly, then looked back up.

She was different somehow. Her physical presence. And then I realized I was seeing her somewhere she was comfortable. Somewhere she was at ease and not the least bit anxious. I was seeing Mae as only her family and friends had seen her.

She was home at her house and little office and barn, where she had her vet practice in Strawberry Plains, Tennessee.

'New barn,' she said, waving an arm, and she smiled and transformed into a woman I did not recognize. She held a hand out, and an ancient horse shuffled close. Mae was sitting on a hay bale, camera propped up somewhere or other, and the horse snuffled her neck. Mae reached for a bucket of carrots and fed her, and I could actually hear the crunch as the horse ate. 'This is Zu Zu,' she said with a smile. 'She's thirty-three, which is really old for a horse, and I leave her stall door open, because she likes to wander around. She's a little claustrophobic, so I give her some space. She's had a pretty hard life, but she's good now. Aren't you, baby?' She gave the horse a kiss on the nose.

Then Mae reached out a hand, and a low-slung dog wandered into view and jumped up on to the hay bale. The dog took one of the carrots out of the bucket, then settled down beside Mae with the carrot between her paws.

'This is Piggy. She is very sweet, but opinionated. She is jealous of Zu Zu. She does not really like carrots, but if Zu Zu has one, she wants one, too.'

Zu Zu swung her head and looked at the camera. She sagged a bit, around the middle, and held herself as though she was very tired. She was a dark bay, and her coat was shiny, she was well fed, and it was clear that she considered herself queen of the barn. The carrot was gone, and the horse ambled off, and I wished so hard that Mae was still there in that barn, instead of incinerated in France, and I wondered what would happen to her horse, and all the animals she had rescued, and her vet practice, and her barn.

Mae rubbed her fist on the knee of her jeans and looked up at the camera. 'So this is for you, Junie Lagarde, if you are somehow still alive. I'm planning on letting you live. This is an apology for what has happened already, what is coming, and I need to tell you how sorry I am for causing you so much pain, which you did not deserve. I know that pain. So I'm not going to ask forgiveness. But I was grief-crazy when I sabotaged the plane and caused the death of your husband. Somehow, I thought I could fix my grief, that what I was doing would make the world better and me better. But it didn't.

'You might say I went down the rabbit hole, and when that happens, there are always people who are happy to catch you. People I will deal with later. On my own, I'm not sure I would have done anything so very awful. But somehow . . .' She took a breath, shrugged.

'You'll know by now what happened to my family. They will have told you about all the comments in the newspapers after the fire. You . . . you live in Kentucky. Did you and . . . and . . .' She looked away. Caught her breath. 'Did you and your husband ever come down to Gatlinburg? I bet he liked to ski.' She rubbed her eyes. 'Do you remember that fire in the Smoky Mountains, the Gatlinburg fires? Did you read any of those horrible things people said?'

I sobbed. Grabbed a wad of tissues from my purse.

Madame Reynard said something softly I could not hear. Philippe took my hand, but I pulled it away and shook my head fiercely. This was for no one else. This was between me and Mae.

'I love the EU. I love France. I imagine you do, too. I imagine you get it. How it really is different over there. I mean . . . health care is for everyone, not just the rich, and you don't lose your house to bankruptcy because of an ER bill. People can go to school if they pass the tests, without going into indentured servitude. It's just . . . it's just basic common sense, and everyday . . . humanity. I mean they are a long way from perfect, but most of them don't remove the sex organs of their pets just because they find it convenient, like we do here. Those kinds of things just add up, don't you think?' She looked up at the camera. 'I don't do that. In my practice. By the way.'

'After your husband died in that crash, I saw the pictures of you coming back to France for his body, out on the trails on Mont Blanc looking for your dog.' She shuddered and bit the back of her hand. 'I thought nothing could be worse than how I felt when my family died, but *this was worse*. So much worse. This was *my* fault. I took my grief and gave it to you. That made me wake up. I got homesick and I came home. And here I am.

'But I had to go and see you in person. I watched your house. I saw you go for a walk every morning. Sometimes you had an empty leash in your hand, and I couldn't tell if that was on purpose or if you were even aware you had it. I felt really bad. I followed you to the garden center one Friday afternoon. You go there a lot. And that pot you bought – it was a big one, three feet high, slate-blue and heavy. I don't know if you remember me helping you put it in your car. It was all I could do. That one little thing. But then I thought I could do *one more* thing: I could get you back your dog.

'So I went back to Chamonix, and I found him in the old shed where . . . I found him in that old shed, and he was tied up out of reach of his food.' She frowned hard. 'I cut him loose, and he didn't even eat; he just took off. I knew he would find you somehow.' And she smiled. Because he had.

'And then the court rulings came out – did you hear about those? The justice department threw out the lawsuit on the Gatlinburg wildfires on a technicality, even though we had a slam dunk against the National Park Service. Letting that fire burn for five days, *hoping* it would go out, worrying about budgets and doing pretty much nothing. You know, I have to tell you that wishful thinking does not put out a fire. And they didn't warn anybody. Didn't evacuate just to be on the safe side. *Didn't give anybody a chance.* Why not? They do that

in other parts of the country – people are always being evacuated. Were the people in my town just not worth the trouble?

'And that's why it got thrown out, right? Because it *was* a
slam dunk. And then all those comments again. We deserved
what we got because we live in Tennessee.' Her face went
hard, and then I saw her. The terrorist. She held herself differently. All of the anguish and the softness got buried under the
facade. The warrior was back.

'You know, if it happened in France, at least there would
have been a big protest and they'd have shut the park services
down, and there would have been a *thing* of some kind – a
lot of noise and inconvenience; trash pick-up would probably
be delayed, which is better than nothing. But here, of course,
we got nothing, because *here* we *mean* nothing.

'After everything goes down, and when this is all over, I
want to be buried with my family. I have a plot and a tomb-
stone ready; all it needs is a date and me buried there. I want
to be with my family. I don't want to be all alone.

'But in the meantime, I just wanted to say . . . sorry. I
thought . . . I thought I might just stop and pull out. But once
that ruling came down, I realized. I just don't have a choice.'

The horse ambled back into the pathway of the camera,
nosing into the carrot bucket, and Mae wiped tears out of her
eyes and laughed.

The screen went black. I took a shuddering breath. I thought
about how Olivier and I rambled around Gatlinburg on New
Year's Eve. Walking Smoky Mountain trails with Leo, who,
never satisfied with a mere stick, would hike with a tree branch
in his mouth. Had we seen her and not noticed? Had she seen
us? How odd it was that we had been wandering around in
the same places, completely unaware.

Why did she have to do it? Why did it have to happen?
Couldn't we just somehow go back and change everything.
And why did I even want impossible things?

Madame Reynard had opinions. On the psychology of
terrorists, the American South that seemed to get blamed for
everything, the odd and bitter division of the US into reds
and blues, a division dictated by a flawed voting system that

seemed convoluted and manipulative. I didn't disagree, but I could not bear to listen.

I squeezed Philippe's hand, made my apologies and ran out of Madame's office, Leo trotting beside me, bewildered. It was a relief to be outside, and I sank on to the front stone steps of the building, feeling the wind in my hair and the sun on my face. I put my head in my lap, arms wrapped tight around my middle, and focused on one breath after another. Leo sat beside me, nuzzling my neck, giving me kisses.

They were all dead now – the ones who had murdered Madame Fournier, Laurent and my beloved Olivier. St Priest, Béatrice . . . Mae. They made their choices, and I made mine. I did not regret Béatrice or the vile St Priest. They would have found trouble no matter what; it was embedded in their DNA.

But Mae. A beloved equine vet, graduating from the University of Tennessee, one of the best vet schools in the country. The media had been full of the details of her life. Sifting her mutism, hungry for the details of a woman who had spent years fiercely going after cruel training methods for show horses, taking in abandoned, abused or aging horses on her small farm and practice in Strawberry Plains, Tennessee, halfway between Knoxville and her family in Gatlinburg.

It was seared in my memory how gently she held Leo, all one hundred pounds of him. How she tucked him into the Z4 with his new pink bear, given to him by the daughter of Madame Fournier, another of Mae's victims. And it was not the twisty Béatrice who rescued Leo from St Priest, but Mae.

And yet . . . I had watched the sabotage video, once only. Seen how coldly Mae sabotaged my Olivier's plane, and sent Olivier, Leo and the pilot, Madame Fournier, who had a husband, a daughter and three cats, spinning down to crash on Mont Blanc and burst into flame. I thought of Mae's family – her big brother, her mom and dad, their ancient Standardbred bay mare, their Rottweiler/cattle dog mix – overtaken and consumed in a wall of fire while running from their family home on a steep, twisty road in the Smoky Mountains of Tennessee . . . no warning, no hope of rescue. I saw it in my mind's eye, all of them running together, all of them burning, three hundred yards from their house. Horse on a lead rope, dog on a leash, mom, dad and big brother, all heaped together in the middle of the road, unrecognizable after the fire. There was no chance of safety or sanctuary, no matter how fast they ran. And all that was left of her family were the blackened bones of their two-story chalet, nestled in a thicket of trees that were now skeletal, stunted and dead.

I could hear Madame Reynard's voice echoing in my head as she summed it all up, her opinions lacing through the facts, about the makings of an eco-terrorist. Grieving Mae, shaken and enraged by the vile trolling of a Southern tragedy in all the major newspapers, a piling on of vitriol by frenzied people, drinking the Kool-Aid of an electoral college system of voting that manipulated them into seeing red and blue states and not people.

And yet Mae had changed her mind. She had tried to make amends. She had been haunted by Olivier's death, by the family of Madame Fournier, by the media photos of me walking into the morgue to identify Olivier's body, of me on the trails trying to find my dog.

And yet. It was a violation, the way she had haunted my life. How she had come to Kentucky and tracked me down, helped me put that giant pot into my car. How she had appropriated my grief and mixed it in with her own. Laurent would call her a vulture of grief. He would be right.

But I well understood her traumatized fury, the rage of all of us who don't matter, who die when fires are swept into the winds of mountain waves that erupt in a tsunami of fire.

I did not blame Mae for giving up and heading for France. Had I not done the same? I wish I did not understand what she did, but I do.

And she was right about one thing. The fires are coming for all of us.

And I can still see her so clearly, waving me away as she clutched the Torvex dynamite to her chest and disappeared in a blaze of fire, smoke and pain. It is over for her now. And I wonder if I am the only person who envies the dead.

* * *

I do not know if there was a gathering or anyone there to wish her well, but Madame Reynard sent what little was left of Mae's ashes sealed into a little bronze square box, via FedEx, to a small cemetery office in Sevierville, Tennessee, entrusted to the cemetery owner, who said everything was paid in advance. I admit I liked the idea of her family all being buried in one place. And the bottom line was that at least I'd know where she was. Maybe it would help get her out of my mind. It was an end to her. Sometimes you take what you can get.

But I was not sorry she died.

FIFTY-SIX

Days later, back home in Annecy, in the apartment above Chez Eugene, where Philippe and I had come to gather up more of my clothes and the things we wanted for our place in Provence, the weather in Annecy turned cold and the temperatures began their precipitous drop on Mont Blanc . . . and I dreamed of Laurent.

He was wearing that hunter-green sweater I remembered from the night when he cooked me dinner at his cabin in Chamonix. And I remembered how we had sat and talked in front of the fire, about grief and Violette and Olivier. I felt sad for the woman I was then, who thought she knew everything and really knew nothing at all. So overwhelmed with sadness she could barely breathe.

In the dream, Laurent sat in a chair, and his hair was long and greasy, and his face looked like a vase that had shattered and been glued back together.

'Why are you here?' I asked him. I knew that he was dead.

He tilted his head to one side. 'Because I *see* you, Junie. I think of you driving up to my cabin that day. How it shook me. The *coup de foudre* – the thunderbolt of love. And *les vagues de culpabilité* – the waves of guilt. Terrible guilt.

'I caused you so much pain, you and Olivier. You had what Violette and I had. I did not see, until Olivier's funeral, what a dangerous thing I had done, to drag the two of you into my terrible mess. I opened my eyes to it then. Too late. Too late.

'So I am here now to sit with you, and to comfort you.'

I felt a wail of anguish rising inside of me, thinking of Olivier, how I missed so much the life we had had. 'And you, Laurent? Have you found your Violette?'

'The thing is, Junie, I never lost her.' He cocked his head to one side. 'But I hear you when you cry out, Junie. When you say sorry to me, when you ask, *Why am I here?* Every single thing, Junie, is awake at every level. And all things are possible.'

'What does that even mean?'

And he smiled. 'It is the answer to your question.'

I woke up crying, wondering why all of it had to happen, thinking if only we could go back and make it all right again. And Olivier would be alive. He would never have gone down on the plane, burning, burning, burning. He would be here beside me, safe, familiar, my heart.

Philippe, warm and drowsy, pulled me close, and I turned toward him and tucked my head on his shoulder.

'What is it, Junie?' His voice was thick with sleep.

I traced my finger along the skin of his bare chest, feeling, as I did so often, a grateful contentment that he was here beside me, and I wondered if I would ever take him for granted, that privilege of time and familiarity. I wanted not to, but I knew that surely someday I would.

'I was dreaming of Laurent,' I said, with a catch in my voice.

Philippe paused and stroked my back.

'Do you have dreams like that, Philippe?'

'I was just now having a dream. I was dreaming of coffee and baguette.'

Leo, stretched across the foot of the bed, lifted his head, and I pushed Philippe sideways. 'Now you've done it.'

Philippe sat up and rubbed the stubble on his face. 'The bakery will be open. Leo and I will go.'

But I did not want to be alone. Not with that image of Laurent in my head.

'I'll go with you, and we'll take a walk first. Can I borrow your sweater?'

He sighed. 'Can I stop you, Madame?'

Then we both smiled. Because we knew the answer to that.

Leo, Philippe and I were walking away from the bakery, Leo on my left, Philippe on my right, holding my hand and the paper bag that held the baguette we would all share. And I was becoming happy in Annecy, a city that worked like magic on my soul. It all seemed somehow miraculous, the three of us together. One of the gifts of grief is to know these moments and hold them.

We sat on a worn wooden bench right off the path, green paint fading, leaves layering the ground, gravel beneath our feet. The bench faced the lake, and there were swans, and the water looked clean and cold. Mesmerizing. Philippe was eating bread and feeding bites to Leo and then to me. We were sharing a cup of coffee and steamed milk.

How could this be, I wondered. How did I get here? How is it I could be so sad and so happy all at once? Simple moments were now such a strangeness to me. They felt unreal, like a memory. So often, I was afraid. Because you never know when the last time is. You never can know that.

Philippe was explaining something, and I could not make out exactly what he said. He asked me a question, and I pulled my hair back to show him that I had forgotten to put my hearing aids in, and I tensed up, felt my face grow warm and flushed.

He handed me a chunk of bread and gave me an amused smile.

That smile.

No annoyance. No impatience. No contempt.

And I knew that smile, oh, I knew it. I thought of Olivier chuckling when I told him what I *thought* I heard. Of him explaining how my hearing loss meant my music was better.

Philippe squeezed my hand, and his touch was warm, his fingers strong, and this too made me think of Olivier. And I knew that feeling of being anchored, seen . . . safe.

And I thought of my dream. I thought of Laurent. His grief that was so like mine. The terrible places it took him. I could hear his voice in my head, yet again.

That is when I had hope again, Junie. At Olivier's funeral. When I held your hand and told you to breathe. I think you had given up, Junie, and my soul called out to Violette. How he had touched my hair. How he had looked at me, as if I were someone else. Someone he loved. Someone who had come back to him.

I had been so angry with St Priest, who had appropriated

the concept, pretended he was somehow and some way my husband. I had known how wrong it was. Still, it tortured me. How had he known about the wedding bouquet, the secret *muguet* hidden in the middle? And I saw him again, looking at me with such love, right before I shot him. *Junie, mon amour.*

And when I thought of Laurent and the gentle smile on his face, I had seen the lure of it. The idea that if such a thing were possible, that, somehow and some way, Olivier and I had another chance. And I had known very well how dangerous it was to even think such a thing, when I was so vulnerable in my grief.

It was nothing more than the way you see the long-dead person you love on a crowded street, in a restaurant, out of the corner of your eye. This happened to everyone. Who would know if they were seeing only a memory or a brief flash of presence?

I thought of the night Philippe had come to the apartment. How we had danced and held hands. How he had spoken of a heart attack, happening when he had been tired of his life, three weeks after Olivier's death. How the illness had changed him. How estranged he had been from his old life. How different he was now, the changes he would make. He wanted me, and that was that, as long as I wanted him.

And he watched me now, perplexed. 'What is it, Junie? What is in your head?'

'I was thinking of that night when everything blew up. When you left me in the apartment, with L'agent Durand out front. When you said, *You won't lose me twice.*'

And he gave me that smile that felt like a future memory and a glimpse of my past. He was so familiar to me. He was so new.

He looked at me steadily. 'You know me now, Madame?'

I nodded, tears running down my cheeks. 'I know you.'

Proof and facts are nothing more or less than an ever-changing and evolving sidebar in the ebb and flow of life.

What I know is that the last year had changed me in ways that were profound. So much of grief was love, overlaid with the shock of absence. And maybe absence is the only way we can truly know the depth of our love.

I am grateful for the places that grief takes me, while I despair over the anguish it fuels. What an extraordinary thing it is to be human, to feel both things at once. And sometimes, still, I feel so lost. Like I am a ghost . . . haunting my life . . . and nothing more than a memory from a long, long way away.

Some things you cannot know. Some things are just mystery. Some things are just . . . a beautiful risk.

Milton Keynes UK
Ingram Content Group UK Ltd.
UKHW011834240124
436635UK00004B/390